Strange Tales

Strange Tales

Hanns Heinz Ewers

Introduced
by
Stephen E. Flowers

With a Foreward
by
Don Webb

Introduction
Copyright © 2014
LODESTAR

Stories © Wilfried Kugel, Berlin 1993

This edition has been produced in cooperation with the estate of
Hanns Heinz Ewers

"C.3.3." 1903 Translated by O.F. Theiss
"The Water-Corpse" (Die Wasserleiche) 1904 Translated by Stephen E. Flowers
"The White Maiden" (Das weiße Mädchen) 1904 Translated by Erich Posselt and Sinclair Dombrow
"From the Diary of an Orange Tree" (Aus dem Tagebuch eines Orangenbaumes) 1905 Translated by Stephen E. Flowers
"Tomato Sauce" (Die Tomatensauce) 1905 Translated by Erich Posselt and Sinclair Dombrow
"Fairyland" (Feenland) 1907 Translated by Hanns Heinz Ewers
"Mamaloi" (Die Mamaloi) 1907 Translated by Erich Posselt and Sinclair Dombrow
"The Spider" (Die Spinne) 1908 Translated by Walter F. Kohn
"The Box of Counters" (Der Spielkasten) 1908 Translated by Hanns Heinz Ewers
"The Execution of Damiens" (Die Hinrichtung des Damiens) 1922 Translated by Hanns Heinz Ewers

1901 Photo of Hanns Heinz Ewers owned by Wilfried Kugel, with permission.

Published by
LODESTAR
P.O. Box 16
Bastrop, Texas 78602

www.seekthemystery.com

Acknowledgments

Special thanks go to Dr. Wilfried Kugel, Dr. Bernd Kortländer, Don Webb, Dr. Claus Laufenburg, Jim Rockhill and Bouton Jones.

Contents

Strange Tales

The Dark Side of Wonder

Adolf Hitler, Aleister Crowley, Dashiell Hammett and H.P. Lovecraft all agreed on one thing – Hanns Heinz Ewers was a scary guy and a gifted writer. But the first name on that little list is why you have never heard of him.

I'll tell you my own Ewers-saga. I feel I have to, since I ripped the guy off once. Er, created a literary homage. Now the sad part of my tale is I'm too early in the Ewers Renaissance, somebody will make big money doing the screenplay of *Vampir*, but I doubt it will be me. I'm doing this little squib for Love of the Weird . . .

I am writing this little essay ninety-three years after Ewers went through this part of the world. I have three degrees of removal from Ewers, since I once met a man that rode with Pancho Villa. In a charming little bookstore in Austin, Texas called Adventures in Crime and Space, I encountered a rather musty hardback anthology edited by Dashiell Hammett called *Creeps by Night* (World Publishing Co., 1944). My woebegone purchase was three-quarters full of classics of the weird tale – "A Rose for Emily" by William Faulkner, "The Music of Erich Zann" by H. P. Lovecraft, "The King of the Cats" by Stephen Vincent Benet and so forth. I really wanted to read the other stories, to see if they were of the same level; this introduced me to William Seabrook and HHE, who certainly belonged in such august company.

Hammett also introduced me to the Scots word "Weird" meaning "something that really happened." This led to a fascination with the word, which in some sense I have come to represent.

Ewers' story, "The Spider," was powerful, and I soon found a reprint collection of three of his stories called *Blood*. I enjoyed the last one "Tomato Sauce" so well, that I ripped off its plot for "Letter from Bemi III" that I cowrote with Rosemary Webb, for *Infinite Loop* (1993). I didn't feel bad about this, Guy Endore, who translated *Vampir*, completely ripped off its plot for his own *The Werewolf of Paris*. *Vampir* remains one of the best studies of the interplay of the sadistic and Loving impulses in mankind – its atmosphere being the most resonant of the cinematic works of David Lynch of anything else I've ever read.

I was so taken with his dark vision, I dedicated my first book in German *Märchenland ist abgebrannt* (1989), to him. Then I read a piece of trash journalism called *Morning of the Magicians* that insinuated that Ewers wrote the Horst Wessel song. On no, I thought, I've dedicated a book to a Nazi, the worst sort of Nazi.

So I stopped recommending this very fine writer to my friends, and I hoped that no one would notice my "borrowings" from him. But weirdly enough, I joined an esoteric study group here in Austin, and looking over its journal noticed a translation of one of Ewers' stories. I asked the translator, a Dr. S. E. Flowers, about Ewers, and learned not to trust trash journalism. I told Dr. Flowers that I thought his translation was good, a little too good for a newsletter that went to 30 people; he should do a book.

Little did I know that he would found a press to do so.

Soon the braver people who have picked up this book will be plunging into the Dark Wonder of HHE. Now, what they don't know is they will be a little *different* after swimming in this sea.

This is a Good thing, since the Weird always makes people a little richer and stranger. . .

Don Webb
Austin, Texas
1999

Introduction

The Life and Times of Hanns Heinz Ewers

I. Reputation

Hanns Heinz Ewers (1871-1943) was at one time one of the best known and most popular of German writers. His works abound in images and ideas that readers, even in today's jaded climate, often find disturbing. But then he was more than a writer. He was a poet, dramatist, film-maker and performance artist, who at one time in the early part of the century had a hit play, a best-selling book and an acclaimed film before the public simultaneously in the metropolis of Berlin. But what happened to this artist's reputation? To some extent that is the story of this introduction.

Ewers, it appears, was even more than an artist, although it is as an artist that his reputation must rest. He was a man of mysterious connections: he met and worked with notorious occultists of his day (e.g. Guido von List, Aleister Crowley and Erik Jan Hanussen), and he at one time had access to the highest echelons of political power – he was inducted into the National Socialist Party by none other than Adolf Hitler himself – who was an avid reader of his fiction.

Up until now Ewers has perhaps been best known in English-speaking horror and fantasy circles through a brief quote in H. P. Lovecraft's *Supernatural Horror in Literature* (1927) where Lovecraft says of Ewers' work:

> In the present generation German horror fiction is most notably represented by Hanns-Heinz [sic] Ewers, who brings to bear on his dark conceptions an effective knowledge of modern psychology. Novels like *The Sorcerer's Apprentice* and *Alraune* and short stories like "The Spider" contain distinctive qualities which raise them to a classic level.

Another place where we find an intriguing quote about Ewers is in *The Morning of the Magicians* (p. 281), where it is said that Ewers "was an enthusiastic member of the [Nazi] Party because he saw in it, at the beginning, 'the strongest expression of the Powers of Darkness.'" The veracity of the entire paragraph in which this quote appears is, however, open to question. For example, it implies that Ewers *wrote* the "Horst Wessel Lied," the "Party anthem," when in fact that song was written by none other than Wessel himself! Ewers did write the "official biography" of Wessel, and worked on a motion picture meant to portray the life and death of this Nazi "martyr." Ewers' cooperation with the Nazis was to turn out badly for him eventually, as he was rejected– first in life by a faction of the National Socialists for being "too decadent," and then in death by politicized literary critics for being a "Nazi."

These mysterious and intriguing flashes of information do much to enhance fascination with Ewers and his work. However, until recently little but fragments of such information and mythology were available. This situation has largely been remedied by the brilliant work of Dr. Wilfried Kugel: *Der Unverantwortliche: Das Leben des Hanns Heinz Ewers*. This is a treasure-trove of precise information and biographical detail from which this introduction has largely been drawn.

Ewers presents a fascinating study to the student of horror and fantasy literature. His tales rarely contain what could be called "supernatural" events. They are usually more dependent on the psychological quirks of the characters or uncanny twists of fate.

In the final analysis it is as an innovative artist as well as a psychologically and ideologically complex poet and author that the reputation of Hanns Heinz Ewers is to be evaluated. His popularity and original contributions to the artistic and literary world of the first half of the twentieth century can not continue to be ignored simply because his ideas and certain biographical details perpetually disturb every one from middle-class shop-keepers to Marxist ideologues.

In the course of this introduction we will see how much of Ewers' *sinister* reputation is well-deserved, and how perhaps it has even been *understated* by sensationalistic, yet uninformed writers up to now, but how too his reputation as a "Nazi" is in certain essential respects undeserved. For example, he was no anti-Semite and with his influence even helped Jewish friends escape persecution in Nazi Germany. In life his fate was sealed by his own irresponsible actions, but in death, and in the fullness of time, his larger fate can be rewritten based upon the original raw power of his art.

II. Early Life
(1871-1898)

Birth and Youth

In the early years of Ewers' life lie the roots of his later literary work– which he was not to begin in earnest until he was 27 years old. In this early period Ewers pursued two obsessions– sex and the occult. Themes which were to find expression in his written production of later years. But without an understanding of their origins, certain nuances of meaning will be missed.

Hans Heinrich Ewers – a name he later modified to "Hanns Heinz" – was born in Düsseldorf, Germany on 3 November 1871. Both his parents were artistically inclined. His father, Heinz, was a singer and painter, and his mother, Maria, *née* aus'm Weerth, was a painter and talented story-teller. Heinz Ewers was a court painter for the archduke of Mecklenburg-Schwerin and the young Hans often had to pose for his father as a substitute model for the children of the court of Friedrich Franz II. These tiresome sessions of posing in royal costumes – as a model for the bodies of the children whose faces would appear in the final portrait – were only made bearable by his mother reading to him or telling him stories.

His "Mother Maria," as he would address her later in life, was apparently at least one source of Hans' later "diabolism." Even as a young girl she expressed the fervent wish that it would make her happy to be able to meet the Devil in person. She was also given to writing lively descriptions of the tortures of hell for her school work. Maria was an intellectually rebellious girl– and later encouraged this in her son.

The Ewers household was very much dominated by the feminine. Until she died in 1890 Hans' maternal grandmother, who was by all accounts a domineering woman, lived in the Ewers' large home at Immermannstrasse 22. Because his father's duties at the court of Mecklenburg-Schwerin kept him away from home for extended periods the early influence of his mother was dominant. This influence naturally became even more prevalent when Heinz Ewers died in April 1885.

Maria Ewers remained single and raised her children in a worldly atmosphere of intellectual liberality. Hanns Heinz developed a strong relationship with his mother, which is reflected in many of his works.

Earlier interpretations of Ewers' works had it that he received his sensitive nature from his mother, and the more demonic aspects from his father. However, more recent evidence shows that it was his mother who encouraged him in the pursuit of his literary career and who imparted an interest in the fabulous and fantastic to her young son.

In order to earn money his mother rented rooms to borders in the large family home. These borders, often from foreign countries, served to stimulate Hans' imagination and curiosity. School certainly did not do this for the young man. However, due to his mother's influence Hans was an enthusiastic reader– especially of Romantic literature (e.g. Heine and Hoffmann) and philosophy (e.g. Kant, Spinoza, Stirner and Nietzsche). He thought: "Philosophy is good – precisely because it is good for nothing."

Early on his attitude of cynical detachment was pronounced. But this, he freely admitted to himself, was a *mask* for his underlying personality which was painfully shy. In fact, he was so shy he had difficulty just going into a shop to buy school supplies. This almost debilitating shyness, coupled with a tremendous interest in women and girls made for a painful combination in adolescence. He wanted to approach girls with his desires, but was prevented from doing so by his inhibitions– and this led to a deep sense of self-loathing. It also inspired some of his earliest efforts at poetry.

His greatest inspiration – and source of years of the tortures of unfulfilled love – was a girl who began to board in his mother's house at this time: "Lili" (Helene Schleifenbaum). She inspired a whole cycle of youthful poems. But because he could not early on muster the courage to pursue sexual relations with her – something he desperately wanted – she became a source of not only inspiration but torment and self-hatred.

By this time in his life he was already alienated from any orthodox notions of "God"– and often contemplated suicide. A passage from an early diary reveals: "How happy it makes me when I can make people believe I'm cold and cruel and cynical, I always think: that suits me! But it's all just a pitiful lie." (See Kugel 1992: 31)

The Lilith-Theme

Throughout his life Ewers was to have an ambivalent attitude toward the feminine– which he tended to view as a dichotomy between the Virgin Mary and Lilith. Both of these archetypes were embodied from an early time in both his mother and "Lili." Lilith is a figure from Hebrew mythology who is seen as Adam's disobedient first wife and who ultimately becomes a dangerous force– an archetype of the *femme fatale*. The symbol of Lilith would recur overtly and covertly in Ewers' work, e.g. "Von Hella" (1904) and "The Spider" (1908). In *The Sorcerer's Apprentice* he would wrap his Lilith-cult in Christian garb.

This *femme fatale* is both an object of veneration or a source of artistic inspiration and an agent of ruination. This conflicted relationship with the

[3]

feminine was first made conscious in Ewers' experience with "Lili." He became obsessed with her because he desired sexual relations with her– but because he could never actualize these desires he grew to hate himself and to fear women on some level. Eventually she, of course, turned away from the hesitant suitor and towards other men– but he put some measure of the blame of the failure of their relationship on her.

This complex and deep-seated attitude toward *das ewig Weibliche* ("the Eternal Feminine") would be the fuel of artistic inspiration and personal unhappiness throughout his life.

Early Adulthood

On 12 March 1891 Ewers passed his college preparatory exam (*Abitur*)– unexpectedly, it seems, as he had been a bad student and even prepared for his suicide in the likelihood of his failure of the exam. Before entering the university, however, he had to fulfill his obligation for military service. He joined the Kaiser-Alexander-Gardegrenadier-Regiment Nr. 1 in Berlin– but was discharged after only 44 days due to his poor eyesight.

It was that spring, in Berlin, when Ewers had his first "complete" sexual encounter. It was with Illa Lampe– an older married friend of the family with two children. Subsequently he began to keep company with prostitutes– who suited him very well.

Immediately after his discharge from the military he entered the Friedrich-Wilhelm University, Berlin. At the insistence of his mother – but also in imitation of his literary heroes Heinrich Heine and E. T. A. Hoffmann – he studied law. He at once joined the "Normannia" student association and threw himself into the student life. Although Ewers' face was soon to show the results of repeated sword-duels – facial scars referred to as *Schmisse* – he would eventually be expelled from the "Normannia" for insufficient performance in fencing. He subsequently studied in Bonn, Brünn and Geneva. His experiences in the student corps, while not entirely successful, would be used in his literary and cinematic work, e.g. "From the Diary of an Orange Tree" and *The Student of Prague.*

From 1894 Ewers began legal work in the civil service in Düsseldorf, while haphazardly continuing his studies. His university work in the law never inspired him– he dedicated most of his time and effort to fleeting love affairs (one resulting in an illegitimate child, Victoria), pining for "Lili," reading literature and philosophy– and studying the *occult sciences.*

Spiritualism and Occultism

In the late 1890s Ewers was much involved with occultism, hypnotism and spiritualism. He was influenced by the literary and mystical ideas of Stefan George (1868-1933)– especially his "mystification of the blood." Ewers turned his practical studies in hypnotism to acts of seduction by hypnotizing potential sexual partners. By 1895 he had joined the "Psychological Society" of Düsseldorf– a branch of a spiritualistic movement founded by Maximilian Ferdinand Sebaldt (von Werth) (1859-1916). Sebaldt was a Berlin Theosophist and pioneer of sexual magic and sexology who worked cooperatively with the Viennese mystic, Guido von List.

Ewers was considered a "talented medium" in séances conducted by the "Psychological Society"– but his cynicism and open discussion of "tricks" used by spiritualists caused him to be expelled from the society in 1896.

At the end of 1897 Ewers was released from his position in the civil service– which he later characterized as "the most decisive moment of my life." As a matter of prestige Ewers went on to complete a doctorate in jurisprudence at the University of Leipzig in November 1898– but this was the *end* and not the beginning of his legal career.

III. Early Writing Career
(1898-1918)

This twenty year period saw much adventure and success for HHE. His creative star would rise high and at one point he would simultaneously have the most successful book (*Alraune*), film (*The Student of Prague*) and play (*Das Wundermädchen von Berlin*) in the German capital, Berlin. Success never comes "over night." But for HHE it does seem to have come through the night.

In the artistically decisive time before 1900, the chief literary influences on Ewers were, Heinrich Heine, Edgar Allan Poe, E. T. A. Hoffmann, Villiers de l'Isle-Adam, J.-K. Huysmans, G. d'Annunzio, J. Troop, Maurice Maeterlinck and August Strindberg. Additionally, the personality and work of Oscar Wilde played an important role. Ewers later claims to have been so disgusted by the treatment Wilde received at the hands of the "law" that he decided to give up its practice. He even wrote a fictionalized account of his meeting with Wilde on the island of Capri in 1898 or 1899– "C. 3. 3."

His first publication was the poem "Mutter" ("Mother") in the journal *Frühling* (March 1898). This was written under his artistic form of his name: Hanns Heinz Ewers. Other of his earliest publications appeared in periodicals such as *Der arme Teufel*, a German language journal produced in Detroit, Michigan by Robert Reitzel, *Der Kunstfreund* which Ewers edited with his friend Theodor Etzel, and *Der Eigene*– "the first homosexual magazine in the world" as it called itself. These publications were poems, short stories and fables. The fables were to be collected in his *Fabelbuch* (1901)

It was this volume of fable which brought Ewers to the attention of Ernst von Wolzogen (1855-1934), who in the early part of 1901 was in the process of establishing a cabaret in Berlin– to be called the *Ueberbrettl*. On the stage Ewers became a sensational performer of his poetic fables. Here he broached taboo subjects and often humorously addressed previously forbidden themes. He was most renowned for his use of the word "*Popo*"– a slang term for the buttocks or anus. Another of his fables performed at this time was "Im Karpfenteich" ("In the Goldfish Pond")– later worked into the story "The Water Corpse" (1904). In this tale he explores the idea of the creative process within a social context, the nature of the mass-mind which is the audience– and its stupid and fickle quality. By 1904 Ewers had become well-known as a teller of gruesome, yet humorous, tales, and so he had some experience in the kind of ultimate reaction to his work displayed in the story.

By the end of 1901 Ewers had become at least a moderately celebrated poet and performer. But he was dissatisfied with this kind of success– as reflected in the tone and theme of "The Water Corpse." His interests ran deeper than superficial entertainment and he longed to be taken seriously as an artist. Although he continued to perform in cabarets for years, he set his course in a different direction over the coming years.

In May 1901 Ewers married the painter and illustrator Caroline Elizabeth (Ilna) Wunderwald (1875-1957), to whom he had been engaged since 1897. Ewers' mother much supported this marriage, which would eventually end in 1912. Ilna worked with Ewers at the cabaret and illustrated some of his early works.

The years leading up to the publication of Ewers' first major collections of short stories, *Das Grauen* (1907) and *Die Besessenen* (1908)– both published by Georg Müller in Munich – were filled with a variety of experiences reflected in the tales contained in these collections.

Ewers spent most of the time between the end of 1902 and the middle of 1904 with his wife on the island of Capri. Here HHE developed an interest in nudism and wrote the essay "Nackte Schönheit" (Naked Beauty).

In this period, too, HHE was involved in the cause of homosexual emancipation. He worked on the journal *Der Eigene*, a periodical of the *Gemeinschaft des Eigenen*. The aim of this community was to spread the idea that young men should only have sex with other men until the time of their marriage to a woman. Ewers himself had homosexual affairs throughout his adult life. This he saw as an expression of the androgyny of his own creative soul.

After their travels to Capri Hanns and Ilna, with their companion Albert Hubert, left for Spain and southern France in February of 1905, and would not return to Germany until June. On these travels Ewers visited the Alhambra and Granada and other cities in Spain. He is supposed to have written his essay "Edgar Allan Poe" in Granada in 1905. He also attended a cock-fight in Malaga on 20 March 1905, and saw bull-fights in Toledo. Ewers was a dedicated animal-lover and found these displays disgusting and disturbing in the extreme– yet he used his feelings in his artistic productions which were to come out of these experiences, e.g. in "Tomato Sauce" (1905). In the south of France on the island of Porquerolles– there was a camp of the French Foreign Legion. His experiences and stories he heard there helped him write the "Box of Counters" (1908).

In southern France, too, Ewers continued his experimentation with various drugs. He had drunk alcohol regularly from his school days and had experimented with hashish since 1893. In this he was inspired by his literary role models such as Poe, Baudelaire and Gautier. During the time spent on Capri, Ewers began to experiment more widely with various kinds of drugs. This he conceived of as "research" for a work to be called *Rausch und Kunst*(Intoxication and Art)– which now exists only as a manuscript fragment. He experienced opiates, (opium and morphine) as well as hallucinogens (mescaline) and absinth and remained a life-long proponent of the use of drugs in enhancing the development of artistic inspiration. This use also, according to Dr. Wilfried Kugel's research (1992: 401-410), heavily contributed to Ewers' later debilities and loss of contact with reality.

Despite a difficult financial situation, Ewers arranged for an extended trip to the Americas. On the ship over to Cuba in March 1906 he began work on his first novel originally to be titled *Der Meister*(The Master)– which became *Der Zauberlehrling* (The Sorcerer's Apprentice). His travels took him through Cuba, various locales in the Caribbean (Cuba, Puerto Rico, the Dominican Republic and Haiti), Mexico, various Latin American countries and even the southern part of the United States, where he visited San Antonio, Texas and New Orleans, Louisiana. In Haiti Ewers was able to observe voodoo ceremonies– including one in which a young boy was sacrificed. His observances of the voodoo-cult are reflected in his story "Mamaloi" (1907). He is also thought to have been involved in voodoo practices in the southern U.S. (1914-18). The American trip ended in September 1906. Many of his experiences and observations of both Spain and America were chronicled in *Mit meinen Augen. Fahrten durch die lateinische Welt* (1909).

The tales published in *Das Grauen*(1907) and *Die Besessenen* (1908) marked for Ewers a new artistic beginning, as previous efforts were even withdrawn from the market. These incorporated experiences and ideas gathered over the ten year period since he had dedicated himself to writing. The later collection contains Ewers' most famous story: "The Spider." This tale carries an alternate title: "Lilith." This is the key to the symbolic interpretation of the story. In a rare example of Ewers discussing the symbolic content of one of his own stories, he wrote in the journal *Zeitgeist* (Dec. 7, 1908):

> Lilith, that is: Adam's first wife. Or: the serpent of the Garden of Eden. Or: the great grand-mother of the Devil. Or: the eternal feminine. Or: the inadequate which becomes a phenomenon. Thus the "Spider" is a symbol, perhaps indeed an inadequate one. However, – here – this inadequacy becomes a phenomenon, and grows into fact and beyond that. Thus the entire thing is a symbolic poem: the eternal victory of woman. In connection with this I was especially overcome with the idea of a strange force, which is capable of exercising some sort of an exterior, dark will upon us. This is why I placed the following epigram before the "Spider":
> "And a will therein lieth, which dieth not. Who knoweth the mysteries of a will with its vigour?" (Glanville)

Here Ewers harkens back to the Lilith motif and his complex relationship with the "Eternal Feminine."

In September 1909 Ewers finishes his novel: *Der Zauberlehrling: Oder die Teufelsjäger*. Certain aspects reflected in the novel are loosely based on historical events which happened in a Swiss mountain village, Wildisbuch (Kanton, Zürich) between 1817 and 1823. (See Kugel 1992: 418-19) Ewers naturally reshaped the events to fit his own artistic and philosophical purposes. The novel appears to be in fact a symbolic explanation of Ewers' idea on race, the nature of the human species and the role of the creative genius in the world. It contains numerous digressions into many of Ewers' favorite theories– often apparently loosely drawn from nationalist thinkers such as Guido von List or Lanz von Liebenfels. The ideological link between Ewers' ideas and those of the German nationalists was so pronounced that even several years later communist journalists would draw parallels between the *Sorcerer's Apprentice* and the ideas of National Socialism!

Satanism and the "Occult"

Ewers had long evidenced an interest in occult matters in his personal life. He had been a member of the "Psychological Society" and in 1897 in Paris he attended a lecture by Leo Taxil, who was famous for claiming a Satanic purpose behind Freemasonry. But this had only found moderate expression in his written works until the period following 1904. The stories collected in *Das Grauen* reflect a certain melding of his newer artistic style with the substance of a deepening interest in the occult, magic and esoteric racial doctrines. These interests would continue to develop over the years punctuated by contact with well-known occultists such as Aleister Crowley and Erik Jan Hanussen.

Earlier Ewers had certainly had some contact with the circles surrounding Guido von List. He contributed to List's earlier journal *Der Scherer* and the two shared many acquaintances in Berlin. It is not unlikely that Ewers had some contact with Theodor Reuss, head of the sex-magical order *Ordo Templi Orientis*, as they tended to run in similar social circles—which included Stanislaw Przybyszewski, Gustav Meyrink and Max Ferdinand Sebaldt. The latter had been the founder of the spiritualistic "Psychological Society" and was an esoteric sexologist, who apparently first inspired in Ewers the idea for a common German-Jewish heritage (in connection with the Ostrogoths) as the "chosen people(s)." This idea would find expression in Ewers' 1920 novel *Vampir*.

Later I will return to Ewers' relationships with Crowley and Hanussen, as they belong to different times in Ewers' life. However, it is important to understand Ewers' own deep and long-standing involvement with the occult before the full scope of his relationship with these occultists can be appreciated.

In Berlin on Friday 4 February 1910 Ewers held his lecture "The Religion of Satan" for the first time. He would give this lecture many times in the years to come (until 1925) all over Europe. These lectures won him great notoriety– as he became known as "Satan's advertising manager." This was because these lectures actually *promoted* the idea that Satanism was the basis of all science, art, philosophy, human discovery and evolution. His lecture was heavily based on Przybyszewski's text entitled *Die Synagoge Satans*, with extensive use of the poetry of Johann von Goethe (*Faust* and *Prometheus*) and Giosué Carducci ("Hymn to Satan") as well as references to the Satanic influences of Friedrich Nietzsche, Max Stirner, and E. T. A. Hoffmann. It was widely suggested to Ewers that he write a major manuscript based on the content of his "Religion of Satan" lectures. This was never done, as Ewers preferred to work his own ideas into his own fictive creations rather than publishing them in historical-critical form. A fragment of the lecture manuscript for the "Religion of Satan" survives in the Ewers archive in Düsseldorf.

Clearly Ewers' interests in the occult run deep and were first instilled in him by his mother, as was his Romantic and revolutionary image of Satan as a liberator of man. Maria Ewers was an atheistic "nature worshipper" who was thought of as a "witch" by those who knew her best. Ewers' own bewitching account of his mother is found in his story "Meine Mutter die Hex" (My Mother the Witch) (1922). However, it is unlikely that Ewers ever much involved himself with organized occultism, but rather developed his own synthetic esoteric ideology based on the many personal and literary influences on him through the years.

On the whole topic of the "occult" he also took a somewhat rational position:

> The occult is the unconscious, it is that which we do 'not know.' Or, as I conceive of it, what we do not yet know. Therefore there are still doubtless many things that remain 'occult.' However, from the moment that we become aware of this or that, it ceases to be something unconscious, and becomes much more something of which we are very conscious. It is this that the investigator strives after– and at the same time it is that which the fanatics never want to see.
>
> *Indien und ich*, p. 85

Travels and Further Transformations

From as early as 1906 Ewer's marriage to Ilna had reached a crisis point. Although they usually travelled together, they had generally lived apart, he in Berlin, she in Düsseldorf in his mother's house. It seems he increasingly retreated behind a "mask" to guard his true emotions and nature in order to make it possible for him to find the inner condition needed for his creative work. This, of course, caused him to become increasingly cold and distant from his wife. Sexual relations between them probably ceased two or three years after they were married. Each of them had lovers – probably of both sexes – through the years.

A final attempt at reconciliation came in connection with a trip to India and the South Pacific. Then Hanns and Ilna left for Ceylon in April 1910. They first visited this island extensively, then spent two weeks travelling through India itself on a train with luxurious accommodations. HHE's observations and experiences on these journeys were first published in periodicals, then collected into the volume *Indien und ich* (1911). This trip took them further on to Australia, islands of the South Pacific, and south-east Asia. By October Ewers was back in Berlin.

Shortly after their return, Hanns and Ilna separated for good– although the divorce would not be final until 1912. In the end the marriage eventually failed due to personality conflicts, to some degree centering on a sense of artistic competitiveness. Financial problems stemming from the separation and divorce would plague Ewers throughout the 1920s.

In the summer of 1911, while travelling in the Adriatic, Ewers finished his second novel– *Alraune*, published later that year. This was to become Ewers best-known work– an international "best-seller" translated into 20 languages and filmed five times. This novel is a prequel to *Der Zauberlehrling*, which, with *Vampir* (1920), forms part of the "Frank Braun trilogy." Frank Braun is the fictionalized alter-ego of HHE.

Alraune, or "Mandragora," is an *unnatural* humanoid creature – a beautiful, yet soulless girl – engendered from the sperm of a hanged criminal in the womb of a prostitute. This *artificial entity* brings happiness to those who possess it, but destroys those who fall under its spell. This became a common theme in German art – including the political art – in the years to come.

HHE and Film

The cinematic success of *Alraune* is only the most conspicuous aspect of Ewers' involvement with film. As early as 1908 he realized the *artistic* as well as pedagogical – possibilities of film when he first began his experiments in Film while in France. Ewers was always interested in translating his ideas into new forms of media. The Wagnerian concept of a *Gesamtkunstwerk* (total work of art) had possessed him from early on.

The years 1913-1914 were extremely active ones for Ewers' cinematic endeavors. In connection with Deutsche Bioscop, Ewers collaborated on as many as eleven films– providing the scripts and even directing many of them himself. His chief co-workers in these early films were the actor Paul Wegener, the Danish director Stellan Rye and the cameraman Guido Seeber.

Der Student von Prag(The Student of Prague) [1913] stands as the first true *Autorenfilm*, a true *art film*, conceptualized from its beginnings as a cinematic work of art by a reputed artist. It is based on certain ideas pioneered by Adelbert Chamisso, E.T.A. Hoffmann and Oscar Wilde surrounding the *Doppelgänger*, which had been further refined by Ewers in his 1908 stories "The Spider" and "Der Tod des Barons Jesus Maria von Friedel." In the latter tale, the division in the soul is between masculine and feminine sides. In *The Student of Prague* we see once more the Lilith-motif– where the homicidal priestess of Lilith; in the form of the gypsy girl, Lyduschka; sews discord in the soul of the main character– and thus destroys him. This film was perhaps the most critically acclaimed film of its time.

In 1913 Ewers stood at the height of his popularity. His books were best-sellers, his film successful – both financially and critically – and his plays were staged on multiple stages in Berlin. His popularity was punctuated on 1 April 1914 when he was awarded a prize at a Berlin artists' festival for his masculine beauty– leading ladies of the city sat as judges. This "media-event" was widely covered by the press and would later come back to haunt him, as it would make him the butt of humor in many circles, artistic and political.

IV. The First World War and its Aftermath (1914-1920)

At the height of his popularity Ewers undertook another trip to South America in May 1914. Europe stood on the eve of the "Great War." Soon after the assassination of archduke Francis Ferdinand, Ewers made his way to New York. He arrived on the day Austria declared war on Serbia (28 July 1914). In New York Ewers began to devote himself to the cause of Germany, which entered the war in August 1914. He put himself in the service of the German Ambassador, Count Bernstorff, in the production of pro-German propaganda. This work was essentially directed at making the case for Germany in America, and attempting to prevent the entry of the USA in the war on the side of the British and French.

To this end Ewers collaborated with a group of German-American writers and businessmen to publish the magazine *The Fatherland*. Its publisher was George Sylvester Viereck, who also put out *The International*, a monthly literary magazine. *The Fatherland* found contributors from among those promoting German, Austrian, Hungarian, Irish and Jewish interests. Viereck was a member of the German propaganda cabinet and received $100,000 from the German government for his effort. In the years between the beginning of the war in Europe and the American entry into the war in early 1917, Ewers was free to speak and travel, and he enjoyed great popularity in New York.

Apparently his efforts at aiding German interests were not limited to writing. He made at least three mysterious trips through the southern part of the U.S. into Mexico contributing to efforts to stir up Mexico against the U.S. in an attempt to distract the Americans from the situation in Europe. In these efforts Ewers visited Francisco "Pancho" Villa, whom he had first met in 1906. Even in these times, however, HHE never seemed to pass up an opportunity for strange experiences. In the spring of 1917 he is said to have attended voodoo ceremonies in New Orleans, and it was during one of these trips that he engaged in an adventure in voodoo-esque grave-robbing. In the exhumation of the human corpse Ewers touched it with his hands– shortly thereafter he began to suffer from eczema on his palms. In the coming years, whenever he was asked about the sores on his hands, he would nonchalantly reply: "Oh, it's just from working in the garden."

In spite of – or perhaps *because* of – Ewers' involvement with voodoo, and his frequent trips to countries where non-Caucasian races were in the majority, he was, at least from the time of his travels to the Caribbean in 1906, a dedicated racist. He considered the "colored" races to be inferior to the Aryan/Caucasian, and especially to the Germanic– which he identified as the "German, English, Scandinavian and American." It is difficult to believe this racism was not a part of his background before his travels, given his early exposure to the philosophies of List, Liebenfels and Sebaldt. Despite this general approach to *groups* of people, he could always respect *individuals* whose *greatness* or *beauty* elevated them to a higher status– regardless of race. Aspects of this general attitude are expressed in tales such as "Fairyland" (1906), "Mamaloi" (1907), and "Box of Counters" (1908).

Hanns Heinz Ewers and Aleister Crowley

HHE had made the acquaintance of the British poet and magician Aleister Crowley (1875-1947) at least by the spring of 1915. During the war years Crowley worked with *The Fatherland* and *The International* for the common interests of Ireland and Germany against England. Later, it appears, Crowley would try to change this story. However, all of Crowley's actions at this time – including his magical declaration of an independent Irish Republic on Liberty Island, New York, to his pro-Irish-German activities in England, for which he was deported from England – point in the direction of his dedication to anti-English interests. It is likely that Ewers and Crowley got to know each other quite well in these years. Ewers even attempted to have Crowley's work published in Germany, but the publishers found the work "too long." Crowley and Ewers shared common interests in the esoteric as well as political and cultural matters.

During this time Ewers also made the acquaintance of Ernst ("Putzi") Hanfstaengl, who was the center of an artistic circle in New York. They probably knew each other from as early as 1914. Hanfstaengl would later be an early supporter of Hitler and the National Socialists and would certainly aid Ewers in his efforts to become influential in artistic circles in Nazi Germany.

Over the years 1915-1916 Ewers wrote most of his third Frank Braun novel– *Vampir*, which was not able to be published until 1920. This is a heavily autobiographical work set in New York during the time of the outbreak of the First World War, and is in part inspired by Ewers' relationship with the half-Jewish Adéle Guggenheimer-Lewisohn, whom he had known since 1891. When they again met in 1914, and became lovers, she was the widow of Randolph Guggenheimer (1848-1907). She recurred in Ewers' works under the name "Lotte Lewi" (e.g. in "Der letzte Wille der Stanislawa d'Asp" [1908] and *Der Zauberlehrling* [1909]). Ewers sent some of the profits from his writings to aid the Jews of Poland– a cause for which Adéle worked at the time.

At the end of 1916 Ewers met a 19 year-old actress and singer, Josephine Bumiller, in New York. She would later become Ewers' second wife.

Internment and Return to Germany

The United States entered the war against Germany in April 1917, whereupon Ewers' propagandistic efforts were brought to an end and he was put under close observation by the Secret Service. In the summer of 1918 Ewers was finally arrested as an enemy agent and eventually sent to Fort Oglethorpe internment camp in Georgia (POW #1587). The conditions in the camp were good, but rather hard on the almost 50 year-old Ewers. He especially suffered from having no access to drugs and little access to alcohol.

In November 1918 the hostilities of WWI ceased. Ewers would not be released from custody until August 1919, however, and then he was only paroled. He finally received permission to leave the U.S. in the summer of 1920.

Ewers returned to a Germany in economic and political chaos. He was at once beset by legal and emotional claims made on him by his first wife. The financial costs of these claims would make life difficult for him for the next ten years or so.

Toward the end of 1920 *Vampir* was published by Müller. As the third of the Frank Braun trilogy, it actually marks the end of Ewers' best writing period. In this novel Frank Braun, a German, discovers that he is suffering from a disease– a thirst for blood. His lover, Lotte Lewi, a Jewess, is able to save him by sacrificing her own blood, and hence her life, to him. In the process of doing so she transforms him from a cosmopolitan into a nationalist. This is mirrored in Ewers' own personal development at the time the novel was written.

The philosemitism of *Vampir* had been evolved by Ewers over the years. In 1905 he wrote an essay: "Der Jude ein Pioneer des Deutschtums" (The Jew: A Pioneer of German Culture) and in 1916 he wrote an English-language essay: "Why I am a Philosemite." Probably originally based on the esoteric ideas of Ferdinand Sebaldt, Ewers developed the concept of a German-Jewish "cultural-nation." He felt that the Jews were the only race equal to the Germanic (i.e. Germans, English and Scandinavians). He even put forward the idea that there was an almost "chemical attraction" between members of the Jewish and German races. These writings were noted by antisemitic philosophers such as Adolf Bartels and Theodor Fritsch (*Germanenorden*), who would mount continuing opposition to Ewers in later years.

At least on one level the whole "Frank Braun trilogy" is interpreted by Wilfried Kugel (1992: 428) as a prophecy of the Third Reich. *Der Zauberlehrling* portrays "the establishment of a dictatorship of religious

[12]

madness," while *Alraune* introduces the idea of the "breeding of a new man." In this context then, *Vampir* is a prediction of the destruction of the Jews as human sacrifices. Ewers was, after all, described in his younger days as a "talented medium"!

V. New Beginnings
—and the Beginning of the End
(1921-1930)

From Cosmopolitan to Nationalist

The experience of the war – both psychologically and physically – had taken its toll on Ewers. Germany was in a downward spiral economically, which affected the writer's prospect for creative work. But he was determined to pick up where he left off, and from his first post-war effort it is easy to see his ego was still firmly intact.

Friedrich von Schiller (1759-1805), together with Johann Wolfgang von Goethe, is one of the demigods of German letters. His work had long since formed a canon of German *Klassizismus*. Schiller had left a work, *Der Geisterseher* (The Visionary) as an unfinished fragment. Ewers undertook the bold, even impudent, idea that he could "collaborate" with Schiller and "finish" the Classical master's fragment. The resulting work was published in 1922 by Müller and caused a storm of controversy among critics and Germanists. The same year work was completed on another collection of short stories: *Nachtmahr* which contained "The Execution of Damiens."

When Ewers left New York he was undecided as to whether he should marry the wealthy Adéle Lewisohn or the young pretty singer Josephine Bumiller. He carried out a regular correspondence with Josephine who had to remain in the U.S. due to health problems. His letters to her from this time contain numerous references to American comic book and cartoon characters which Ewers had come to love while in America. By February 1921 Josephine was in Berlin and she and HHE were married on 15 October of that year.

Immediately after the marriage, however, HHE headed out on a 34 city tour of his "Religion of Satan" lecture, which would keep him on the road until December. From the beginning there were problems in the Ewers' marriage. Josephine always (rightfully) suspected Hanns of having affairs– but the often homosexual nature of these liaisons were difficult for her to understand. After approximately two years of marriage Hanns and Josephine ceased having sexual relations. The reason for this recurring pattern in Ewers' marriages are complex, but certainly his intimate relationship with his male secretaries, Rolf Bongs and Bruno Jahn, cannot have helped matters. Josephine tended to blame Ewers for holding her back in her singing career– even though he paid for her singing lessons and outwardly supported her in her endeavors.

The chaotic political and economic situation in Germany during the 1920s is reflected in Ewers' own search for a political identity. Previously he had been uninterested in partisan politics, but the times increasingly seemed to demand a more partisan approach. At first Ewers gravitated in the direction of his old dream of a German-Jewish *Kulturnation*. He took up his relationship with Walther Rathenau, with whom he had become acquainted in 1911. He and Rathenau, who was a Jewish industrialist,

[13]

politician, homosexual – and German patriot – exchanged ideas in correspondence. Rathenau was named Foreign Minister of the Weimar Republic in February 1922, after having served as the Minister for the Reconstruction of Germany. On 24 June 1922 Rathenau was assassinated by agents of the antisemitic "Organisation Consul," a division of the esoteric *Germanenorden.*

Ewers' reaction to the murder of Rathenau was something other than one might expect. Without understanding the antisemitic intentions of the assassins, Ewers seemed to have been awakened to their nationalist motivations and to some understanding of why they despised Rathenau and the Weimar Republic. However, Ewers never gave up his philosemitic attitudes – even after he joined the Nazis – which would cause him problems in the years to come. From this time forward Ewers became increasingly nationalistic in his politics. The German economy continued to suffer, his home town of Düsseldorf was occupied by French and Belgian troops– all as a result of the Treaty of Versailles. In April 1925 Ewers voted for the conservative Paul von Hindenburg (1847-1934) for president– which was the first time he had ever voted in his life. At the time Ewers was hoping for a return of the Kaiser from exile in Holland.

To this political situation was added the fact that his old friend, Ernst Hanfstaengl, had been back in Germany since the summer of 1921 working tirelessly for the fledgling National Socialist German Workers' Party (NSDAP) and its leader, Adolf Hitler. Through this personal connection Ewers began making contacts among the National Socialists as early as 1921– and by 1923 he was collecting material from among the young men of the *Freikorps*/Storm Troopers for his novel *Reiter in deutscher Nacht* (*Rider of the Night*) [1932]. Circumstantial evidence shows that Ewers even played some supporting role in the attempted Putsch by Hitler on 9 November 1923.

In the mid-1920s the situation in Germany began to look better and Ewers found more time and energy to devote to various projects. These included a popularized scientific book about the life of ants *Ameisen* (1925), a romantic opera *Iva's Tower*, the first German musical *Das Mädchen von Alaska*, and a new filming of his film script *The Student of Prague* (1926). Curiously, a young friend of the Ewers' family named Horst Wessel appeared as a student extra in the film.

On 18 July 1926 "Mother Maria" Ewers died at the age of 87. She had been ill for some time and Hanns travelled to Düsseldorf to visit her often in the time leading up to her death. However, at the time of her actual passing away Ewers was on Capri. Frau Ewers' explicit wish was to be cremated as soon as possible, so HHE could not be in Düsseldorf at her services. She also explicitly asked that her children not be called for any funeral. Her ashes were interred in her husband's grave in the Nordfriedhof. Ewers only regretted not being able to prevent churchmen from being present at her services. In an obituary written by family friend Herbert Eulenberg, he poetically describes how he imagined that the smoke rising from the crematorium where Maria was being cremated turned into the shape of a broom– on which Mother Ewers would ride off to a Walpurgisnacht celebration on the Blocksberg!

Ewers had always been interested in the concept of androgyny. His own bisexuality was but one manifestation of this. He thought of himself as having an androgynous soul– which found expression in his physical sex-life. He explored the idea of psychological androgyny in his story "Der Tod des Barons Jesus von Friedel" (1908). However, advances in medical science being made in the 1920s, along with legal reforms, began to make surgical and hormonal transformation of individuals from one gender to the other possible for the first time. Ewers was fascinated with this, investigated the medical cases, and from his research wrote a new novel– *Fundvogel* (1928), about such a sexual transformation. For this book Ewers produced the first filmed advertisement for a book. The film is now lost, but notes for its production survive.

Since his cabaret days at the turn of the century Ewers had been acquainted with some of the leading researchers and pioneers in the emerging field of *Sexualwissenschaft* (sexology) – such as Magnus Hirschfeld and Albert Eulenburg. Both Hirschfeld and Eulenburg founded a journal for the study of sexuality and were involved with the "Medical Society for Sexology and Eugenics" headquartered in Berlin. Ewers based the character of Dr. Magnus in *Fundvogel* on Hirschfeld, who was active in trying to get laws against homosexuality repealed in Germany. The artist, Ewers and the scientist, Hirschfeld, collaborated on the three volumes of *Liebe im Orient* (Love in the East) [1929], for which Ewers wrote introductions. These volumes were translations of Hindu and Arabic sex-manuals. Ewers hoped to be able to inspire more "art" in the practice of erotic techniques.

In 1928 Ewers became very ill. He was diagnosed with polyneuritis– an inflammatory disease of the peripheral nervous system. This was, no doubt, the effect of chronic alcoholism and drug usage on his 57 year-old body. About the same time he and Josephine separated for good. Although they would remain married, because she would not give him a divorce, until Ewers' death in 1943. All of these events left Ewers extremely depressed and he even contemplated suicide during the latter part of 1929 and the beginning of 1930. On top of this he was even suspected by some in the rash of murder of women and children then taking place in Düsseldorf. Investigations proved that Ewers could have had nothing to do with these killings. (The murders were committed by Peter Kürten – the so-called vampire of Düsseldorf – who was arrested in May 1930 and executed in July 1931.)

VI. A Ride into the Night
—Involvement with National Socialism and Death—
(1931-1943)

In the midst of Ewers' life-crises of the late 1920s and early 1930s, he began to make ties with the Nazis– a move which would on the one hand prolong his life, but at the same time seal the fate of his creative career. His final years were marked by a continual pattern of his offering his services to the National Socialist cause, only to be scorned and rejected by ideologically rigid elements within the Party which knew him well as both a philosemite and writer of intentionally decadent literature– such as *Fundvogel* and *Vampir*. The basic contradiction between the biologically based antisemitism of National Socialist doctrine and Ewers' deeply rooted idea of some esoteric connection between the Germans and Jews made his acceptance as a propagandist for the NSDAP all but impossible.

[15]

Ewers had been a member of the right-wing and monarchist DNVP (Deutschnationale Volkspartei = German-National People's Party) since the mid 1920s. He had also maintained close personal relations with his old friend "Putzi" Hanfstaengl, who was an essential operative for the National Socialists. In the late 1920s also, Ewers increasingly began to socialize with young men belonging to the paramilitary *Freikorps* movement and the S. A. (*Sturmabteilung*) of the NSDAP. His circle included the young S.A.-man Horst Wessel, who was to be shot by an assassin's bullet on 23 February 1930, and die shortly thereafter. In connection with this circle he researched and wrote a novel: *Reiter in deutscher Nacht*. This novel was finished in the spring of 1931, and began to be serialized in a periodical in September. At once NS-ideologues found fault with it– chiefly for elements which portrayed the right-wing protagonist in less than glowing terms morally. The book itself is a testament to the transformation of the cosmopolitan, citizen of the world, Ewers, into a nationalist. According to a theory made explicit in the book, when things are going well for a people the best among them feel cosmopolitan, but if things go badly then only the worst elements in society feel that way. (Kugel 1992: 299) Many National Socialists, and other nationalists, were impressed by the book, but the "politically correct" ideologues found only fault with it.

A number of factors led to HHE becoming a member of the NSDAP itself. This happened in the fall of 1931. The Party was gaining momentum for its assumption of power in the first month of 1933. In October the NSDAP absorbed the DNVP, to which Ewers belonged. Ewers' own personal contacts with Party members had increased since the publication of *Reiter in deutscher Nacht*.

Accounts differ as to the exact circumstances of Ewers' induction into the National Socialist Party. (Kugel 1992: 302-309) It appears that Ewers was invited by Hanfstaengl to be inducted into the Party by Hitler himself on Ewers' 60th birthday, i.e. 3 November 1931. Also present were Rudolf Hess and S. A.-chief Ernst Röhm. It is likely that Ewers' "celebrity status" interested Hitler and other NS-leaders, and it is also true that Hitler had been an admirer of the writer's work for years. However, ideological opposition to Ewers from other corners was unrelenting.

At the meeting in which Hitler inducted Ewers into the NSDAP, the idea was expressed (most likely by S.A.-chief Röhm) that Ewers should write a novel about the S.A. martyr Horst Wessel. Röhm had been a friend of Ewers since perhaps as early as 1923. Wessel had become a quasi-religious martyr to the cause of National Socialism since his death in 1930. In fact the circumstances of his death remain somewhat mysterious: perhaps he was killed by a criminal rival, or assassinated by the Communists, or even perhaps liquidated by the Nazis themselves. He is credited with writing a marching song which bears his name and which became the anthem of the NSDAP.

Ewers researched the book on Wessel and finished the manuscript in the summer of 1932. There was pressure from Wessel's family to make the subject of the book more upstanding morally than he appears to have been in real life. (Wessel lived with a girl-friend who was a prostitute.) Ewers was forced to make changes in the text. It is noteworthy that even in its final version the book is pointedly lacking in antisemitic sentiments. The novel finally appeared at the end of 1932.

The increased attention the novel *Horst Wessel*, and subsequent film based on it, brought Ewers in NS-circles continued to lead to resistance to him at higher and higher levels. He was regularly attacked in the press– from both right and left-wing perspectives. But his connections at the highest level of the Party continued to protect him– at least temporarily.

Ewers and Hanussen

The times were dangerous– especially for men such as HHE. He used many tricks to stay ahead of his detractors. There was another man in Berlin at the time who was an even bolder trickster– a stage hypnotist and astrologer calling himself Erik Jan Hanussen. Hanussen was actually a Viennese Jew, born Herschmann Steinschneider (1889-1933).

Hanussen had built up a sizable following as a performer of stage magic and hypnotism, as well as through private astrological consultations. He had been an early supporter of the Nazis, and especially of the S.A., which he in part financed. But it was probably Hanussen's demonstrated ability to manipulate crowds that was of greatest interest to Hitler himself. Some have speculated that Hitler actually consulted Hanussen on techniques for the hypnotic manipulation of crowds.

Ewers and Hanussen may have become acquainted in the 1920s in Berlin as Hanussen plied his hypnotic trade in cabaret acts. Later on both ran in the same circles among members of the S.A., and socialized at Hitler's Berlin headquarters at the Hotel Kaiserhof. Hanussen was secretly known in S.A. circles as a provider of erotic entertainment, especially orgies on his yacht "Ursel IV" which sailed the lakes in and around Berlin. He supplied willing women and boys for his special guests. But all this was apparently understood in some esoteric context by Hanussen himself– as Bruno Frei wrote in 1934: "Hanussen showed himself to be inexhaustible in the invention of games of love. He called this a celebration of the Indian Goddess of Love, Sarasvati, according to the Aryan service to Shakti by Shiva. In holy ecstasy they worshipped the lingam, the divine phallus. Hanussen portrayed himself as a yogin of the Gods, a conjuror of the lord, a priest of the diabolical ritual."(See Kugel [1992, p. 336.)

Despite Hanussen's attempt to disguise his genealogy and in spite of his relationship with Hitler, his true heritage was soon discovered and shortly after the rise to power by the Nazis Hanussen was arrested and secretly executed 24 March 1933. Ewers' enemies in the NSDAP spread rumors concerning "non-Aryan" elements in his family as well.

Ewers Banned

It appears that Ewers became a pawn in a political game between propaganda chief Josef Goebbels and the head of ideological education, Alfred Rosenberg. Rosenberg chided Goebbels for accepting the known decadent author of works such as *Vampir* and *Fundvogel* in his office. Goebbels' best excuse for this was that Hitler had asked Ewers to write the *Horst Wessel* novel. By 1934 the impulse to purge the Party of perceived "decadent" elements had reached a critical juncture. Beginning on 30 June 1934 the Party began a blood-purge against S.A. leadership circles. Publicly Hitler pretended to be outraged by revelations of homosexual conduct within this group– although such behavior had been known and tolerated from the beginning. The time had come to consolidate political power and individuals who might have been useful in the beginning had outlived their usefulness. Ewers' name even appeared on a death-list, but he was at the time in the remote location of Bad Eilsen and his influential friends were able to save him from eventual liquidation.

In the wake of the "Night of the Long Knives" all of Ewers' written works were generally banned, and he was subsequently prohibited from writing for publication. Only *Reiter in deutscher Nacht* escaped the ban. Even *Horst Wessel* was banned *de facto* as permission was never given to reprint it after 1934. Ewers was accused by Goebbels of enriching himself at the expense of the life of Horst Wessel– which is to a degree true as the initial royalties on the book were substantial. Goebbels even brought a legal case against Ewers to recover monies earned– but Hitler intervened and put a stop to the case.

"Putzi" Hanfstaengl fled Germany in March 1937, as it appeared elements in the NSDAP wanted him dead. He ended up in London, and eventually in the U.S., where he acted as an advisor to Franklin Roosevelt during the war.

By 1937 none of Ewers' works were available in Germany and perhaps his best connection to the Party elite had vanished. Inwardly he turned away from National Socialism. Despite his own rather precarious situation Ewers extended what help he could to friends and acquaintances of German-Jewish heritage to help them obtain exit visas and so escape the impending storm.

At about this time Ewers had the foresight to collect much of his literary estate together – manuscripts, prints, photographs, letters, etc. – and sent them in seven boxes to the Düsseldorf City and State Library on 26 March 1938. These documents survived the war intact and are now, along with additional material, in the Heinrich-Heine-Institut, Düsseldorf.

The last love of Ewers' life was Rita Grabowski (1912-1989), whom he met in 1939. He was 68, she 27. Rita was of half-Jewish ancestry and so lived under dangerous circumstances within the Third Reich.

Throughout the last years of life Ewers struggled with authorities and bureaucrats concerning permission to write again and tried to publish what he could– but very little was accomplished. 1942 saw a decline in his physical health as he began to lose weight rapidly and suffer from a chronic cough. Later that year he was diagnosed with tuberculosis. As his health deteriorated he also began to suffer from heart failure. In his last months Rita and his secretary Jenny Guhl kept him company. On 12 June 1943 at 10:15 a.m. Ewers died in his apartment at Cornelius Str. 4a. His last words were reportedly spoken to his secretary: "Jennylein, what an ass I was!" On the same day his boyhood home at Immermannstrasse 22 would be destroyed by allied bombs.

Hanns Heinz Ewers was cremated in Berlin and his ashes sent to Düsseldorf where they were interred together with those of his mother in the Nordfriedhof in that city.

In November 1943 the apartment building at Cornelius Str. was destroyed by bombs as well. Thus were lost many of Ewers own personal papers, library and antiques.

As he died without a recent will, a will from 1928, in which he bequeathed his inheritance to his wife, Josephine, remained valid.

VII. A Final Assessment
The Ideas and Art of Hanns Heinz Ewers

Post-war cultural politics and artistic fashion practically dictated a catastrophic turn in the direction of Ewers' reputation as an artist. An essential focus of this essay has been to put the multifaceted artistry and ideology contained in the life and work of HHE into a more objective perspective.

As an artist who worked in original ways in a wide variety of media Ewers deserves considerable attention as a pioneer. In his own life-time he was often compared to Edgar Allan Poe, who is another whose artistic reputation has suffered from similar considerations of fashion passing for criticism. As Poe might be praised for inventing various *genres* of literature– the science fiction novel or detective story – Ewers should be remembered, if for nothing else, as an innovator in a wide variety of media– the printed word, film, lectures, performed poetry, drama and musical drama.

In the field of the written word – the medium in which he produced the majority of his work – Ewers might be counted as one of the most imitated writers of the century. This despite the fact that he seldom received acknowledgment for the inspiration he provided. His originality perhaps stemmed from the roots of his unusual, complex and conflicted personality. Similar to the 19th century French Decadents, whom he so admired, Ewers could give expression to a deep-seated neurosis and antinomian feelings. Yet more like the English and German Romantics of his own heritage, Ewers exuded a superhuman exultation in these feelings. HHE was one of the true *Neuromantiker**) of the 20th century. He created from within himself a unique synthesis of elements and developed an artistic voice in order to give expression to this synthesis– though, like all true artists, his seeming inability to give *perfect* expression to his ideas was a source of personal torment.

As a film-maker Ewers was a visionary. From his first exposure to film he saw its potential as a tool for the creation of a new level of the Wagnerian *Gesamtkunstwerk* ("total work of art"). Typical of the way in which Ewers' work as been parenthetically dismissed is a passage found in Lotte Eisner's *The Haunted Screen* (p. 39):

> As early as 1913, some writers started campaigning for the *Autorenfilm*, that is, the idea of a film being judged as the work of an author. This is not surprising in a country with so marked a literary bias as Germany. . . . there was . . . Hanns Heinz Ewers, author of strange tales of blood and lust. (Nobody was surprised when this even then over-rated individual turned his hand to the *Blut und Boden* – blood and soil – conception of the Nazis.)

---

*) This word is, in German, loaded with a double-entendre. It can be parsed as *Neu-Romantik*, i.e. Neo-Romantic, or as *Neuro-Mantik*, i.e. "Neuro-Mancy"– the art of eliciting "occult" knowledge from the human nervous system.

Here Ewers is grudgingly given credit for originating the *Autorenfilm* – the idea of creating a script of "literary" merit originally *for the screen* - and not an adaptation from another medium. Certainly, if it were not an objective fact that *The Student of Prague* (1913) was the first of its kind, Ewers' name would have been happily expunged from the cinematic record by the academic fashion police.

But with the printed word and film the media explorations of HHE were far from exhausted. His humorous cabaret act performances, which focused on taboo subjects, even made him a pioneer in the art of "stand-up" comedy. Later, in his more serious phase, the lectures on "The Religion of Satan" must have been more effective as performance art, than as objective information. In many respects HHE was born too soon. His visions of multi-media shows and creative uses of new media technologies was not something that would be fully appreciated until the latter half of the 20th century.

Clearly, both in his own day and subsequently, the *perspective* from which HHE created his material has gone relatively unappreciated. To understand that perspective we have to read his voluminous output for clues to the mystery of his *persona*. By closely reading his works – fiction as well as essays – his perspective can be reconstructed to provide the *Eureka* to the world-view from which his literary production was created. Although that exceeds the limitations of this introduction, I refer the dedicated reader to Dr. Wilfried Kugel's book for a broader summary of themes in Ewers' works.

The World-View of HHE

"I am a king, I am a god. I create. I create a great and strange world."

Ewers' works are thought of as disturbing because he created from a perspective which those subscribing to consensus reality find unnerving. Quite intentionally Ewers left his world-view inexplicit and mysterious. Had he written it, a book developed from his lectures on "The Religion of Satan" might have come as close as possible to such an explicit statement of his world-view. But he rejected the idea of making such an explicit declaration, preferring instead to embed his ideas here and there in his fictive works– with fragments also being represented in essays.

HHE's world-view divides things into two categories – that which is *natural* and that which is *against nature*. The latter he clearly identifies as being "Satanic." But in the natural world, that which is significantly *beautiful* or *great* transcends the confines of what is ugly and small in ordinary nature. He did not necessarily ascribe mankind to a higher category of being. In a letter to Ilna in 1908 he wrote: ". . .and ultimately there is not such a great difference between any old plant and a human being."

Ewers' philosophy can only be fully understood as a philosophy of art, or an artist's philosophy. He lived at a time when the idea of Expressionism held a broad sway in German art. Expressionism presents things not as they appear objectively, but rather as the artist subjectively, and idiosyncratically, sees them. Things appear to be "distorted" because the subjective, inner reality of the artist may be significantly other than that of the average *reader*.

[20]

The *writer* (i.e. active *creator*) of art must be able to withdraw – behind a mask – into an inner, subjective space in order to engender a vision– which he will then *write* upon the world. This process can be done through a variety of media. So for Ewers creativity begins with an *inner thought*– or "dream."

> Deed is nothing– thought is all. Reality is ugly– and to the ugly is denied all right of existence. Dreams are beautiful, and are true because they are beautiful, and therefore I believe dreams as the only reality.
>
> *Edgar Allan Poe*, p. 50

That into which the artist withdraws is the soul or psyche. The psyche is for Ewers an androgynous entity– and so in order to be able to create in a real sense the artist must also become androgynous. Male and female parts blended in order to engender a work in the world. This is the process of artistic creation.

The artistic ego – the self-created self – becomes, and is, something quite apart from the ordinary collection of human-kind. Ewers used a variety of techniques to attain his level of creativity. These included, but were not limited to, the reading and writing of imaginative fiction, travel, interaction with those travelling a similar road, use of drugs, and experimental sexuality (especially bisexuality).

Once the artistic ego has been realized it can truly *create*– independent of the constraints of nature. Ewers ecstatically proclaimed these ideas in 1915 in a letter to his wife:

> And when the most beautiful thing stands right alongside the ugliest thing, the most repulsive, the most disgustingly perverse next to the purest and most holy– then I think I'll take this world! there is nothing – nothing!! – that simply cannot be, which does not exist– and there is nothing that my art can not express, and if it's possible at all, then it's art as well, and the most "individualistic" art, is to sanctify the most repulsive thing and to make the purest thing into that which excites the greatest disgust! whether evil is good – or the good is evil – it's all the same! it's the same on both sides: seen by God or the Devil!

Here we see Ewers expressing a kind of artistic alchemy whereby base things can be made noble, and to prove the independence of the will of the artist, noble things can be rendered base, all according to the will of the creator– the artist.

The true artist creates a subjective reality– marked by beauty and greatness – and from behind his mask, or stage *persona* – he is able to *write* (project) this reality onto the objective universe. This was the magic conceived by Hanns Heinz Ewers.

Ewers was a difficult individual who lived a fascinating life. As an artist he was extremely thoughtful and original. His enormous artistic legacy includes ten novels (one unpublished), 113 short stories (21 unpublished), 15 dramas, 79 essays (22 unpublished), hundreds of poems and numerous fairy-tales, translations, introductions and editions— as well as a couple of dozen films. Woven into this body of work is an underlying mysterious world-view which acts as a matrix for all his individual creations. To penetrate into this mythos would be perhaps even more disturbing than are the tales manifested out of the mythos.

In the end the reputation and regard for HHE will in the future have to rest, as it has for all artists throughout history, on his creativity, originality and technique – on the genius (or lack of it) inherent in his work – and not on the company he kept or the unpopular opinions he might have held, or his "immoral life-style." A hundred years after he began writing seems a good time to begin to view the creation of this disturbing artist with a renewed and more objective eye.

Stephen E. Flowers
Woodharrow 1999

Bibliography for Introduction

Eisner, Lotte. *The Haunted Screen*. Berkeley: University of California Press, 1969.

Ewers, Hanns Heinz. *Edgar Allan Poe*. Berlin/Leipzig: Schuster & Loeffler, 1906.

----------------------. *Das Grauen*. Munich: Müller, 1907.

----------------------. *Die Besessenen*. Munich: Müller, 1908.

----------------------. *Der Zauberlehrling oder die Teufelsjäger*. Munich: Müller, 1909.

----------------------. *Grotesken*. Munich: Müller, 1910.

----------------------. *Alraune*. Munich: Müller, 1911.

----------------------. *Indien und ich*. Munich: Müller, 1911.

----------------------. *Vampir*. Munich: Müller, 1920.

----------------------. *Nachtmahr*. Munich: Müller, 1922.

----------------------. *Fundvogel*. Berlin: Sieben-Stäbe Verlag, 1928.

----------------------. *Reiter in deutscher Nacht*. Stuttgart: Cotta, 1932.

----------------------. *Horst Wessel*. Stuttgart: Cotta, 1932.

Kugel, Wilfried. *Der Unverantwortliche: Das Leben des Hanns Heinz Ewers*. Düsseldorf: Grupello, 1992.

Lovecraft, H. P. *Supernatural Horror in Literature*. In: *Dagon and Other Macabre Tales*. Sauk City: Arkaham House, [1927].

Pauwels, Louis and Bergier, Jacques. *The Morning of the Magicians*. New York: Avon, 1963.

Strange Tales

C.3.3.

»Logos«

To the Memory of Oscar Wilde

Mimes, in the form of God on high,
Mutter and mumble low,
And hither and thither fly;
Mere puppets they, who come and go
At bidding of vast formless things,
That shift the scenery to and fro,
Flapping from out their condor wings
Invisible Woe!

But see, amid the mimic rout
A crawling shape intrude!
A blood-red thing that writhes from out
The scenic solitude!
It writhes! It writhes!

E. A. Poe: "Ligeia"

The Isle of Capri, May 1903

C.3.3.

For about a quarter of an hour I had stared down from the Punta Tragara upon the sea, of course, upon the sun, and upon the rocks. I rose, and turned to leave. A man sitting beside me on the stone bench suddenly clutched me by the arm.

"How do you do, H.H.!" he exclaimed.

"How do you do," I said, looking at him. Surely I knew him, most assuredly I did. But who was he?

"I suppose you don't remember me?" the voice stumbled. The voice, too, I knew, surely! But in a different fashion— flying, soaring, as if gliding in lancers. But now the voice sounded quite sticky and pimping, as though on crutches.

At last:

"Oscar Wilde?"

"Yes," the voice stumbles, "almost! Say C.3.3., that is what the prison has left of Oscar Wilde."

I looked at him. C.3.3. wasn't very much, only a trace of smut, an ugly memory of O.W.

As I was about to hold out my hand to him I thought. Five years ago you refused to give him your hand. That was very stupid of you, and Oscar Wilde laughed when his friend Douglas flew into a passion of anger. If you give your hand today it would seem as if you were giving it to a beggar, to C.3.3.— out of pity. Why tread upon a sick worm?

So I did not give him my hand. I believe Oscar Wilde was grateful to me for this. We walked down the steps without saying anything to each other. I didn't even look at him. It seemed to do him good.

At a cliff I asked: "Up there?"

His laughter crept out of his mouth like legless toads. He moved his head to and fro, very slowly, looked up and mocked:

"C.3.3.?"

Now. This wouldn't do; I laughed. And O.W. was happy that I showed no trace of pity for him.

We went around the hill, sat down upon the rocks, and stared at the Arco.

Suddenly I said: "Years ago I went over this road with the massive Annie Ventnor. And here we met Oscar Wilde. His upper lip rose then, his eyes shone and looked at me, so that my hands twitched and I quickly had to break my cane, not to strike him in the face— At the very place I am sitting again today. Lady Ventnor is dead, and beside me stands C.3.3. It is like a dream."

"Yes," said O.W.

"Like a dream which some stranger dreams of us."

"Yes— what is that you are saying?" Oscar Wilde called out quickly, abruptly, anxiously, visibly excited:

"* * * *Like a dream, which some stranger dreams of us.*"

My lips merely uttered it. I hardly know what I was really thinking.

[29]

Oscar Wilde leapt up. This time his voice again had the old ring of the man whose proud spirit flew so high above the contemporary rabble.

"Beware of ever becoming acquainted with the stranger, not every one may meet him."

I didn't understand him, and was about to ask, but he made a gesture, turned, and walked away. I looked after him.

He stood still, coughed slightly, but did not turn. Slowly, bending forward, limping, almost creeping, he went— this demi-god out of whom the hypocritical carrion vultures of his country had made C.3.3.

Three days later I received a card:

"Oscar Wilde would like to speak with you. He will expect you at eight o'clock in the evening in the Grotta Bouemarina."

I went to the shore and whistled for my boatman. We sailed through the summer evening. In the grotto Oscar Wilde was crouching on a rock. I stepped out of the boat, and sent the boatman away.

"Sit down," said O.W. A last gleam of the evening sun fell into the dark ocean grotto against whose walls the green waters wept and wailed like little children.

I had often been there. I knew perfectly that it was only waves striking against the stones, and yet I could not rid myself of the sensation that it was impaled naked little children wailing for their mothers. Why had O.W. asked me to come to just this place?

He felt, it seemed, my thoughts, and said:

"It reminds me so much of my prison."

He said "my" prison, and his hobbling voice sounded as if it were a dear memory to him.

Then he continued: "You said something the other day— I do not know whether you attached any particular significance to it. You said: 'It is all like a dream which some stranger dreams of us.'"

I wanted to reply, but he would not let me. He continued:

"Tell me— no doubt many shook their heads, when I allowed myself to be imprisoned? They thought why does Oscar Wilde go to prison? Why doesn't he put a bullet through his head?"

"Yes, many probably thought so."

"And you?"

"I thought, he had his reasons, no doubt."

He continued:

"Oscar Wilde was no longer young, he was not of the people, and he was as delicate as some are strong. Oscar Wilde, the finest aristocrat since Villier's death, Oscar Wilde, who made an art of life as none other before him in the three kingdoms. And yet he went to prison, an English one at that, in comparison with which your German prisons are benevolent institutions. He knew that he would be tortured to death, slowly, painfully, gruesomely, and yet he went— and did not kill himself."

"Why then?" I asked. O.W. looked at me. He evidently had wanted me to ask this question.

Slowly:

"You yourself gave the reason the other day, because everything is only a dream which some strange being dreams of us."

I looked at him; he answered my look.

"Yes," he continued, "that was it. I have asked you to come here to explain it to you."

He stared down upon the water and appeared to listen to the gurgling sounds it made. Several times he rubbed with the index finger of the left hand over his knee, as if he were about to draw letters. After a while, without looking up:

"Do you care to hear?"

"Of course."

O.W. breathed deeply several times.

"It wasn't necessary for me to go to prison. On the very first day of the trial a friend had passed me a revolver, the very one with which Cyril Graham killed himself. It was a very beautiful little revolver with a coat of arms and signature of the Duchess of Northumberland set in rubies and chrysoberyls, an admirable little revolver, fit to have been used by Oscar Wilde. When after the session I was led back to prison I played with it for a full hour. I took it to bed with me, placed it beside me, and fell asleep happy in the thought to have a sure friend who could snatch me from the bailiffs at any moment; even should the jury find me guilty, which at that time I believed impossible.

"I had a mad dream that night. Beside me I saw a strange being, a soft, mollucous mass, which appeared to branch out at the top into a grimace. The creature had neither arms nor legs. It seemed like an elongated, roundish head, which might suddenly extrude slimy limbs on all sides if it desired. It had a whitish-green, almost transparent color, which mingled in a thousand lines. And with this thing I talked, I no longer remember about what. Yet momentarily our conversation became agitated. Finally the grimace laughed contemptuously and said:

"'Trot off, it isn't worth while to chat with you.'

"'What?' I replied. 'That's pretty strong! A creature which is nothing but a mad dream figment of mine dares be so impudent.'

"The grimace transformed itself into a broad leer, bowed several times, and chuckled:

"'Well, well, look at him! I am a dream figment of yours? No, my poor friend, the matter is the other way around. I *dream* and you are nothing but a little point in *my* dream.'

"Saying this the thing grinned all the more, it seemed to have become a broad leer. Then it disappeared, and I saw nothing but the broad leer in the air.

"On the next day the presiding judge asked me in reference to Parker:

"'So it pleases you to dine with young persons of the people in the evening?'

"I said:

"'Yes! Certainly much more than to be cross-examined here.'

"At this reply the audience in the courtroom broke out into loud laughter. The court resented this and threatened to have the room cleared on repetition. It was only then that I turned my eyes toward the rear of the room which was open to the public. I was unable to see a single human being. The entire space was occupied by the horrible, malformed creature. The malevolent leer which had tortured me throughout the night spread broadly across the grimace. My hand went to my head. Is it possible that all this is merely a comedy, a harlequin, which the creature dreams.

"In the meantime the court put some question or other to which Travers Humphreys, one of my attorneys, replied. In the rear of the room suppressed laughter sounded again. The grimace seemed to dissolve, and utter gurgling sounds. I closed my eyes, and convulsively kept them shut for a while, and then again looked sharply toward the rear. I now noticed people on the benches; there sat John Lane, my publisher, there Lady Welshbury, and beside her young Holms. But beyond them, in them, above them, spread the mysterious creature. The sleepy laughter seemed to come from it.

"I forced myself to turn my head, and did not look back again. Yet it was impossible for me to follow the proceedings carefully. I always felt the infamous leer in the nape of my neck.

"Then the gentlemen of the jury found me guilty. Four jobbers, five dealers in cotton, flour, or whiskey, two schoolmasters, and one most honorable master butcher sent Oscar Wilde to prison. It was really very droll!"

O.W. stopped and laughed and threw little pebbles into the water.

"Really very droll! The little bits of heads. Do you know that court procedure, every court, is the most democratic and plebeian institution that exists on this earth? Only the ordinary man has a good court, capable of judging him. The judges are far above him, and that is how it should be. But we! I should never have exchanged a word with any one of my judges. Not one of them knew a single line of my works. Why should he? He would not have understood it anyhow. And these good citizens, these impoverished little worms, creeping on the earth, by law and authority were allowed to send Oscar Wilde to prison. Most droll, indeed!

"It was solely this thought which occupied me, when I was back in my cell. I played with it, composed variations on it, I made half a dozen aphorisms of it, each one of which was worth more than the lives of all the jurymen in England throughout the entire glorious reign of our virtuous queen. And much amused and quite content I fell asleep. My aphorisms were excellent, they really were.

"People say that waking hours are a torture and sleep is a blessing for some one just condemned to several years' imprisonment. It was just the opposite with me. Hardly had I fallen asleep before the intolerable grimace stood beside me.

"'You,' it said to me and grinned with keen delight, 'you are a very merry dream.'

"'Trot off,' I said, 'you bore me. I cannot bear such conceited dream grimaces.'

"'Still the same delusion,' the creature laughed good-naturedly. 'You are my dream!'

"'And I am telling you, that the reverse is the case,' I screamed.

"'You are mistaken, that is all,' said the grimace.

"Now a long explanation began in which each of us tried to convince the other. The creature refuted all of my reasons. The more excited I became the more it laughed in silent self-satisfaction.

"'If I am your dream,' I cried, 'how does it happen that you are talking with me in English?'

"'What am I talking with you?'

"English! My language!' I said triumphantly. "And that proves—'

"'Have you lost your wits?' laughed the grimace. 'I talk your language? You are speaking my language— of course! Pay close attention.'

"It was only now that I noticed that we were not conversing in English. We were speaking an idiom which I didn't know and yet understood and used perfectly. It certainly had no affinity with English, or any other language of this earth.

"'Do you see now, that you were wrong?' the round creature grinned.

"I did not reply, and for several minutes there was silence.

"Then it spoke again:

"'You have a pretty little revolver. Take it. I would love to dream how you kill yourself. It would be very gay.'

"'I will not do anything of the sort!' I said, took the revolver, and hurled it backward into the corner.

"'Better think it over!' said the grimace, and turned around and brought back the revolver. 'It is a very pretty weapon,' it said, and again placed it beside me on the bed.

"'Kill yourself if you wish!' I roared in anger, turned over, and put my fingers in my ears. But it was of no avail. I understood every word as before. Throughout the entire night the grimace stayed with me. It laughed and grinned and begged me that I should finally kill myself.

"When I awoke the guard was just opening the door to bring my breakfast. Wildly I leapt from the bed and put the revolver in his hand.

"'Take this thing away, quickly, quickly! The dream grimace must not carry its point.'

"* * * On the next night the grimace came again.

"'It is too bad,' it said, 'that you have given away your pretty little revolver. But you might hang yourself by your suspenders. That too, would be gay.'

"In the morning I tore and gnawed my suspenders into tiny pieces with endless trouble.

"So I went to prison. To take up the struggle with the world's stupidity, to play the hero and martyr before wretched little tortures— Oscar Wilde had no ambition for that. He lived as he always had lived, or rather, he did not live. But there was a new stimulus and a new struggle, a struggle the like of which hardly any other mortal went through. I wanted to live in order to show a dream grimace that I was alive; to prove by my existence the non-existence of another being.

"The Carthaginians had a torture— the breaking of bones. The condemned man was bound to a stake. The executioner then broke the first joint of the little finger of his right hand and went on. After exactly an hour he returned to break the little toe of the delinquent's left foot. And after another hour he broke the first joint of the little finger of the left hand, and after another hour the right little toe. Immediately in front of the prisoner was a large hour glass, so he could mark the time himself. When the last grains of sand had run out, he knew that another hour was run, that now the man would come to break his thumb. And then the large toe— and the middle finger, and the ring finger— limb after limb, very carefully, so that not too much might go to pieces at one time. And then the bridge of the nose and the lower arm and the thigh, every bone nicely by itself. It was a somewhat circumstantial procedure, lasting several days, until the executioner broke the spine.

"Today a different method is employed, a better one. They take a longer time, and this is the height of art in all torture. You see, my limbs are whole, and yet everything of me and in me is broken, body and soul. It needed two years in Reading Gaol to break Oscar Wilde.

"They knew their art well there. C.3.3. is a good advertisement for them.

"I am telling you this to show that my struggle was not quite easy. All the chances really were in favor of the grimace. It came to me every night, and frequently enough during the day. It so much wanted to dream that I kill myself, and always suggested new ways to me.

"After a year its visits grew less frequent.

""'You are beginning to bore me,' it said one night, 'you no longer deserve to play a principal role in my dreams. There are other things which are much gayer. I think I am slowly forgetting you.'

"* * * And you see, I also believe that it is forgetting me slowly. Now and then it still dreams of me for a moment, but I feel how my life, this dream-life, slowly glides away. I am not ill, but my vital force grows less and less. *The beast no longer wants to dream of me!* Soon it will have quite forgotten me, then I shall go out.'

Oscar Wilde leapt up. He supported himself against the wall of rock, his knees trembled, his tired eyes protruded far from their deep caverns.

"There, there it is!" he cried.

"Where?"

"There, down there!"

He pointed with his finger. The greenish-blue water surged over a rounded rock, and slowly flooded back. And actually, in this deep half-darkness the wet stone showed a face— a malevolent good-natured grimace with a broad leer over the entire mouth.

"A rock!"

"Yes, of course, a rock! Do you imagine I do not see that? But it is the grimace nonetheless. It can give its form to any object it desires. See how it laughs."

It did laugh, there was no denying it. And I had to admit it. The rock with the water slowly running from it looked exactly like the creature which Oscar Wilde had described to me, exactly like it.

"You may believe me," said Oscar Wilde as the fisherman rowed us back to the boat, "you may believe me, there is no room for doubt. Give up your magnificent thoughts of humanity. Human life and all the history of the world is nothing else but a dream, which some absurd creature dreams of us."

The Water-Corpse

Mir ist mîn êrriu rede
enmittenzwei geslagen

Walter. v. d. Vogelweide

Berlin, Dec. 1904

The Water-Corpse

Once upon a time there was a young man who looked at the world with eyes slightly different from those of other people living around him. At noon-time he dreamed and at midnight he let his thoughts run free— thoughts that others sitting around him found quite foolish. They called him a fool; he, however, believed himself to be a poet.

When they laughed at his verses, he would laugh along with them. Because then they might not notice just how much it hurt him.

It hurt him so badly that he once went out along the Rhine, which was tossing its muddy high March water, slapping up against the old customs house.

It was actually only by coincidence that he didn't jump in the river that day. It was really only because he met some friend who said to him:

"Come on along to the tavern!"

In the tavern he sat and drank, first with his friend Josephshöfer, and after that with Maximi Grünhäuser and Foster Kirchenstück. All of a sudden a few lines of poetry came to him and he wrote them down on the wine list with a pencil. But when his good colleagues the junior barrister, the assistant judges, the prosecuting attorneys, and the two county court judges came, he read them out loud:

> "...in the pond of goldfish
> Once swam a blanch and bluish
> And slimy-soft water-corpse."

Water-corpse, slimy, squish.

He told about how the goldfish talked about the corpse, and indulged in speculations about it, how one would say something good, and another something bad about it. He went on:

> But an old, centenarian boy
> Rejoiced over God's good gift,
> He spoke not a word. He ate and ate,
> Such that he forgot the world up above
> And thought: "Not often is there in the pond
> Such a nice, slimy soft
> And bluish blanch water-corpse.

You should have seen the good colleagues then! The junior barristers, and the assistant judge, the prosecuting attorney and the two county court judges!

"Man!" the state's attorney said. "I hope you don't think badly of me because I was always making fun of you before! You're a genius, you'll make a name for yourself yet!"

"Gweat," cried the blond county court judge, "gweat! That comes fwom twaining in the law! Fwom such stuff awe Goethes made!"

"Habemus poetem!" the butterball of a junior barrister rejoiced. And all of them told him he was a poet, a real poet, a unique poet, a poet "fit" for our time and "up to date."

The young man laughed and jostled those around him because he thought they were just playing a joke on him. But when he saw they were really serious, he left the tavern. At that moment he was sober— so sober in fact that he almost went back to the Rhine. So that's the way it was to be: when he felt like a poet, they yelled that he was a fool; now when he plays the fool, they declare him to be a poet.

Of course, the state's attorney was right: The young man was to make a name for himself. On billboards and placards, on signs large and small— everywhere his verses would be seen. Then his mouth got round, like that of a fish and he puckered up, like he thought a goldfish might pucker, and would begin:

"In the pond of goldfish
Once swam a blanch and bluish
And slimy-soft water corpse."
"In the pond of goldfish
Once swam a blanch and bluish
And slimy-soft water corpse."

Water-corpse, slimy, squish

It's a sure thing that his good colleagues hadn't said all that much— the junior barrister and the assistant judge, both of the state judges and the prosecuting attorney. It's well known how much he was recognized and praised and how people cheered and applauded him in every German city. And since actors and speakers, as well as lecturers, snatched up his poetry everywhere his fame spread even further. And that composers set it to music and had it sung and tried to intensify the smacking of the goldfish by means of natural sounds.

All that is well-known.—

The young man thought: "That's really fine. Just let them cheer and clap and acclaim as great poetry your verses inspired in a tipsy mood. Just let them! — You'll get known, known everywhere, and after that you'll easily be able to succeed with what you can really do." Or so the young man thought.

And so he revealed to the delighted ears of many thousands the story of the blanch and bluish and slimy-soft water corpse, and didn't tell anyone how revolting all of it was to him. He bit his lip, first made a kind expression and then puckered up in the goldfish-face.

The young man forgot that the highest virtue of the German is his faithfulness. And that he expected from poets above all else to be faithful: They were to sing and sing again and again in the same tones in which they first sang, and not anything else. If they sing something else, then it is false and unfaithful and reprehensible and the German disdains it.

And just as this young man was dreaming of asphodels, and of orchids, of yellow mallows and tall chestnut blossoms, people turned their backs and laughed at him.

Not everywhere. The fashionable world is so civilized— right from the nursery onward. When he was recently to perform at a place on the Ringstrasse, following the court opera singer and the long haired composer, and was to speak with a tired voice of the souls of flowers, people didn't laugh. The people even applauded and thought it all very nice. The people are just that cultured there. But the young man nevertheless felt that the ladies and gentlemen were bored, and was not surprised when one of them cried.

"The water-corpse!"

He didn't want to do it; until the lady of the house insisted:

"Yes, please, Herr Doktor, the water-corpse!"

He sighed, bit his lip, made the goldfish-face and performed his horrible story for the threethousand twohundred and twenty-eighth time. He almost choked on it.

But the ladies and gentlemen applauded and cheered him. Then he saw an old lady had lept up from her easy-chair — screamed sharply and hoarsely — and then sank back down into her seat.

The men brought Eau de Cologne and washed the forehead and temples of the unconscious lady. But the young man knelt at her feet and kissed her hand: He felt, as if she were his mother, and loved her.

As her eyes opened, he was the first person she saw. She pulled her hand away as if he were an unclean animal, and screamed:

"Get him away!"

He then jumped up and ran off. Back in the corner of the hall he sat down and rested his head in his hands. While they led the old lady down the stairs to her couch. He sat there: He knew everything exactly, very exactly before, before any body had said a word to him.

It was an expectation fulfilled, he had always felt it would eventually have to come to this.

And when they came to him with their "Terrible!"

— "Really frightful!" — with their "Tragedy of life!" and "Cruel accident!" — he was really not surprised.

"I already know," he said. "The old lady lost her only son a few years ago; he drowned in the lake, and it was only after some months that they found the horrible unrecognizable corpse. And she, the mother herself, had to identify the body —?"

They nodded. Then the young man straightened himself up. He almost screamed:

"And to amuse you asses, I — what a fool — caused an unfortunate mother all this pain! So, laugh if you will! Go on, laugh!"

He made the goldfish-face and smacked:

"In the pond of goldfish
Once swam a blanch and bluish
And slimy-soft water-corpse."

But this time they didn't laugh, they were much too civilized for that.

The White Maiden

A mi me gusta el blanco!
Viva el blanco, muera el negro!
Porque el negro es muy triste
Yo soy allegre! Yo no lo quiero!
                    Andalusian copula

Naples, May 1907

The White Maiden

Donald McLean was waiting for him in the café. When Lothar entered, he cried:

"At last! I thought you would never come."

Lothar sat down, aimlessly stirring the lemonade the girl brought him.

"What is it?" he asked.

McLean leaned slightly forward.

"It should interest you," he said. "You are studying the transformations of Aphrodite, are you not? Well, there may be a chance of your seeing the foam-born goddess in a new guise."

Lothar yawned.

"Ah, really?"

"Really!" said McLean.

"Just a moment, please," Lothar proceeded. "Venus is Proteus' true daughter, but I flatter myself I know all her disguises. For more than a year I was in Bombay with Klaus Petersen—"

"Well?" asked the Scotchman.

"Well? Obviously you don't know Klaus Petersen? *Herr* Klaus from Hamburg is a talented man; perhaps a genius! The *Maréchal* Gilles de Rais was a charlatan compared to him!"

Donald McLean shrugged his shoulders.

"That isn't the only art!"

"Certainly not! But, just wait. Oscar Wilde was a good friend of mine, as you know, and I knew Inez Seckel for many years. Each one of these names ought to give you a wealth of sensations!"

"Not all of them," the painter remarked.

"Not all of them?" Lothar drummed on the table. "But the best, no doubt! In short: I know the Venus who changes into Eros; I know her when she clothes herself in furs and swings the scourge. I know Venus as a Sphinx, thrusting her blood-thirsty claws into the flesh of children. I know Venus when she wallows lustfully in decay. And I know the black love-goddess who, at Satan's masses, squirts the priest's revolting sacrifice over the body of a virgin. Laurette Dumont took me into her private zoo. I know what few others know; the rare delights that Sodom offers! More than that. In Geneva I fathomed lady Kathlin McMurdoch's secret, of which no other living person was aware! I know the vilest Venus— or shall I say the purest?— the one which weds man to the flower. Do you still believe that Venus could choose a mask unknown to me?"

McLean slowly sipped his *strega*.

"I promise you nothing," he said. "I only know that the Duke Ettore Aldobrandini has been in Naples again these last three days. I met him yesterday on the Toledo."

"I should be glad to meet him," Lothar replied. "I have heard of him often enough. He is said to be one of the few men who knows how to make of his life a work of art,— and has the means to do it."

"I don't believe they have exaggerated," the Scotch painter continued. "You can convince yourself; the day after tomorrow the Duke is giving a reception at which I shall be glad to introduce you."

"Thank you," Lothar replied.

The Scotchman laughed.

"Aldobrandini was in excellent spirits when I met him. Besides, the extraordinary hour for which he invited me — five o'clock in the afternoon — indicates that something unusual is in the air! For this reason I believe that the Duke has a special surprise for his friends; if this be the case, you may rest assured that we shall see something unheard of. The Duke never follows the trodden path."

"Let's hope that you are right!" Lothar sighed. "In that case, I shall have the pleasure of calling for you at your home the day after tomorrow?"

"LARGO SAN DOMENICO!" McLean instructed the driver. "Palazzo Corigliano!"

The two men mounted the broad baroque stairway; an English butler led them into the salon. They found seven or eight gentlemen, all in full dress; the only exception was a priest in a violet soutane.

McLean introduced his friend to the Duke, who shook hands with him.

"Thank you for coming," he said with a charming smile. "I hope you won't be entirely disappointed."

He bowed and, in a somewhat louder voice, addressed all those present.

"Gentlemen!" he said. "I beg your indulgence for having disturbed you at such an unusual hour. But it is a case of necessity; unfortunately, the little doe that I shall have the honor of presenting to you today comes from a very good, respectable family. She can come to me only under great difficulties, and must positively be home by half past six, so that her father and mother and the English governess will not notice her absence. These, gentlemen, are things which a cavalier has to reckon with! And now I shall ask you to excuse me for a few minutes, as I still have a few preparations to make. In the meantime I hope you will partake of a little refreshment."

The Duke motioned to his servant, bowed again and left the room.

A gentlemen with huge Victor-Emanuel mustachios approached Lothar. It was di Nardis, the political editor of the "Pungolo," who wrote under the pseudonym "Fuoco."

"I wager we shall witness an Arabian joke," he laughed. "The Duke has just returned from Bagdad."

The priest shook his head.

"No, Don Goffredo," he said, "we shall see a piece of Italian Renaissance. For the last half year the Duke has been studying Valdomini's secret history of the Borgias, loaned to him after long entreaties by the director of the royal archives in Severino e Sosio."

"Well, we shall see," answered McLean. "Will you give me, meanwhile, the racing tips, which you promised me?"

The editor drew out a notebook and entered into a long conversation on the turf with the Scottish painter and the priest. Lothar slowly sipped orange ice from a crystal plate. He studied the pretty golden spoon which bore the arms of the Aldobrandinis; a ragged cross-beam surrounded by six stars.

After half an hour a servant drew back the curtains.

"The Duke prays you to follow me," he announced. He led the guests through two small rooms, then opened a double door, had them all pass through it, and quickly shut it behind them. They found themselves in a spacious, extremely long hall, sparingly lighted. The floor was covered with a wine-red rug, and the doors and windows were hung with heavy curtains of the same hue, in which the ceiling, too, was painted. The walls, absolutely bare, were also overlaid with wine-red cloth; and the same material covered the few armchairs, sofas and lounges which stood around the room. The far end of the room was in complete darkness; it was barely possible to distinguish a grand piano decorated with red damask.

"Please be seated, gentlemen," cried the Duke. He himself took a chair and the others followed suit. Quickly the servants moved from one wall-bracket to the other, extinguishing the few burning candles.

When the room was in utter darkness, a soft chord from the piano became audible. Softly, a sequence of moving cadences floated through the hall.

"Palestrina," the priest murmured under his breath. "You see that you were wrong with your Arabian idea, Don Goffredo."

"Well," the editor answered in the same tone, "was yours a happier guess when you thought of Cesare Borgia?"

They recognized, incidentally, that the piano was an old spinet. The simple chords awoke a strange sensation in Lothar, but he was unable to determine exactly what it was. At any rate, it was something he had not felt for a long time.

Di Nardis leaned toward him so closely that his mustachio tickled Lothar's cheek.

"I have it!" he whispered. "I did not know that I could still be so ingenious."

Lothar felt that he was right.

After a while the quiet servant lit two candles. A pale, almost uncanny sheen fell upon the hall.

The music played on.

"And yet," Lothar whispered to his neighbor, "there is a curious cruelty in these tones. I might say, an innocent cruelty."

Again the quiet servant lit a few candles. Lothar stared into the red glow which filled the entire room like a mist.

The blood-color almost stifled him. His soul clung to the tones which awoke in him the sensation of a faint shimmering white. But the red obtruded itself, gained the upper hand; always new candles were lit by the quiet servant.

"This is unbearable," Lothar heard the editor hiss through his teeth.

Now the hall was half lit. The red seemed to cover everything with a stifling pall, and the white of the innocent music became ever fainter — fainter —

Then, from behind the spinet, emerged a figure; a young girl wrapped in a great white shroud. Slowly she walked to the middle of the hall, a shining white cloud in the red glow.

There the maiden stopped. She spread her arms so that the shroud fell to the floor. Like silent swans the cloth kissed her feet, but the white of her body shone more brightly still.

Lothar leaned back and involuntarily raised his hands to his eyes.

[45]

"It almost blinds you," he breathed.

She was a young, adolescent girl, with the charming unripeness of a bud— a sovereign innocence that needed no protection; and, at the same time, sure promise that called forth a boundless wish for fulfillment. Her blue-black hair, parted in the middle, waved over temples and ears, and was caught in a heavy knot at the back. The big black eyes looked straight at the men, indifferently, without seeing anyone. They seemed to smile like her lips: a strange unconscious smile of cruelest innocence.

And the gleaming white flesh shone so brightly that all the red about her appeared to recede. The music seemed to throb with exultation.

Only now did Lothar notice that the girl carried a snow-white dove on her hand. She bent her head slightly and raised her arm, and the white dove stretched its little head.

And the pigeon kissed the white maiden. She caressed it, stroked its head, and pressed the bird gently to her bosom. The white dove lifted its wings a little and cuddled close, closer to the gleaming flesh.

"Blessed dove!" whispered the priest.

And then, with a sudden quick motion, the white maiden lifted the pigeon with both hands high above her head. She leaned far back and, with a strong jerk, tore the dove in two. The red blood trickled down without splattering her face, flowing down in long streams over her shoulders and breast, over the gleaming body of the white maiden.

All around the red mist closed in again; it was as if the white maiden were drowning in a bath of blood. Trembling, anguished, she cowered down. And from all sides the lustful glow crept near; the floor opened like a maw of fire; the frightful red engulfed the white maiden.

The next instant the trap door had closed again. The silent servant tore back the curtains and quickly led the guests back to the reception room.

No one seemed to want to say a word. Silently they took their coats and went downstairs. The Duke had disappeared.

"GENTLEMEN!" said the editor of the "Pungolo" to Lothar and the Scottish painter, when they reached the street. "Will you dine with me on Bertolini's terrace?"

They drove together to the terrace. Silently they drank their champagne; silently they stared down on cruelly beautiful Naples bathed by the last rays of the evening sun in a luminous glow.

The editor took out his notebook and jotted down a few figures.

"Eighteen—blood, four—dove, twenty-one—maiden," he said. "A fine *terno*; I shall try it in the lottery."

From the Diary of an Orange Tree

"O, how many sorcerers, how many sorceresses
Are there among us, who no one knows about!"
Ariosto: Orlando Furioso. Ges. VIII, 1.

Isle of Porquerolles, June 1905

From the Diary of an Orange Tree

If I follow your wishes, my dear Director, and fill out the pages of the notebook you gave me, then you'd believe me that I am doing it only after careful consideration and with well thought-out intentions. For in principle we are just dealing with a struggle between us two, you, the head doctor of this private mental institution, and me, the patient, who was committed here three days ago. The complaint which was the cause of my involuntary committal here — please excuse this student of law who likes to use legal terminology! — charged that "I am '*suffering from the* idée fixé *that I am an orange tree.*'" Now my good Director try to furnish the proof that this is a "delusion of false pretenses" — if you could succeed in convincing me of this, your opinion, then I would be "healed," wouldn't I? If you prove to me that I am a man, like all others, that I was only seized by a malignant monomania due to a number of agitations that unsettled my nerves — just like the many thousands of sick people in all the sanitariums in the world — then with this proof you will have at once delivered me back to the living: the "nervous breakdown" would be instantly eradicated by you.

On the other hand, I have the right, as the defendant, to request the presentation of the factual evidence. The purpose of these lines, my most honored Director, is to convince you of the irrefutability of what I am saying.

You will see that I think quite soberly, every word is quietly weighed. I sincerely regret the scene I made the day before yesterday; it distresses me greatly that my silly behavior disturbed the peace and quiet of your house. You ought to take a lenient view of the earlier excitement, just think, if someone suddenly and deceitfully put you, most honored Director, or some other healthy person, in a mad-house, he wouldn't act much differently than I did. But our hour-long interview of yesterday evening put me completely at ease; I realize my relatives and fraternity brothers merely wanted what was best for me when they brought me here. And it's not just what they "wanted"; I believe it's really for the best. Because if I am successful in convincing a psychiatrist with a high reputation throughout Europe, such as yourself, Herr Director, of the correctness of my assertion, then the greatest skeptic must bow before the so-called "miracle."

You asked me to write as complete an autobiography as possible in this notebook, as well as all my thoughts concerning what you call my *idée fixé*. Of course, I understand, even if you didn't express it, that for you, a responsible servant of science, it all has to do with "getting as accurate a picture as possible of the disease from the mouth of the patient himself." I want to follow your wishes in their smallest details, in the certain conviction, that you, after you have recognized your mistake, will be able to lend me a helpful hand during my evolution into a tree, as I, hour by hour, take on more and more the form of a real tree.

[49]

You will, Herr Director, as you look through my papers, which I know you now have in your possession, find along with my registration for the exam for the doctor's degree in jurisprudence, a detailed *curriculum vitae*, which contains all the external particulars. I can therefore summarize here quite briefly; you will be able to tell from the documents that I am the son of an industrialist from the Rhineland, graduated from the gymnasium when I was 18, absolved my year-long military service obligation in a regiment of the Guards in Berlin, enjoyed my youth as a student of law at various universities, in the meantime took a series of long and short journeys, and finally completed my internship and doctor's exam in Bonn.

All of that, Herr Director, is of just as little interest to you as it is to me. The story that interests us first begins on February 22nd of this past year. On this day — at a Fasching ball — I made the acquaintance of the — at the risk of appearing ridiculous I'll write it anyway — *sorceress*, who transformed me into an orange tree.

It is perhaps necessary to say a few words about the lady, to whom I was introduced at this party. Frau Emy Steenhop made a very remarkable appearance that irresistibly drew the attention of every eye. I will resist describing her charms, you would only want to smile at the portrayal of a lover as an extreme exaggeration. Nevertheless, it is a fact that among my friends and acquaintances there was not one who was not enthralled at first sight, who was not happy for every glance, for every word, she directed toward him.

Lady Emy Steenhop had been living for about two months on Koblenzstrasse in a spacious garden villa, which she had furnished extremely tastefully. She had an open house in which the officers of the royal hussars and the members of the most prestigious corps gathered every evening. It is correct, that no other ladies were present at her place, nevertheless I am convinced, that this was only because Frau Steenhop, as she often laughingly explained, for the life of her couldn't stand the idle chatter of women. Neither did the lady visit any other family in Bonn.

It is understandable that the gossip of the small city was soon concerned with the conspicuous strange lady from out of town, who drove her snow white Mercedes through the streets each day. Soon the most fantastic rumors were circulating by word of mouth about the nocturnal orgies on Koblenzstrasse. The little clerical rag even brought out an absurd article entitled "A Modern Messalina" and whose lead-line — "*Quosque tandem*" — was at least supposed to have indicated the "higher education" of the editor. I can assure you — and I am convinced, that all the gentlemen who ever had the honor to be received by Frau Emy Steenhop — that at no time did anything happen in her house which would offend the strictest social formalities — even in any slight way. A kiss of the hand — that was the only thing the lady would allow her worshippers — and that was allowed to all. Only the short colonel of the hussars had the privilege of being allowed to press his martial moustache on her white forearm. Frau Emy Steenhop had us all on a leash, such that we were as well-behaved as pages and served our lady in an almost chivalrously romantic form.

In spite of this it came to pass that her house was suddenly deserted. I had gone home for my mother's birthday on the 16th of May and when I returned I heard to my surprise that by order of the colonel the officers of the hussar regiment were forbidden to visit the lovely lady's house any more. The members of the corps immediately followed this precedent. I inquired after the reason, my corps brothers informed me that as far as their procedure was concerned the regimental order was authoritative for them as well; it was impossible for corps students to go to a house that had been put off-limits by the regiment of the hussars. In fact both institutions showed consideration for the other, actually, because every year so many members of the corps served with the hussars or belonged to the regiment as reserve officers.

It was said that the reason for the colonel's action was not known, even to the officers themselves it was unknown. Nevertheless it was speculated that it was connected to the sudden disappearance of lieutenant Baron Bohlen— and no one could come up with the slightest reason for this either.

Since Harry von Bohlen was personally close to me, I went that very evening to the barracks of the hussars to try and find out some details. The colonel received me quite kindly, invited me to take a glass of *sekt*, but avoided coming to the point of the visit. When I finally came right out and asked him my question, he quite politely, but very curtly, refused to answer it. I made a final attempt and said:

"Herr Colonel! Your regulations and those of the corps are, of course, binding for your officers and the corps-students. They are not for me. I can, this very day, resign my association and then I will be the master of my own actions."

"Do whatever you want," the colonel answered nonchalantly.

"I only ask you to listen to me patiently for a moment," I went on. "It might not be so hard for any of the others to miss out on going to the house on Koblenzstrasse. They will sometimes recall with some slight regret the nice evenings and ultimately forget them. But I—"

He interrupted me.

"Young man," he cried, "you are the fourth one to give me this speech! Two of my lieutenants and one of your corps-brothers were already in here the day before yesterday. I gave the two lieutenants leave, and they've already left; I also gave your corps-brother the same advice. I can only tell you to do the same. — You must forget, do you hear! — One victim is enough!"

"Well then at least enlighten me as to what's going on, Herr Colonel!" I pressed. "I certainly don't know, and I can't find out anything anywhere. Is Bohlen's disappearance in any way connected with your orders?"

"Yes!" the colonel said.

"What became of him?"

"That I don't know," he answered. "And I'm afraid I'll never know."

I grasped both his hands.

"Tell me what you know!" I demanded, and felt a quiver in my voice which must have forced him to answer. "For God's sake tell me what's become of Bohlen, and why you issued the order."

He pulled away and said:

"My stars, it really seems to be worse with you than with the others!"

He filled both our glasses and slid mine over to me.

"Drink, drink!" he cried.

I poured the champagne down and bowed to him.

"Tell me," he went on, as he looked me over keenly, "weren't you the one who read the poems that time?"

"Yes," I stammered, "but . . ."

[51]

The colonel stroked his moustache.

"That time I was almost jealous of you," he said reflectively; "our nymph allowed you to kiss her hand twice. — Were they your own poems? There were all kinds of flowers mentioned in them."

"Yes, I wrote the poems myself," I responded.

"It was a terrible bunch of nonsense!" he said as if to himself. "Excuse me," he went on out loud, "I don't understand a thing about poetry. It's possible they were very beautiful. The nymph found them to be so."

"But Herr Colonel," I interjected, "what about my poems anyway? You wanted ..."

"I wanted to tell you about something else, of course," he interrupted. "But it's because of the poems that I'm doing it. It's said that people who write poems are dreamers. — I believe, that poor guy, Bohlen, also wrote poems in secret."

"What about Bohlen then?" I pressed.

He paid no attention to the interjection.

"And dreamers," he explained his train of thought, "dreamers, are those who apparently get involved with them most easily. — I want to warn you, sir, as well as I can."

He straightened up.

"So listen!" he said seriously. "Seven days ago today lieutenant Bohlen didn't show up for duty. I sent somebody to his apartment, he had disappeared. With the help of the police and the district attorney's office, we took every step, without any success. And despite the short time, that's passed since then, I am for my part convinced of the uselessness of any further efforts. No objective reasons are present. Bohlen was very able, had no debts, was very healthy and very happy in his profession as a cavalry officer. He didn't leave behind anything but a brief note to me— the details of which I cannot reveal to you."

A great sense of disappointment seized me, which my face betrayed at once.

"Wait!" the colonel continued. "I hope that what I tell you will be enough at least to save you. I believe that lieutenant Bohlen is dead, that he took his own life in a dark mood of mental derangement."

"Did he write that?" I interjected.

The colonel shook his head.

"No!" he said. "Not a word! He only wrote: *I am disappearing now. I am no longer a man. I am a myrtle tree.*"

"What?" I cried.

"Yes," said the colonel "a myrtle tree! He believed that he had been turned into a myrtle tree by the sorceress— Lady Emy Steenhop."

"But that's just a load of stupid fantasies!" I cried.

The colonel again directed his investigative, pitying gaze toward me.

"Fantasies?" he repeated. "You call them fantasies. It could also be called madness. But one thing is certain: Our poor comrade was destroyed by it. He believed himself to be enchanted. Weren't we all a little bit bewitched by the beautiful lady? Wasn't I an old ass, just like a school-boy, fawning all over her? I'll tell you every evening an incredible longing came over me to go to her villa and to press my gray moustache upon her soft skin. And it wasn't any different for my officers. The lieutenant colonel, Count Arco, whom I sent on leave day before yesterday, admitted to me that he had walked up and down in front of her house for five hours

[52]

in the moonlight, and I'm afraid he wasn't the only one. I would be the last one in the officers' mess every night still drinking— a good example of what I mean. I assure you I haven't drunk so much champagne in years as I have in the past week — but it didn't taste a bit good. — Drink, drink! Bacchus is the enemy of Venus."

He again poured our glasses full and went on:

"Now you see, young sir, when such a prosaic guy as myself can't get rid of the itch, when such a blasé ladies' man like Arco makes lonely moonlight jaunts, don't I have to fear that the Bohlen case wouldn't remain the only one. And I'd have her to thank for turning my whole officer corps into a forest of myrtle trees!"

"I thank you, Herr Colonel," I said.

"Without question you acted correctly from your perspective."

He smiled.

"Very kind of you to recognize that!" he said mockingly. "But you would oblige me more if you would follow my advice. I was at one time the elder, in a certain sense the leader, of the witch's cult on Koblenzstrasse; now it's as if I were responsible for everybody, not just my officers. And I have the feeling — nothing more than a feeling, but I can't get rid of it — that some further misery will come from that beautiful woman. Call me an old fool, but promise you will never again step foot in that house!"

He spoke so seriously, so intently, that suddenly a strange fear gripped me as well.

"Yes, Herr Colonel!" I said.

"It would be best if you went on a trip for a few months like the others did. Arco went with your corps-brothers to Paris, why don't you go too? That'll distract you, you'll soon forget the sorceress."

I responded: "Yes, Herr Colonel!"

"Your hand on it!" he cried.

I held out my right hand, which he shook forcefully.

"I will pack my things right away and take the midnight train," I said firmly.

"All right!" he cried and wrote a few words on his calling card. "Here's the name of the hotel where Arco and your friend are staying, give my best to them both, have fun, do a little slumming for me, but come back to me — without this — dejected smile."

With his index finger he stroked the corner of my mouth as if he wanted to smooth it out.

I ran home right away with the firm intention to depart in three hours. My bags were already packed and ready when I took a few things out and put others in. Then I sat down at the desk and wrote my father a note in which I informed him about my trip, and asked him to send me money in Paris. As I was looking for an envelope my gaze fell upon a small stack of letters and cards which had arrived while I was away. I thought: "They can just stay there until I get back from Paris." But nevertheless I stretched my hand out and pulled it back again. "No, I don't want to read them," I said. I took a coin out of my pocket and thought: "If it's heads, I'll read them, tails, I won't." I tossed the piece of money on the table, it came up tails. — "Well, then," I said, "I won't read them." In the same moment I became annoyed with this stupidity and reached for the letters. A few bills, invitations, advertisements— then a violet envelope, which bore my name in large bold upright characters. I knew right away: This is why I wanted to look at the letters. I tested the weight of the letter in my hand, but certainly I felt I would have to read it. I had never seen the handwriting before, and I knew at once it was hers. Suddenly I said under my breath:

"*Now it begins.*"

I didn't mean anything by it, I had no idea what was supposed to begin. But I was afraid.

I ripped open the envelope and read:

"My friend! Don't forget to bring orange blossoms this evening.
Emy Steenhop"

The letter had been written ten days earlier, on the day I'd gone to my parents. I had told her the evening before, that I'd seen blooming orange blossoms in a gardener's greenhouse, and she expressed the wish to have some of these blossoms. Right away the next morning, before my departure, I went to the gardener and contracted for him to deliver the blossoms to her by cart that evening.

I read the lines very calmly, then put the letter in my pocket. I tore up the letter to my father.

To the promise I made to the colonel, I didn't give another thought.

I looked at my watch— nine-thirty; that was the time when she usually received her entourage. I called for a cab and changed.

I went to the gardener and had blossoms cut. And then, at last, I was in front of her villa.

I had myself announced, and the maid conducted me into the small parlor. I sat on the divan and stroked the soft guanaco hide lying over it.

Then she came in, in a long, yellow silk dress. Her black hair fell from the smooth crown of her head over her ears, and there was spun into little ringlets— like that worn by the women of Lucas Cranach. She was a little pale, a violet light shown from her eyes.

"That's because she's wearing yellow," I thought to myself.

"I was out of town," I said, "for my mother's birthday. I just got back this evening a few hours ago."

She hesitated for a moment.

"Just this evening," she repeated, "then you don't know— " she interrupted herself: "But of course you know!" she smiled. "In these few hours they've probably told you everything."

I was silent and twirled the blossoms.

"Of course they did!" she went on. "And you found your way here anyway? I thank you."

She offered her hand to me, and I kissed it.

Then she said very softly: "I really knew you would come."

I straightened up.

"Gracious lady!" I said. "I came across your letter upon my return. I hurried to bring you the blossoms."

She smiled.

"Oh, don't lie!" she cried, "you know I wrote you that letter ten days ago, and you sent me the blossoms right away."

She took the branches out of my hands and drew them to her face.

"Orange blossoms, — orange blossoms," she said slowly "how glorious is their scent."

[54]

She looked at me intently and went on:

"You don't need an excuse to come here. — You came because you had to, didn't you?"

I bowed.

"Sit down, my friend," said the Lady Emy Steenhop, "let's drink some tea."

Then she rang for the servants.

*   *

*

Believe me Herr Director! I could recount each of the many evenings I spent with the lady in great detail, I could repeat our conversations word for word. All that is chiseled into my memory as if in stone, I wouldn't forget a movement of her hand, or the light play of her eye brows. — I want to pick those details that appear essential for the picture you wish to get from me.

Once lady Emy Steenhop asked:

"Do you know what became of Harry Bohlen?"

I replied: "I know what people say."

She asked: "Do you believe I turned him into a myrtle tree?"

I grasped her hand and kissed it.

"If you wish it, beautiful lady," I laughed, "I would very much believe it."

But she pulled her hand back. She was speaking — and in her voice there resounded such conviction, that I trembled:

"*I believe it!*"

*   *

*

She expressed the wish that I bring her orange blossoms every evening. One evening when I again handed her the white blossoms, she whispered:

"Astolf."

Then she went on out loud:

"Yes, I will call you Astolf. And if you want, you may call me Alcina."

— I know, honorable Herr Director, how little leisure we have nowadays to concern ourselves with old sagas and stories. So these names will likely not mean anything to you, while to me they instantly revealed an immanent wonder — horrible and yet sweet. If you knew Ludovico Ariosto, if you had read any of the heroic tales of Cinquecento, then the beautiful fairy Alcina would be as well-known to you as she is to me. She caught Astolf of Angel-Land in her net, the mighty Rudiger, the son of Haiman Reinold of Montalban, the knight of Bayard and many another hero and paladin. And it was her habit to turn her lovers into trees after she became weary of them.

She laid both her hands on my shoulders and looked at me:

"If I were Alcina," she said "would you like to be my Astolf?"

I didn't say anything, but my eyes answered her. And then she said:

"Come!"

*   *

*

You're a psychiatrist, Herr Director, and I know that you're a recognized authority. I often read your name in all sorts of newspapers, it is said of you that you have actually developed some new thoughts. And now, since I believe that it is never the case that one man alone has these

[55]

so-called new ideas, but that these come into being in different brains simultaneously, I have the hope that your new ideas relating to the human psyche will be able to coincide with mine. It is only this feeling that allows me to give you such unlimited trust.

Thought is the primary thing, or more to the point it is *the only thing that is real*, isn't it? It is childish nonsense to conceive of matter as something real. That which I see, touch, and feel can be, by virtue of the most imperfect instruments, recognized as something completely different from that perceived by my few senses. A drop of water appears to my miserable human eye as a small, clear, transparent ball; but a microscope of the type children use as toys teaches me that it's the playground of the wildest battles of infusoria. That is a higher perspective— but not the highest; for doubtless in a hundred years people will be equally amused by our splendid scientific instruments, just as we are by the tools of Asclepius. Therefore, perception, which I count as the most wonderful of instruments, has just as little reality as that of my poor senses. How ever I might conceive of matter, it is always something different from what I understood it to be. But it is not only that I can never completely perceive the essence of matter, but also it's that it has no being. Spray water on a hot oven and it is instantaneously vaporized, if I throw a lump of sugar into a cup of tea it melts. If I break the cup I'm drinking out of, I'll have nothing but shards— but no longer a cup. If, however, being can be turned into not-being with the flip of the wrist, then it is not worth talking about it as being. Not-being, death, is the real essence of all matter, *life is only a negation of this essence for an infinitely short span of time.* — But the thought of the drop of water, or the lump of sugar remains immutable, it can never be broken, evaporated, or melted. So isn't this thought to be spoken of with much greater right as reality, than fluctuating material is?

Now, Herr Director, if we humans are just as much material as everything around us, every chemist can easily prove to us what the percentages of oxygen, nitrogen, hydrogen are that we consist of. But if thought is revealed in us — what right do we have to assume that it couldn't be manifested in other forms of matter?

I always use the word "thought," Herr Director, only because this word fits the concept that I have in mind for me personally. Just as different languages have different words for an idea, as the Italians call the organ with which we speak "bocca," while the Englishman calls it a "mouth," the Frenchman "bouche," the German says "Mund," the different arts and sciences have different words of the same idea. What I call "thought," could be called "God" by the theosophist, "soul" by the mystic, "consciousness" by the physician; you, Herr Director, would perhaps call it "psyche." But you will agree with me that this idea, whatever one may call it, is the original, and at the same time only real, thing.

Now if this isolate idea, which has all of the characteristics the theologians attribute to the so-called personal God, and which is therefore unending, eternal, unlimited, is manifested in our brain, why shouldn't it be at liberty to appear in everything else as well. At least I can conceive of more comfortable places to live than in the brains of a lot of people.

All this is certainly nothing new, billions of people throughout time have believed — and still believe today — that the soul can also appear in animals. The teachings of Buddha, for example, accepted the theory of metempsychosis. What prevents us from going a step further and include

[56]

springs, trees, and rocks as was done — perhaps only for poetic and aesthetic reasons — in Hellas. I really believe the time has come in which the human mind has evolved so far, that it is able to recognize the souls of many organic entities.

I already spoke to you about my poems that I once read to the lady, and that the colonel called such terrible nonsense. That may be— I don't have a judgment on them. They're nothing more than a stammering attempt to reflect the souls of a few flowers in human language.

Why is it that a eucalyptus tree raises the thought in every artist of a woman longingly spreading out her naked arms? That daffodil irresistibly warns us of death? That wisteria conjures the image of a little blond pastor's daughter, that the orchid reminds us of the witches' sabbath and black masses.

It is because *the thought of these things live in these flowers and trees.*

Do you believe it's a coincidence that the rose is the symbol of love and the violet is that of modesty among all peoples of the world? There are hundreds of small fragrant flowers which bloom in equally concealed and hidden ways, none of them exercises a similar effect on us. If we pick a violet, however, we will instinctively think: modesty. This strange feeling doesn't actually come from what we find most characteristic about the little flower, that is, from its fragrance. For if you take the perfume "vera violetta," whose smell is so deceptive that you wouldn't be able to tell the difference between it and a large bouquet of violets in the dark, you will never have the same sensation.

Just like the feeling which overtakes us, against our wills in the vicinity of a blooming chestnut tree — the thought of eternally victorious masculinity — doesn't have the least bit to do with what first binds our sense: the powerful trunk, the broad leaves, the thousands of shimmering stems of flowers. Only after reflection do we come to the realization that here it is the aroma, hardly noticeable, which reveals the soul of the tree to our thoughts.

Apparently, the idea I am calling "thought," takes on all forms and shapes; merely the fact that I, or anyone else, can think this way is already a valid proof of it.

Because thought knows absolutely no boundaries, matter is no barrier for it at all. No insightful person can run away from the truths — which are certainly relative as are all others — of the monistic world conception, and it teaches us, that as matter we humans are in no way different from any other material form. If I have to admit this and be on the other side of the "thought" of being— in its true and powerful sense — constantly forcing me to this realization, I can only come to one conclusion, otherwise confirmed by a thousand examples, that if *"thought" is able to penetrate not only humanity but also every other material then why not also the branches, leaves, and blossoms of an orange tree?*

For the philosopher's Faustian nature a doctrine of faith, accepted among primitive peoples, is only found in its beginning formula: "In the beginning was the word." And they all falter and their ideas will never amount to anything more than the mysterious "logos," until it is revealed in its complete magnitude one day in somebody's head or another. Because the human brain is the most perfect among all material things on this dead little star we call Earth, this revelation will probably only come into being for us there.

But those people are wrong, who, like the mystics, believe in such a revelation of the "logos" and concern themselves with it, consistently assume that it will come suddenly, like a bolt of lightening. It will come, as it came, slowly, step by step, as the sun evolved from a cosmic cloud, or humans from the *amoeba primitiva. It is eternal and never completed, and therefore it will never be perfect.*

No hour, no second, goes by in which the thought does not reveal itself, greater, more glorious than before. More and more we are recognizing this idea *that is all and everything.*

And it is such a greater awareness, in which I believe, that is being reflected in my brain. O, I don't imagine myself to be the only one; I already told you, Herr Director, that I believe a thought never bears fruit in a single brain alone. But in many the seed of the spirit will dry up, in only a few may it come to blossom.

*   *
*

One night, the woman I called Alcina had completely covered the couch upon which we rested with orange blossoms. When she embraced me, her delicately flaring nostrils trembled against me as she pressed them closely to my neck.

"My friend," she said, "you smell like the blossoms!"

I laughed; I believed she was making a joke. — But later I was convinced she was right.

*   *
*

One day my landlady came into my room. She sniffed around in the air and said:

"O, how good that smells! Do you have more orange blossoms in here?"

But I hadn't had any blossoms in my room in days.

I said to myself: We could both be fooling ourselves, the human nose is such a poorly evolved organ.

But my hunting dog can not be fooled; his nose is infallible.

So I did an experiment. I often had my dog fetch an orange branch in my apartment or garden; when I did this I carefully hid the branch and taught him to bring it when I called: "Get the blossoms!" He always brought the branch back from its hiding place after a short while.

Then I waited a few days, during which time I had no blossoms in my apartment. One morning I took the dog to the swimming pool. When I got out of the water I cried:

"Ali, fetch! Get the blossoms!"

The hunting dog raised his head up high, sniffed a few times around in the air and then came without hesitation over to me. I went to my locker and showed him the clothes, that could have perhaps held some kind of fragrance. But the hunting dog hardly smelled of them, he kept sniffing of me: *It was from my flesh that he smelled the fragrance.*

Now, Herr Director, if that can happen to the dog with his highly developed organ, don't you need to wonder if you have entertained the same deception when you thought I had branches with me. After you left me yesterday evening, I heard how you told the orderly in the hall to search through my room carefully and remove the orange tree branches. I don't think badly of you because of it; you believed I'd hidden such

[58]

blossoms in my room and considered it your duty to keep away from me everything that might remind me of "my *idée fixé.*" Herr Director, you could have saved your orderly the trouble: he can look every day for hours and won't find a single blossom. *But when you visit me again you will again smell the fragrance that exudes from my flesh.*

*   *

*

Once I dreamt I was going through a wide garden at noon time. By the round fountain, through a pagoda with broken marble columns. And over long, smooth lawns. I saw a tree that shimmered all over with blood red fiery oranges. Then I knew *that I was that tree.*

The gentle wind played in my leaves, and in an infinite passion I expanded and stretched my full branches. Over the white gravel path there came a tall woman walking, in a broad yellow raiment. From deep violet eyes her gaze caressed me.

Then I rustled from my dense branches:

"Pick some of my fruit, Alcina!"

She understood this language and raised her white arm. Broke off a branch with five or six golden pieces of fruit.

There was a gentle, sweet pain; and I woke up from it.

I saw her crouching down beside me on the soft yellow-white guanaco hide. Her eyes stared at me so strangely.

"What are you doing?" I asked.

"Quiet!" she whispered, "I am listening to your dreams."

*   *

*

On one afternoon we had traveled over the Rhine, gone from Drachenfels down to the cloister of Heisterbach. Behind the ivy-covered ruins she threw herself down on the grass. I sat beside her, took deep breaths of the mild air, lifted my chest and stretched out my arms wide.

"Yes," she said and covered her eyes with her deep eyelashes, "yes, spread out your branches! How cool it is resting here in your shade!"

Then she told me—

*   *

*

Oh, throughout the nights she told me tales. Ancient sagas, fairy tales and stories. She always closed her eyes as she told the tales. Only slightly did she open her elegant lips, words dripped from her mouth like the little ringing bells.

"You robbed me of my sash," Flordelis said to her knight; "so bring me another worthy of me!"

"Then the blond Gryph saddled his horse and hunted through all the world to get a sash for his mistress. Battled with giants and knights, with witches and necromancers and won the most glorious sashes. But he threw them all in the dust, or on the laps of beggars and declared that they were all only poor rags and were not worthy to decorate the loins of his lady. And when he had wrested the sash of Venus herself from the mighty Rodomont, he tore it to shreds and swore that he wanted to get her a sash such that had never been worn by even a goddess. He defeated the giant Atlas and stole his wingéd steed; through storm and wind he rode in the air and with his bold hand he ripped the Milky Way down from the heavens.

"He came back to his mistress and kissed her white foot. Around her hips he wrapped the sash, upon which many thousand stars shimmered as jewels.—

*   *
*

"Read me what you wrote about the orchids!" she said.

So I read to her:

"When the Devil was a woman,
When Lilith wound
Her ebony hair in heavy braids,
And framed
Her pale features all'round
With Botticelli's tangled thoughts,
When she, smiling softly,
Ringed all her slim fingers
In golden bands with brilliant stones,
When she leafed through Villiers
And loved Huysmans,
When she fathomed Maeterlinck's silence
And bathed her Soul
In Gabriel d'Annunzio's colors,
She even laughed—

—— —

And as she laughed,
The little princess of serpents sprang
Out of her mouth.
Then the most beautiful of she-devils
Sought after the serpent,
She seized the Queen of Serpents
With her ringed fingers,
So that she wound and hissed,
Hissed, hissed
And spit venom.
In a heavy copper vase;
Damp earth,
Black damp earth
She scattered upon it.
Lightly her great hands caressed
This heavy copper vase
All around,
Her pale lips lightly sang
Her ancient curse—
Like a children's rhyme her curses chimed,
Soft and languid
Languid as the kisses,
That the damp earth drank
From her mouth,
But life arose in the vase,
And tempted by her languid kisses,
And tempted by those sweet tones,
From the black earth slowly there crept,
Orchids —

When the most belovéd
Adorns her pale features before the mirror
All 'round with Botticelli's adders,
There creep sideways from the copper vase,
Orchids—
Devil's blossoms which the ancient earth,
Wed by Lilith's curse
To serpent's venom, has borne to the light
Orchids—
The Devil's blossoms—"

"That's beautiful," Alcina said.

*　　　　*

*

"Yes, Herr Director, such was our life: a fairy tale woven from the rays of the sun. We inhaled a past lost in time; an unsuspected future grew out of our kisses.

And more and more clear, more and more crystalline became the harmonies of our dreams. Once she interrupted me in the middle of a poem.

She said: — "Quiet!" and pressed her face to my chest. I felt how her fine nostrils trembled on my flesh— minutes on end.

Then she raised her head and said:

"You don't need to speak — *I can smell your thoughts.*"

She closed her eyes — *and slowly she finished speaking my verse.*

Or she held my head tightly in her arms and stroked my temples with her slim fingers.

It was then I felt how her desires glided over into me, they took possession of my soul like a caress.

It was like a kind of sweet music playing through my temples, like a song of dancing sunbeams:

Where the green lawns expand, where the cool mountain waters flow over snowy marble ledges, where giant moths indulge themselves between magnolia blossoms and white peacocks brood over their lonely dreams, there stands a tree.

It spreads out its branches wide and a fragrance of weddings and love fills the air around it. White blossoms rise from its leaves and between them sparkle golden pieces of fruit.

A fairy rests in the cool shade, she tells tales to the tree, her lover.

She speaks and he murmurs his fragrance to her through the winds.

This is how the couple parley with one another.

*　　　　*

*

Thus the realization grew in me, slowly, gradually, as all revelations come. So harmoniously that I noticed not a single milestone. The few details I have represented to you, Herr Director, have been selected from many thousands. The miracle began when I first saw this woman— but maybe it began earlier. Don't I have to consider my thoughts, for example those, which I expressed in my poems, as the first subtle beginnings?

The miracle will, however, be complete when I am standing outside in the sun with white blossoms and golden red fruit.

[61]

In the meantime there is the evolution: quietly progressing, strong, self-conscious, knowing no resistance.

Not only of the soul but of the body as well. Didn't I already tell you that my whole flesh is soaked with this sweet fragrance? You'll soon be convinced, Herr Director!

* *
*

Then came the final nights. Once she said to me:

"You know, I must leave you soon."

I was not afraid of this. Every second with her was an eternity, and through endless eternities my enraptured arms could still embrace her.

I nodded and she went on:

"You know what will happen then, Astolf?"

I nodded again and asked:

"Where are you going?"

Then two tears rolled across her cheeks. She sat up and her eyes shone like lonely stars in the night over an ice-covered steppe.

"Over the seas," she said, "to that place I came from. — But I want to write you — And then later, when you are blooming outside there, when the gentle breezes are playing in your branches, I will come again. I will come to you, my beloved, and rest in your shade. Rest beside you, my beloved, dream with you our sweetest dreams."

"Beloved," she said, "beloved!" And as the green tendrils of ivy cling to the trunk and branches of a tree, she embraced me— just that way.

* *
*

You, Herr Director, know what happened then. When I went to her villa one night, I rang and no one answered. She was gone, her villa was cleaned out. I put the police and private detectives on her trail, I ran around like a fool for days. I did ridiculous and idiotic things, but I assure you, Herr Director, that all that can be accounted for as the actions of a lover, who had suddenly lost his beauty, as if by a sorcerer's curse.

My corps-brothers again took care of me, more than I liked. They were the ones who sent a telegram to my parents. Then came my outbreak of furious anger, that you call a "breakdown," but which was really a very easily explained natural circumstance. My friends, who, after my idiocies, no longer left me alone for even a moment, noticed that I was always waiting on the postman. And when the letter came, her letter, they took it away from the messenger on the street. Today I know quite well that they had good intentions, that they wanted to keep me from getting agitated again. But in that moment as I watched through the window I saw red— it seemed a sacrilege to me that they touched the paper with their hands, that they were going to read her handwriting. I tore a sharp edged rapier from the wall and rushed out onto the street. I yelled out to them to give me the letter, when they refused I slashed the one holding the letter in the face. The blood splattered and spotted the letter, which I tore from his hands. I ran to my room, locked myself in and read the lines.

She wrote:

"If you love me, you will bring it to an end. —Oh, I will come, come to you, beloved! Will rest in your cool shade and tell you sweet stories.

Alcina."

Now I'm finished, Herr Director. By trickery I was brought here, but now I thank the fate that led me here. The agitations are over with, in this wonderful quiet I have again found peace. I sit in the sweet fragrance *exuding from me*, and feel, know, that I am bringing it to an end. Writing is already becoming difficult for me, Herr Director, my fingers no longer want to stay together, they spread, stretch out from each other *like branches*.

Your institute is in a glorious park-land: I went for a walk there this morning, it is so big and beautiful. I know, Herr Director, that my words have convinced you— oh, yes they have! So when the hour comes, that's now so close, you won't try to prevent its fulfillment. There behind the great meadow I'll stand, where the cascades of water splash. I know you will have me taken care of, Herr Director, the gardener on Bonner Talweg knows what to do with orange trees, he will give you advice. *Because I don't want to shrivel up, I want to grow and bloom, so that she will take pleasure in my splendor.*

She will write, Herr Director, you'll know her address.

And one other thing: Every summer when my crown is shimmering with a thousand golden pieces of fruit, you are to pick the most beautiful of these and put them in a little basket. Send them to her.

A note should be put in with them with the sweet words I heard last time in the streets of Granada:

> *Dearest, take the blood-orange,*
> *I silently picked in the garden.*
> *Dearest, take the blood-orange!*
> *— But cut it not with a knife,*
> *For you'll cut my heart in two*
> *In the middle of the blood-orange*

Tomato Sauce

Chi va lontan dalla sua patria, vede
Cose da quel, che già credea lontane;
Che narrandole poi non se gli crede,
E stimato bugiardo ne rimane:
Chè'l sciocco vulgo non gli vuoldar frede,
Se non le vede a tocca chiare e piane:
Per questo io so che l'inesperienza
Farà all mio canto dar poca credenza.

Poca o molta ch'io ciabbia non bisogna
Ch'io ponga mente al vulgo sciocco e ignoro—

Ariosto, L'Orlando Furioso, Canto VII.

Alhambra (Granada), March 1905

Tomato Sauce

The first time: at the *corrida* five weeks ago, when the black bull of Miura gorged little Quitino through the arm—

And again the following Sunday and the Sunday after— I met him at each bull-fight. I used to sit in front in order to take a few snapshots; his subscription seat was next to mine. A little man with a round hat and the black smock of an English clergyman. Pale, smooth shaven, with a pair of gold-rimmed spectacles on his nose. And something else, too: he had no eyelashes.

I became aware of him immediately. At the moment when the first bull took the horse upon his horns and the tall *picador* fell clumsily off. The nag jumped up painfully again and cantered away, its body torn open, and its legs entangled in its own entrails, which hung down and dragged in the sand. At the same instant I heard a sigh at my side— a deep sigh of content.

We sat together the entire afternoon, never speaking a word. The pretty play of the *bandilleros* interested him very little. But when the *espada* thrust his blade into the bull's neck, so that the handle rose like a cross above the mighty horns, then he gripped the barrier with both hands and leaned far over. And the *garocha*— that was the thing he prized most. When the blood squirted from the chest of a horse in a stream as thick as an arm, or when a *chulo* put the mortally wounded animal out of its misery by driving his short dagger into its brain, or when the maddened bull tore a horse's carcass to shreds in the arena, burying his horns in the lifeless mass— then this man softly rubbed his palms together. Once I asked him:

"You are a bull-fight fan— an *aficionado*?"

He nodded but said no word; he did not want to be disturbed in his enjoyment.

Granada is not a big place, so I soon learned his name. He was the chaplain of the small English colony; his countrymen always called him the "Pope." Apparently he was not held in high regard; nobody had anything to do with him socially.

On Wednesday I visited the cock-fight.

A small amphitheater, perfectly round, with raised benches. In the center, the arena, directly under the skylight. The reek of the rabble, shouting and spitting— it takes some nerve to enter. Two cocks are brought in, looking like hens with their combs and tails cut off. They are weighed, then taken from their cages. And they go for each other without a moment's hesitation. The air is full of flying feathers: again and again the two birds fly at each other, mutilating each other with beaks and spurs— without a sound. Only the human beasts around them cry and shout, curse and bet. Ha, the yellow cock has hacked out one of the white one's eyes, snapped it up from the floor and swallowed it! The heads and necks of the birds, long since plucked bare, sway like snakes above their bodies. Not for

[67]

a moment do they let go of each other. Their feathers are crimsoned. You hardly recognize their forms any more, as they hack each other to bloody chunks. Now the yellow one has lost both his eyes; he hacks blindly in the air while every second the beak of his rival beats down on his head. At last he sinks down; without resistance, without a sound, he permits the foe to finish his task. Nor is this quickly done; five to six minutes are still needed by the white cock, himself exhausted unto death by a hundred spur thrusts and bites.

There they sit around, my fellow men, human beings, all; they laugh at the impotent beak-thrusts of the victor, urging him on and counting each new bite— for the sake of bets.

At last! Thirty minutes, the allotted time, are spent; the battle is over. One fellow, the owner of the victorious cock, rises; with derisive laughter he slays his opponent's bird with a club: this is his privilege. Now they wash the cocks at the pump and count the wounds in order to settle the bets.

I felt a hand on my shoulder.

"How do you do?" the Pope asked. His watery eyes, without lashes, smiled contentedly behind his large glasses. "You like that, don't you?" he proceeded.

For a moment I did not know whether he was in earnest. His question seemed so utterly and stupidly offensive that I stared at him without answering.

But he misunderstood my silence, took it for consent, so certain was he.

"Yes," he said quietly and very slowly. "This is real satisfaction."

We were pushed apart; they brought new cocks into the arena.

A few days later I was invited to tea by the English Consul. I was punctual, the first guest to arrive.

As I greeted him and his old mother, he said:

"I am glad you are early. I want to have a few words with you in private."

"I am entirely at your disposal," I smiled.

The Consul drew his rocking-chair closer and, with strange earnestness, proceeded:

"Far be it from me to dictate to you, my dear sir! But, if it is your intention to remain here longer and to move about generally in society, — as well as in the English colony — I should like to give you some friendly advice."

I was quite curious to hear what he was driving at.

"And your advice?" I asked.

"You have been seen several times in the company of our clergyman—" he continued.

"I beg your pardon!" I interrupted. "I know very little about him. The day before yesterday we exchanged a few words for the first time."

"So much the better!" the Consul replied. "Then I should advise you to shun association with him, at least in public."

"Thank you, Consul," I said. "Would it be indiscreet to ask the reason for this?"

"Of course, I owe you an explanation," he answered, "although I am not sure that it will satisfy you. The Pope— you know they have given him this nickname?"

I nodded.

"Well, then," he proceeded, "the Pope is taboo in society. He attends the bull-fights regularly, — that isn't so bad — he also never misses a single cock-fight; in short, he has tastes which render him impossible among Europeans."

"But Consul, if you condemn him so much for this, why do you permit him to retain his unquestionably honorable office?"

"Well, after all, he has been ordained," the old lady volunteered.

"And, besides that," the Consul affirmed, "in all his twenty years here he has never given the slightest tangible reason for complaint. Moreover, the position of clergyman in our tiny community is the worst paid on the entire continent— it would hardly be possible to replace him."

"Then you are satisfied with his sermons, nevertheless," I said turning to the Consul's mother, making an effort to suppress a malicious smile.

The old lady straightened up in her chair.

"I would never permit him to speak a word of his own in the church," she answered very definitely. "Every Sunday he reads his sermons from Dean Harley's collection."

The answer flustered me somewhat, and I was silent.

"Incidentally," the Consul began once more, "it would be unjust not to mention one of the Pope's good traits. He owns a considerable fortune, and uses his income solely for charitable purposes, while he himself, apart from his passions, lives an extraordinarily modest, even poor, life."

"Nice kind of charity!" His mother interrupted him. "Whom does he assist? Wounded *toreadores* and their families, or even the victim of a *salsa*."

"A— what?" I asked.

"My mother means a *salsa de tomates*," the Consul explained.

"Tomato sauce?" I repeated. "The Pope assists the victims of— tomato sauce?"

The Consul laughed briefly. Then he said very seriously:

"Have you never heard of a *salsa*? It is an ancient, horrible custom of Andalusia, which exists in spite of every punishment by civic and church authorities. Since I have been Consul here, there is proof that a *salsa* has twice taken place. But even in these cases no definite facts were established, in as much as the participants, in spite of the floggings habitual in Spanish prisons, would rather bite off their tongues than reveal even a syllable. Therefore, I could only give you a vague, possibly false, report; make the Pope tell you, if the horrible secret interests you. For he — in spite of the fact that nobody can prove it — is said to be an adherent of this awful custom, and it is particularly this suspicion which causes us to shun him."

A few guests entered; our conversation was interrupted.

When I went to the bull-fights the following Sunday, I brought along a few particularly good snapshots of the last *corrida* for the Pope. I wanted to make him a present of them, but he hardly looked at them.

"Forgive me," he said, "but they do not interest me at all."

I looked puzzled.

"Oh, I did not mean to offend you!" he proceeded. "You see, it is only the redness, the redness of blood which I care for."

It sounded almost poetic the way this pale ascetic said: "The redness of blood!"

At any rate we entered into a discussion. And, in the midst of it, I said without warning: "I would like to see a *salsa*. Won't you take me with you some time?"

He was silent. The pale cracked lips trembled.

Then he asked: "A *salsa?*— Do you know what that is?"

I lied. "Of course!"

Again he stared at me. Then his eyes fell on the old scars of student duels on my cheek and forehead.

And, as if these signs of childish blood-shedding were a secret passport, he stroked them softly with his finger and said solemnly:

"I will take you with me."

A few weeks later, one evening about nine o'clock, there was a knock at my door. Before I could say: "Come in!" the Pope entered.

"I have come to fetch you," he said.

"What for?" I asked.

"You know," he answered. "Are you ready?"

I rose.

"In a minute!" I cried. "Will you have a cigar?"

"Thank you. I don't smoke."

"A glass of wine?"

"No, thanks. I do not drink either. Please hurry."

I took my hat and followed him down the stairs into the moonlit night. Silently we walked through the streets, along the Genil, under pyrrhus-trees in red bloom. We turned to the left, ascended the Moor-mountain and crossed the Field of Martyrs. In front of us glowed, in warm silver, the snow-capped mountains of the Sierra; round about on the hills, fires shone from the caves where the gypsies and other vagabonds live. We circled the deep valley of the Alhambra, filled almost to the brim with a sea of green elms; then through the avenue of age-old cypresses towards the Generalife; and still higher up the mountain, from the top of which the last prince of the Moors, the fair-haired Boabdil, sent his farewell sighs down to lost Granada.

I looked at my strange companion. His glance, turned inward, saw nothing of the glory of this night. As the moonlight played over those small, bloodless lips, upon those sunken cheeks and the deep hollows in the temples, a feeling as if I had known this gruesome ascetic for ages overcame me. And suddenly, like a flash, the solution came: this was the face which the fearful Zurbaran gave to his ascetic monks!

Now the way led through broad-leaved agaves, which lifted the wooden stems of their blossoms the height of three men into the air. We heard the Darro roar as it leaped down the cliffs beyond the mountain.

Three men in brown, tattered coats approached us; already from afar they saluted my companion.

"Guards," the Pope said. "Wait here. I shall speak to them!"

He approached the men, who apparently had been expecting him. I could not understand what they said, but obviously it was about me. One of the men gesticulated vehemently, looked suspiciously at me, threw his arms in the air and shouted again and again: "*Ojo el caballero!*" But the Pope quieted him. Finally he motioned me to come closer.

"*Sea Usted bienvenido, caballero!*" He saluted me and doffed his hat. The two other guards remained at their post; the third one accompanied us.

"He is the patron; the manager, so to speak, of the affair," the Pope explained.

A few paces ahead we reached one of the cave dwellings, distinguished in no way from the hundreds of others along the slopes of Granada. In front of the door-hole, as usual, there was a small, levelled spot, surrounded by dense cactus hedges. There about twenty ruffians stood around, but there was no gypsy among them. In one corner burned a small fire between two stones; above it hung a kettle.

The Pope reached into his pocket and took out one *duro* after the other, which he turned over to our companion.

"These people are so suspicious," he said, "they take nothing but silver."

The Andalusian crouched down by the fire and examined each single coin. He rang them on a stone and bit them with his teeth. Then he counted them— one hundred *pesetas* in all.

"Shall I give him some money as well?" I asked.

"No," said the Pope. "You'd better do some betting; that will give you a safer standing with these people."

I did not understand him.

"Safer standing?" I repeated. "How so?"

The Pope smiled.

"Oh— by betting you come down nearer to their level and make yourself more equally guilty with them."

"Tell me, Reverend," I exclaimed, "how is it, then, that you do not bet?"

He met my glance firmly and replied carelessly:

"I? I never bet! Betting detracts from the pure joy of watching."

In the meantime, another half dozen suspicious-looking individuals had arrived, all of them shrouded in the inevitable brown cloth which serves the Andalusians for a cloak.

"What are we waiting for?" I asked one of the men.

"For the moon, *caballero*," he replied. "It must set first."

Then he offered me a big glass of *aguardiente*. I declined, but the Englishman pressed the glass into my hand.

"Drink! Drink!" he insisted. "It is the first time for you— you may need it."

The others, too, partook of the liquor. However, they made no noise; only hasty whispers and hoarse murmurs penetrated the night. As the moon sank in the northwest behind the Cortadura, they fetched long pitch torches from the cave and lit them. Then they built a small stone circle in the middle; this was the arena. Around this circle they dug holes in the ground and affixed the torches. And, in the red gleam of the flames, two men began to undress; they kept only their leather breeches on. Then they sat down opposite each other and crossed their legs in Oriental fashion. It was only now that I noticed two strong horizontal beams sunk into the ground, each one of which carried two solid iron rings.

Between these two rings the two men had taken their places. Somebody ran into the cave and brought out a few lengths of heavy rope which they wound around the bodies and legs of the two, binding each one to the rings. They were fixed as in a vise; only the upper parts of their bodies could they move freely.

They sat without a word, sucking their cigarettes and emptying the liquor glasses which were filled for them again and again. Clearly they were both quite drunk by this time, their eyes fixed stupidly on the ground.

[71]

And all around them, in the circle of smoking torches, the other men settled down.

Suddenly I heard an ugly screeching behind my back which almost burst my eardrums. I turned around; somebody was carefully sharpening a small *navajo* on a round grinding stone. He tested the knife with the nail of his thumb, and put it aside and took another one.

I turned to the Pope.

"This *salsa* is a kind of— duel?"

"Duel?" he replied. "Oh no. It is a kind of cock-fight."

"What?" I exclaimed. "And why do these men engage in this— cock-fight? Have they offended each other or is it jealousy?"

"Not at all," the Englishman answered quietly. "They have no reason at all. Perhaps they are the best of friends; perhaps they don't even know each other. They only want to prove their— courage. They want to show that they are no worse than the bulls and cocks."

His ugly lips essayed a wry smile as he proceeded:

"Something like your German student duels."

Abroad, I am always a patriot. That much I have learned from the English: right or wrong— my country!

Therefore I answered him rather sharply:

"Reverend, the comparison is ludicrous! That is something which you cannot judge."

"Perhaps," said the Pope. "But I have seen many a fine duel in Göttingen. Lots of blood; lots of blood—"

In the meantime the manager had selected a seat nest to us. He pulled a dirty notebook and a small pencil from his pocket.

"Who bets on Bombita?" he cried.

"I! " – One *peseta!*" – "Two *duros!*" – "No, I'm going to back Lagartijillo!" The drunken voices intermingled.

The Pope grabbed my arm.

"Arrange your bets so that you lose either way," he said. "Give them long odds; you cannot be too careful with this crowd."

So I took quite a number of the bets offered, and always at odds of three to one. Since I bet on both of them, I had to lose necessarily. While the manager was noting down all the bets in clumsy symbols, the sharpened *navajos* were handed round. The blades were about two inches long. Then they were shut, and passed to the two combatants.

"Which one do you want, Bombita Chico, my little cock?" The sharpener laughed.

"Let me have it! No matter which!" grunted the drunkard.

"I want my own knife!" shouted Lagartijillo.

"Then give me mine! It's better anyway!" croaked the other.

All bets were entered. The manager saw that each man was given another huge glass of *aguardiete*, which he emptied in one gulp. Both threw their cigarettes away. Then each one was given a long red woolen scarf, a hip girdle, which he tied around the lower left arm and hand.

"You may start, boys!" the manager shouted. "Open the knives."

The blades of the *navajos* snapped open with a click and remained fixed. A shrill, unpleasant sound. But the two men remained absolutely quiet; neither one made a movement.

"Begin, my little cocks!" repeated the manager.

But the battlers sat motionless; they did not stir. The Andalusians became impatient.

"Get him, Bombita, my young bull! Push your little horns into his body!"

"Ah— you want to be cocks? You are hens! Hens!"

And the chorus howled: "Hens! Hens! Why don't you lay eggs? You hens, you!"

Bombita Chico stretched himself and made a thrust at his adversary. The other lifted his left arm and caught the lazy thrust in his scarf. The two men were apparently so drunk that they could hardly control their movements.

"Wait! Wait!" the Pope whispered. "Wait until they see blood!"

The Andalusians never stopped baiting the two; first with good-natured raillery and then with biting scorn. And again and again they hissed in their ears.

"You are hens! Go lay eggs! Hens! Hens!"

Now they both thrust at each other, almost blindly. The next minute one of them received a small wound in his left shoulder.

"Bravo, darling! Bravo, Bombita! Show him, my little cock, that you have spurs!"

They paused a moment, and with their left arms wiped the dirty sweat from their faces.

"Water!" shouted Lagartijillo.

A large decanter was handed over and they drank thirstily. One could see how they sobered up. The dull glances became sharp, piercing. Hatefully they stared at each other.

"Are you ready, you hen?" asked the little one.

Instead of answering the other lunged forward and cut his cheek open for its entire length. The blood streamed down over the naked body.

"Ah, it begins— it begins," the Pope murmured.

The Andalusians were silent. Greedily they followed the movements of the one whom they had backed with their money. And the two human beings lunged and thrust—

The shining blades flashed like silver sparks through the red gleam of the torches and bit into the woolen guards on the left arms. A big drop of boiling pitch from one of the torches fell upon the chest of one of the men. He did not even notice it.

So rapidly did they flail their arms about in the air that it was impossible to see when one had struck home. Only the bloody rivulets all over the bodies testified to the growing number of cuts and gashes.

"Halt! Halt!" cried the patron. The men refused to stop. "Halt!" he cried once more. "Bombita's blade is broken!"

Two Andalusians rushed up, took an old door on which they had been sitting and ruthlessly threw it between the battlers, standing it on end so that the two could no longer see each other.

Give me your knives, little beasts!" the patron shouted. The two obeyed willingly. His sharp eye had seen correctly; Bombita's knife was broken in half. He had sliced his opponent's ear and against the hard bone of the skull the blade had broken off.

Each one was given another glass of liquor, a new knife, and the door was taken away.

And this time they went at each other like two cocks, without thinking; blind with rage, stab for stab—

The brown bodies became crimson; the blood gushed from dozens of wounds. From the forehead of little Bombita a brown strip of skin hung down; moist wisps of hair licked the wound. While his knife caught the enemies bandage, the latter dug his knife twice, three times, deep into his neck.

Take off your bandage, if you have the courage!" the little one shrieked, as he bore off his own with his teeth.

Lagartijillo hesitated for a moment, then followed suit. Automatically they still parried as before with their left arms, which were soon cut to shreds.

Again one of the blades snapped Again the old door separated them. Again they got liquor and new knives.

"Stab him, Lagartijillo, my strong bull. Stab him!" one of the men shouted. "Tear the bowels out of the old horse!"

Unexpectedly Lagartijillo, at the very moment when the other was whisked away, gave his adversary a fearful thrust in the belly from below, and drew the blade away sharply upward and sideways. A horrible mess of entrails crawled from the huge wound. And then, he stabbed once more from above, quick as lightning, and severed the big vein that nourishes the arm.

Bombita shrieked and doubled up while a stream of blood as thick as an arm gushed from the wound right into the other's face. It seemed as if he must topple over, utterly exhausted; but suddenly he rose once more, expanding his broad chest, raised his arm and lunged at his enemy who was blinded by blood. And struck him, between two ribs, right in the heart.

Lagartijillo beat the air with both arms; the knife fell from his hand. Lifeless the huge body fell forward over his own legs.

And, as if this sight gave new strength to the dying Bombita, whose blood squirted in a horrible stream over his enemy, he stabbed like a madman time and again, thrusting the lusty steel into the blood-soaked back.

"Stop! Bombita, my little brave, you have conquered!" the patron said quietly.

Then came the most horrible thing of all. Bombita Chico, whose life-blood already covered the beaten man in a shroud of red, leaned with both hands upon the ground and lifted himself so high that from the wide gash in his body the yellow entrails crawled like a brood of loathsome snakes. He stretched his neck, lifted his head and, through the deep silence of the night, sounded his triumphant:

"Cock-a-doodle-doo!"

Then he sank down. This was his dying salute to life.

It was as if a red mist of blood had suddenly enveloped my senses. I saw and heard no more. I sank into a purple, fathomless sea. Blood gushed into my ears and nose. I wanted to shout, but, when I opened my mouth, it filled with thick warm blood. I almost suffocated– but worse, much worse, was this sweet, obnoxious taste of blood upon my tongue. Then I felt a stabbing pain somewhere; but it took an eternity till I recognized the cause of the pain. I was biting on something, and it was the thing which I was biting that hurt me so. With an immense effort I wrenched my teeth apart.

When I took my finger from my mouth, I awoke. During the battle I had gnawed off my fingernail down to the root, and now I had bitten into the quick.

The Andalusian touched my knee. "Do you want to settle your bets, *Caballero*?" he asked. I nodded. Then he figured out in many words what I had lost and won. All of the spectators pressed around us; no one bothered about the corpses.

First, the money! The money!

I gave the fellow a handful of coins and asked him to settle for me. He figured it out, and in a hoarse voice arranged matters with everyone.

"Not enough, *caballero*!" he said at last. I realized he was cheating me, but I only asked how much more I had to pay and gave him the money.

When he saw that I still had some in my pocket, he asked: "*Caballero*, don't you want to buy Bombita's knife? It brings luck– much luck!"

I bought the *navajo* for a ridiculous price. The Andalusian shoved it into my pocket.

Now nobody paid any attention to me any longer. I rose, and staggered out into the night. My forefinger hurt; I wound my handkerchief around it. In long, deep draughts I drank up the fresh night air.

"*Caballero*!" somebody shouted. "*Caballero*!" I turned. One of the men came towards me. "The *patron* sends me, *caballero*," he said. "Don't you want to take your friend home with you?"

Oh, yes– the Pope, the Pope! During all this time I hadn't seen anything, hadn't thought of anything.

I turned back again, passed through the cactus hedge. The shackled, bloody corpses were still on the ground. And over them bent the Pope, stroking with caressing hands the pitifully torn bodies. But I saw clearly that he did not touch the blood. Oh no! Only in the air his hands moved to and fro.

And I saw that they were the delicate, fine hands of a woman.

His lips moved. "Beautiful *salsa*," he whispered, "beautiful red tomato-sauce!"

They had to tear him away by force; he did not want to give up the sight. He stammered and tottered uncertainly around on his thin legs.

"Too much booze!" one of the men said. But I knew: he had not touched one drop.

The patron took off his hat and the others followed his example.

"*Vayan Ustedes con dios, caballeros!*" they said.

When we reached the main road, the Pope followed me obediently.

He took my arm and murmured:

"Oh, so much blood! So much beautiful blood!"

He clung to me like so much lead. Painfully I dragged the drunken man towards the Alhambra. Under the Tower of the Princesses we stopped and sat down on a stone.

After a long while he said slowly:

"Oh, life! What wonderful things life gives us! It is a joy to live!"

An icy night wind wetted our temples. I shuddered. I could hear the Pope's teeth chattering; slowly his blood-intoxication evaporated.

"Shall we go, Reverend?" I asked.

Again I offered my arm.

He declined.

Silently we descended toward sleeping Granada.

Fairyland

Port-au-Prince (Haiti), June 1906

Fairyland

While the Hapag steamer lay at anchor in the harbor of Port-au-Prince little "Blueribbon" rushed into the breakfast room. Breathlessly she ran around the table.

"Isn't mama here yet?"

No, mama was still in her cabin. But the officers and passengers all jumped up to take little "Blueribbon" on their laps. Never before had Lady Fair been so feted on board the President as this tot of six laughing summers. He, from whose cup "Blueribbon" drank her tea, was happy for the rest of the day. She always wore a white mull dress and the blue ribbon bow caressed her blond locks. A hundred times a day they asked her: "Why are you called 'Blueribbon'?" Then she laughed: "So that I can be found when I get lost!" But she was never lost, although she ran around all alone in every strange harbor; she was a daughter of Texas and as wise as a little owl.

None at the table could catch her today. She ran to the head of the table and climbed on the captain's lap. Then the big Norseman smiled: "Blueribbon" always showed him marked preference, and that was the one thing of which he was proud. "Want to dip!" said little "Blueribbon," and dipped her biscuit in his tea cup.

"Well, now, where were you going so early?" asked the captain.

"Oh, oh!" said the child, and her blue eyes gleamed even brighter than the ribbon in her hair. "Mama must come along! *We're in Fairyland!*"

"In Fairyland— Haiti" doubted the captain.

"Blueribbon" laughed. "I don't know what they call the country here— but I know that it's Fairyland! I saw them myself, and the wonderful monsters, they're all lying together on the bridge, near the market place. One has hands as big as a cow and the one next to him has a head like two cows! And one has scales like a crocodile— oh, but they're much lovelier and more wonderful than those in my book of fairy tales! Do you want to come along captain?"

Then she jumped up and hurried over to the beautiful woman who had just entered the salon.

"Mama, hurry drink your tea! Hurry, hurry! You must come along, mama; we're in Fairyland!"

They all went along, even the first engineer. He really had no time and had not even put in his appearance at breakfast; something had gone wrong with the machinery, and he had to set it right while they were in the harbor. But "Blueribbon" was fond of him because he carved such pretty things out of tortoise shells. And, therefore, he had to come along, for "Blueribbon" was first in command.

"I'll simply work all night," he said to the captain.

"Blueribbon" heard him, and nodded seriously: "Yes, you can do that. I'll be asleep then anyway."

[79]

"Blueribbon" led the way, and they hurried through filthy harbor streets; from every window and doorway curious negroes peeped forth. They jumped over broad gutters, and "Blueribbon" shrieked with laughter when the doctor stepped into one and the muddy water squirted up high over his white suit. On they went past wretched stalls along the market place, through the ear splitting noise of the screaching negro-women.

"See here they are! O, the darling monsters!" "Blueribbon" tore away from her mother, rushed over to the little stone bridge which led over the arid brook. "Oh, do come, all of you, quick, see the wonderful creatures, the beautiful monsters." She clapped her hands out of sheer joy and bounded with quick steps through the hot sand.

There huddled the beggars, displaying their horrible afflictions. The negro passes them heedlessly, but no stranger can pass them without dipping into his pockets. And they know this well, and know how to appraise each one; he, who recoils at the horrible sight will surely give a quarter, and the lady who is overcome with mal-de-mer, well, at least a dollar.

"Oh, look, mama, that one with the scales! Isn't he beautiful?"

She pointed to a negro whose entire body was deformed by a horrible corrosive scab. He was of a greenish yellow hue and the cicatrized scab really hung in triangular scales over his skin.

"And this one, captain, do look at this one! Oh, what fun it is to look at them! He's got a buffalo's head and the fur cap is grown right onto it!" "Blueribbon" touched a gigantic negro's head with her parasol. He suffered from a frightful case of elephantiasis, and his head was swollen to the size of a giant pumpkin. In addition, the wooly hair had become completely matted and hung down on all sides in ragged clusters. The captain tried to draw the little one away, but she pulled and dragged him along, quivering with delight, to another one.

"Oh, dearest captain, did you ever see such hands? Do you say, aren't they wonder—wonderful?" "Blueribbon" beamed with enthusiasm, she stooped down low towards the beggar, both of whose hands elephantiasis had inflated into awful shapes.

"Mama, mama, just look, his fingers are much bigger and longer than my whole arm! Oh, mama, if I could only have such beautiful hands too!" And she put her little hand in the outstretched ones of the negro, like a tiny, white mouse it trembled on the immense, brown surface.

The beautiful woman screamed piercingly, then fell in a deep faint into the arms of the engineer. They all busied themselves around her; the doctor drenched his handkerchief with Eau de Cologne and put it on her forehead. But "Blueribbon" searched her mother's pockets and brought forth her smelling salts and held them close under her nose. She knelt on the ground, big tears dropped from her eyes and moistened her mother's face.

"Mama, dear, sweet mama, please wake up again! Please, please, please, mama! Oh, do wake up, real quick, dearest mama, and I'll show you many more of these wonderfully beautiful creatures! No, you can't sleep now, mama, because we're in Fairyland!"

Mamaloi

η φυσις δαιμονια, αλλ'ου θεια εστι
Aristotle, De Divinatione, cap II

Ragusa, July 1907

Mamaloi

I received the following letter:

Petit Goaves (Haiti).
August 16, 1906

Dear Sir:

You see, I am keeping my promise. I shall write down everything as you requested, from the very beginning. Do with it as you wish, only don't use my own name for the sake of my relatives. I would like to spare them another scandal; the previous one was a sufficient strain upon their nerves.

Here, as you desired, you will find, to begin with, a very simple story of my life. I came here as a young man of twenty years, to join a German firm in Jeremie. You know the Germans have almost the entire colonial trade in their hands. The salary tempted me– one hundred and fifty dollars per month– and I saw myself already a millionaire. Well, I went the way of all young men who come to this liveliest and vilest of all countries on earth: horses, women, drinking and gambling. Only few are able to tear themselves away; I myself was saved only by my strong constitution. There was no thought of getting on; I lay around for months at a stretch in the German hospital at Port-au-Prince. At one time I did an excellent business with the government; at home, to be sure they would call it an incredibly impudent swindle. There they would have me in jail for three years; here I rose to high honors. All in all, if I had received the punishment provided by the German statutes, for what I and others did, I would have to live five hundred years to be a free man again. But I would gladly serve them if you could point out to me one man of my age in this country who has not an equal score to account for. To be sure, even at home, a modern judge would have to let us go scot free, for we all lack a consciousness of our acts: on the contrary, we look upon our deeds as not only permissible but extremely honest.

Well then, with the construction of the pier at Port-au-Prince– which, of course, was never built– I laid the foundation of my fortune; I shared my booty with a few ministers. Today I own one of the most successful enterprises on the island, and am a very rich man. I barter – or swindle, as you say – with everything imaginable, live in a beautiful villa, promenade in marvelous gardens and drink with the officers of the Hamburg-American liners whenever they call at this port. Thank god, I have neither wife nor child. You, of course, may call the mulatto bastards that run loose in my courtyard my children simply because I begot them – may the Lord keep you and your morals! – but I don't. In fine, I feel excellent.

For years I had a miserable nostalgia. Forty years I had been away from Germany– you understand. I resolved to sell my entire holdings for better or worse, and to spend my declining days in the old country. When I had made my resolution, my longing became suddenly so strong that I could hardly wait for my departure. As a result, I postponed the sale of my property, and with a neat sum of money tucked away, departed helter skelter to spend six months over there.

Well, I stood it three weeks, and, if I had tarried another day, the district attorney would have had to provide shelter for another five years. That was the scandal referred to above. "Another Case Sternberg," the Berlin papers wrote, and my highly honorable family saw their name printed in bold face underneath it. I shall never forget the last interview I had with my brother. The poor man is privy councilor! The face he made when I assured him quite innocently that the girls were at least eleven and possibly twelve years of age! The more I tried to whitewash myself, the deeper I got into the mire. When I finally told him that it really was not so bad and that here in Haiti we prefer the girls even younger, else we would have to be content with sickly specimens and not virgins at all, he stroked his forehead and murmured: "Be silent, wretched brother, be silent. My eyes look into a cesspool of indescribable filth." For three years he raged at me, and I secured his forgiveness only because I bequeathed to each one of his eleven children a considerable sum, and also because I sent him a monthly allowance for his sons. For this he includes me every Sunday in his prayers. Whenever I write him I never fail to mention the fact that another young lady of my neighborhood has reached the convenient age of eight and has enjoyed my favor. I ask him to pray for me, old sinner that I am. Let's hope that it helps! Once he wrote me that he had to struggle with his conscience to accept money from such an incorrigible man; often he was about to send it back: only his consideration and pity for his only brother persuaded him to keep it finally. But now, suddenly, the scales had fallen from his eyes, and he knew that I had been always joking. For now I was ninety-six years of age and for that reason incapable of similar misdeeds. But he begged me insistently to refrain from similar jokes in the future.

I answered him; here is a copy of my letter, which I, as a good business man, kept:

"My dear brother:

"Your letter deeply offended my pride. Under separate cover I am sending you a package of the bark and leaves of the *toluwanga*-tree, which an old negro provides regularly for me every week. The fellow claims to be one hundred and sixty years of age– well, he certainly is a hundred and ten. In any case– thanks to the excellent extract prepared from this bark– he is the stoutest Don Juan of the entire countryside, barring only your brother. The latter, incidentally, is still quite sure of his natural prowess and uses the precious solution only on rare occasions. For this reason he is readily able to grant you part of his store and guarantees its prompt effect. The day after tomorrow, in honor of your birthday, he will arrange a small banquet, and on this occasion he proposes to outdo himself, which is a general practice on memorable days. At the same time he will drink to your health.

"Enclosed, as a little extra for the coming Christmas, find a check for $3000 (three thousand dollars). With my best regards for you and yours, I am,

Your faithful brother.

"P.S. Please inform me if you remembered me in your prayers on Christmas."

Probably my good brother had another serious battle with his conscience, but eventually Christian pity for me, poor sinner, must have conquered in his heart. At any rate he kept the check.

I really don't know what else I should tell you about my life, my dear sir. I could tell you a hundred little adventures and jokes, but they would probably be of exactly the same nature as you heard from every white man, when you traversed our country.

As I re-read this missive, it occurs to me that three-quarters of what I had intended to be a *curriculum vitae* is devoted to the theme "woman";– well, that probably is characteristic of the writer. After all, what interesting thing could I have said about my horses, my merchandise or my wines? And poker I gave up a long time ago. In this village I am the only white man, aside from the Hamburg-American Line agent, and he plays no more than the officers of his line who occasionally call on me.

There remains woman– what will you?

So, now, I shall place this letter in the booklet which is to contain the notes you desired of me, and of which I still have no idea myself. Who knows, then, whether you ever will get it, or if you do– perhaps in an empty booklet?

I salute you, kind sir, and am, Yours very truly, F. X.

The letter is followed by these notes:

August 18.

As I open this empty booklet, I have a feeling as though something new were entering my life. What? The young doctor who visited with me for three days made me promise to investigate a mystery and embark upon a strange adventure; a mystery which, perhaps, does not even exist, and an adventure which may be alive in his imagination only. And I promised so lightly– but I am afraid he will be disappointed.

To be sure, he surprised me. Five months he strolled around in this land of ours and knows it much better than I myself, even though I have been here for fifty years. He told me a thousand things which I have never heard, or else which I had heard and put aside incredulously. Probably I would have paid as little attention to his stories, if he had not extracted from me, by his questions, all kinds of things which were never quite clear to me and which suddenly appeared to me in an entirely new light. And yet, I would have forgotten all that presently, if it hadn't been for the little incident with Adelaide.

What happened? Well, the negro girl – she is the most beautiful and the strongest of all my servants and really my favorite ever since she came to my house – was laying the tea table for us. Suddenly the doctor interrupted the conversation and looked at her attentively. After she was gone he asked me whether I had noticed the small silver ring with the black stone on the thumb of her right hand. I had seen the ring a thousand times, but had never paid any attention to it. Had I seen another one like it on another girl's hand? Well, perhaps; but I could not remember. He shook his head thoughtfully.

When the girl came once more to serve tea on the verandah, the doctor without looking at her, hummed a few notes; an absurd melody backed with a few stupid nigger words, none of which I could understand:

Leh! Eh! Bomba, hen, hen!
Cango bafio tè
Cango mount dè lè
Cango do ki la
Cango li!

Crash! The tea board lay on the stone floor, cans and cups shattered to pieces. With a shriek the girl ran from the house. The doctor stared after her; then he laughed and said:

"I give my word, she is a *mamaloi.*"

We chatted till midnight, until the steam siren called him back on board ship. While I took him back in my boat he almost succeeded in convincing me that I was living like a blindman in a most extraordinary world of horror, the existence of which till then was utterly unknown to me.

Well, I have sharpened my eyes and ears. So far, nothing odd has occurred to me. I am very curious to read the books the doctor proposed to send me from New York. As a matter of fact, I agreed with him perfectly when he said that it is a shame that, in all these years, I haven't read a single book about this country. I didn't even know that such books existed: I never came across one at the house of a friend.

August 27.

Once more Adelaide is away for a week to visit her parents in the interior. She really is the only native girl in whom I ever noticed such a pronounced attachment to her parents. I believe she would run away if I did not give her the desired vacation. For days before she is quite unbalanced, and when she returns, the sorrow of parting always works so severely upon her that she actually breaks down under the strain of her duties. Think of it: a colored girl! Incidentally, I have searched her room during her absence; quite methodically. I prepared myself for the task by reading up on it in a detective story. I found nothing, absolutely nothing suspicious. The only one of her possessions which was not obvious from the very beginning was a black, rounded, oblong stone, lying on a plate bathed in oil. I think she uses it for massaging; all these girls massage their bodies.

September 4.

The books from New York arrived; I want to start reading immediately. There are three German, three English and five French works, some of them illustrated. Adelaide has returned. She is so miserable that she had to go to bed immediately, but, I know her; in a few days she will be all right again.

September 17.

If only one-tenth of what these books contain is true, it is really worth while to pursue the secret which the doctor thinks is so close to me. But these travellers simply must make themselves interesting, so that one copies the rankest idiocies from the other. I am really such a blind ass that never, in all these years, have I noticed anything of the entire voodoo cult, with its veneration of the snake and its thousand human sacrifices. A few small things did occur to me occasionally, but I never paid any attention to them. I must try to remember everything which might have some connection with voodooism.

Once my old housekeeper – I was living in Gonaives then – refused to buy pork in the market. It might be human flesh, she claimed. I laughed at her and reminded her of the fact that she bought pork all year round. "Yes, but never at Easter-time!" I could not convince her, and had to send another girl to the market. I have also seen these *caprelates* quite frequently– *hougons* they are called in this vicinity – decrepit old men who sell *wanges*. These are small bags with shells and multi-colored stones which are worn as amulets. They are divided into distinctive types, such as "points" which render men invulnerable; and for women there are "chances" which secure possession of the naked body of the beloved. But I never knew that these swindlers – or rather, these merchants – are a kind of low clergy of the voodoo cult. Nor did I ever realize that many foodstuffs are taboo for members of the cult. Thus Adelaide never touches tomatoes or *aubergines*, nor will she eat the meat of goats or turtles. On the other hand, she has often said that the meat of a ram is blessed, and blessed also is the *maiskassan*, her beloved corn-bread. I also have learned that twins are greeted with jubilation everywhere; there is always a family banquet when a woman or an ass gets *marassas*.

But, good Heaven, the story of human flesh on the market is certainly a fable; as for the rest, it all seems utterly harmless to me. Small superstitions; where on the entire earth won't you find something similar?

September 19.

So far as Adelaide is concerned, the doctor seems to be right after all, provided that his knowledge is not simply book knowledge. The Englishman, Spencer St. John, does mention a similar ring; it is supposed to be worn by the *mamaloi*, the priestess of the voodoo. Incidentally, I will confess that this term and the analogous one for the chief male priest are in much better taste than I would have believed these niggers capable of using: *papaloi*, *mamaloi*– in their corrupted French the *loi*, of course, stands for *roi*, or king. Can you think of a more beautiful title? Mother and queen– father and king. Does not that sound better than privy councilor, as my god-fearing brother calls himself? I also found mention in the books of the stone which I thought she used for massage. Tippenhauer, as well as St. Méry, knew it. Wonderful! I have a real god in my house; the fellow is called *Damtala*! In her absence I inspected it; the descriptions tally absolutely. It is obviously an old, marvelously well-sharpened axe of the time of the *caraïbs*. The negroes find it in the forest and, unable to explain its origin, think it is a god. They put it on a plate and believe it knows the future and talks by rattling. To keep it in good humor, it gets an oil bath every Friday. I find this utterly charming, and my secret priestess pleases me more from day to day. To be sure, there are still secrets to be fathomed– the doctor is quite right – but there is nothing horrible about it!

September 23.

Now, in my seventieth year, I am forced to realize that it is well to educate yourself in all fields. I would never have had that charming adventure I experienced yesterday if I hadn't studied those books.

I was drinking my tea on the verandah, and called for Adelaide, who had forgotten the sugar. She did not come. I looked in my room, in the kitchen; she wasn't there, nor were the other girls. Moreover, I could not find the sugar. As I walked through the foyer, I heard murmurs in her room. I rushed to the garden – her room is on the ground floor – and looked in. There my pretty black priestess was siting wiping the stone with her best silk handkerchief, putting it back on the plate and carefully pouring fresh oil over it. She seemed very excited; her eyes were full of tears. Carefully she took the plate between two fingers, at the same time extending her arm. Then her arm began to tremble, slowly at first and then faster. Naturally the stone began to rattle. Adelaide talked to it but, unfortunately, I could not understand a word.

But now I am getting somewhere. Fine! the doctor may yet be satisfied. And I, too; for, fundamentally, this is flattering to me. That evening, before dinner, I went to her room, took the talking stone and sat down in my easy chair. When she came in to remove the plates, I quickly put my newspaper aside, took the plate and poured fresh oil over the stone. The effect was remarkable. Crash! went the tray, an habitual occurrence at such moments. Thank God, it was empty this time. I motioned her to be still and said quitely: "Friday! He must have fresh a bath today!"

" You want to ask him?" she whispered.

"Naturally!"

"About me?"

"Of course!"

All this came about very conveniently; now I would certainly learn her secret. I waved at her to leave the room and to close the door behind her. She obeyed, but I could plainly hear her waiting outside and listening. Now I made the god clatter to its heart's content. It skipped about on the oiled plate so merrily that it was really a joy to watch it. The clacking mingled with Adelaide's sighs from behind the door.

As soon as I let the thunder god subside and put down the plate, she slunk in again.

"What did he say?"

Exactly! The devil, what did he say? He clattered, and nothing else. So I remained silent.

"What did he say?" she insisted. "Yes, or no?"

"Yes." I said making a wild guess.

She was jubilant. *"Petit moune? Petit moune?"* In Hatian Creole this stands for *petit mond*, which means "little world," or rather "little child."

"Naturally, *petit moune!*" I repeated.

She jumped around the room, hopping from one leg to the other.

"Oh, he is so good, the dear thunder god! He told me so, too. And now he must keep his promise since he pronounced it twice in one day!" Suddenly she became quite serious again. "What did he say, a boy or a girl?"

At this she fell on her knees before me, crying and sobbing again and again, almost swooning in her joy. "At last! At last!"

September 28.

I know that Adelaide has loved me for a long time and that she wishes for nothing else so much as a *petit moune* from me. She is jealous of the other girls whose brats run around in the courtyard, although, God knows, I don't bother with any of them. I think she would love to scratch their eyes out. So that is the reason why she treated the thunder god so nicely! Incidentally, tonight she was particularly charming, and it seems to me that I have never had so sweet a colored girl. I believe I actually like her a lot, and, so far as I am concerned, everything shall be done to fulfill her little wish.

It is scandalous that I, as a good business man, have never kept account of the extent to which I have contributed toward the betterment of this wretched people. Apparently I have always greatly underestimated my cultural achievements. Today I brought the statistics up to date; it was not very difficult. You know, my thumb has three joints and this is said to be hereditary. In other words, anybody in the village with three joints in his thumb is certainly one of my offspring. In connection with this I made an amusing discovery, so far as little Léon is concerned. I always took the mulatto boy for one of my progeny, and his mother, too, swears to this. But the brat has only two joints in his thumb. Something is wrong here. I suspect handsome Christian, one of the Hamburg-American Line officers; he must have competed with me. As a matter of fact, not less than four of my offspring are missing. Some say they ran away years ago; but nobody is able to tell me anything definite. It is really so unimportant.

October 24.

The clatter-god was right. Adelaide is bewitched, and full of a honeymoon tenderness which is almost disquieting. Her pride and her joy seem contagious; never in all my life have I bothered about the progress of a future pilgrim on earth; while now– what's the use of denying it?– I find myself keenly interested. On top of that comes the closer relationship which has sprung up between Adelaide and me. To be sure there was some resistance and hesitancy, as well as much weeping and coaxing, until I finally won her entire trust. These blacks certainly can be silent if they want to; what they won't divulge you can't get out of them even with red-hot pliers.

Here, again, a particularly happy coincidence provided the means whereby I forced her to remove her last mask.

Adelaide has no parents after all! I learned it from an old woman by the name of Phylloxera, who has weeded my garden these past years. She is a shrivelled old hag who lives with her great-grandchild – a dirty, lousy brat – in a tumble-down shanty in the neighborhood. Once again the little scamp had stolen eggs in my house and faced a severe whipping. Then the old woman came to beg me off. In return she offered me information about Adelaide, since, of course, she too had noticed in what high favor Adelaide stood. And her information – I had to swear by all saints that I would not betray the old hen – was really so interesting that I gave her an American dollar on top of it. Adelaide has no parents and, therefore, could not have visited them. She was a *mamaloi*, a priestess-queen of the voodoo cult. Whenever she took leave, it was for the purpose of rushing to the *honfoû*, the temple situated far away on a little clearing in the woods. And there my little tender Adelaide plays the part of the cruel priestess, invokes the holy snake, chokes children, drinks rum like an old ship's captain and manages unheard of orgies! Small wonder that she always returns home utterly exhausted. Well! You just wait, you little *canaille*!

October 26.

I announced that I was riding to Sâle-Trou and had my horse saddled. The old woman had given me approximate directions to the temple, as well as a negro woman can give directions. Naturally, I lost my way, and had the pleasure of staying over night in the primeval forest. Fortunately I carried a hammock with me. Not until the next morning did I find the *honfoû*-temple, a large, miserable straw hut upon a clearing which had been stamped and smoothed like a dance floor. A rough path led to the temple, and, on both sides, I noticed stakes driven into the earth and adorned alternately with the cadavers of black and white chickens. Between the stakes there were blown-out turkey eggs and grotesquely shaped stones and roots. A big strawberry tree – called *loco*, and held sacred by the believers – stood at the entrance to the temple; and around it were heaped shattered glasses, plates and bottles in its honor.

I entered the room. A few holes in the roof gave sufficient light. Underneath one of them, fastened to a pillar, was a burned-down pitch torch. The interior decorations of the temple were very gay. Against the walls I saw pictures of Bismarck and King Edward VIII from an illustrated weekly. Both of them most assuredly came from me. Who else would have subscribed to the *"Woche"* and to the "Illustrated London News"? Probably Adelaide had generously bequeathed them. In addition there were a few pictures of saints,– horrible oil prints depicting St. Sebastian, St. Francis and Mother Mary– and, next to them, cartoons from *"Simplizissimus"* (mine too!) and from *"L'Assientte au Beurre."* In between hung a few old flag-rags, chains of shells and multi-colored paper garlands.

In the background, somewhat higher up, I noticed a heavy basket. Ah, I thought, that's where *Hougonbadagari*, the great voodoo god, is hidden! Very carefully I opened the cover and jumped back: I had no particular desire to be bitten by some poisonous reptile. But oh! To be sure, there was a snake in the basket, but only a harmless one; and starved to death besides! That is typically nigger; to pray to something as divine and then completely forget it when the festival is over! Naturally a reserve god could be easily procured in the woods. Anyway, *Damtala*, the good clatter-god, was decidedly better off than the mighty *Hougonbadagui* lying miserably shrivelled and dead before me. The former gets oil every Friday, while the latter, who holds the place of John the Baptist in this crazy heathen-Christian voodoo cult, does not even get a little frog or a mouse.

October 29.

When I displayed my new wisdom before Adelaide the next day– I acted as if I had known everything for a long time– she did not even attempt any longer to lie. I told her that the doctor had informed me, he who was a messenger of *Cimbi-Kita*, the head devil. And I showed her an axe over which I had poured some red ink. An axe drenched in blood is the symbol of the devil.

The girl trembled, swallowed hard and could barely be quieted.

"I knew it," she shouted. "I knew it! And I also told the *papaloi* about it. He is *Dom Pèdre* himself."

I confirmed it– why shouldn't the good doctor be *Dom Pèdre* himself? Now I learned that our own village, Petit Goaves, was the headquarters of the devil-sect of *Dom Pèdre*. That was a man – and a nice swindler he must have been! – who came over a long time ago from the Spanish part of the island, and founded the cult of *Cimbi-Kita*, the great devil, and his knight, *Azilit*. He must have made a great deal of money out of it. But he himself and all of his greater and lesser devils may fetch me alive, if I don't make a nice business out of this story. I have an idea already.

Today I heard the *néklésin*, the iron triangle, howl throughout the streets. How often I had heard this childish music before and never thought anything of it! Only now do I know that it is the gruesome signal calling the believers to the temple. I called my little *mamaloi* immediately and informed her that this time I would participate in the rites. She was beside herself; begged and entreated, cried and shrieked. But I did not give in. Again I showed her the old wooden axe with the red ink, which almost froze her with terror. I told her that I was specifically instructed by *Dom Pédre* and that everything would have to be done as usual. She left me to talk with her *houcibossales*, the tattooed voodoo people. I think she is there now; and the *papaloi* himself, too.

I used her absence to read another few chapters in my books; I have here collected a few dates which are probably trustworthy.

Apparently, Toussaint Louveture, the liberator of Haiti, was a *papaloi* himself, as were Emperor Dessalines and King Christoph. Emperor Soulouque was a voodoo priest; I knew the black rotter when I first came to Port-au-Prince in 1858. And President Salnave, my good friend Salnave, in 1868 introduced the human sacrifice in person– the sacrifice of the "hornless he-goat." Salnave! Who would have thought it? The very knave with whom I – in the same year – did not build the pier in Port-au-Paix, which laid the foundation of my fortune. Then came President Salomon, the aged idiot, who was a pious disciple of voodoo. That Hippolyte, his successor, was little less so, I had often heard, but that he preserved as memories the skeletons of his victims is a particularly nice trait about him. When he died ten years ago, they found quite a number of these skeletons in his rooms. He might have left me some of them. I had closed many a good transaction with him – always fifty-fifty – and, besides that, he got all his uniforms free from me, with all the golden tinsel he could wish for! And all the *kapypsos* came out of my pocket, too; and he never had to spend a *centime* for small tips for the gentlemen and deputies.

On the other hand, the two presidents of the sixties and seventies, Geffard and Boisrond-Canal, were opposed to the voodoo cult. The very two with whom it was so difficult to do business! In their days, too, fell the trials against the voodoo people. In 1864 eight prisoners were shot to death in Port-au-Prince because they had sacrificed and eaten a twelve year-old girl. And, in 1876, a *papaloi* was sentenced to death, and, two years later, a number of women. That is not very much, if as Texier has it, a thousand children – *cabrits sans cornes* – were slaughtered and eaten every year.

Adelaide has not returned yet. But I shall insist upon my wish under all circumstances. I belong to this country, and have the right to know it in all its peculiarities.

10 P.M.

The *papaloi* has sent an emissary, an *avalou* – sort of a sacristan – who pleaded for an interview in behalf of his master. I sent him away and refused to listen to anything. Before he left, I showed him my ink-splattered axe, which did not fail to make the desired impression. I notified the *papaloi* that I would shoot him down if he did not live up to my wishes.

At nine o'clock the fellow returned once more to bargain; incidentally, he was filled with wholesome awe and did not even dare to enter my room. In the name of *Cimba-Kita*, the head devil, I did some tall cursing. This man, at least, is as convinced of my devilish mission as Adelaide herself! She has not returned yet and I am positive she is being held. I told the *avalou* that, together with *Dom Pédre* himself, I would call for her if she weren't home within an hour.

Midnight.

Everything is arranged! The expedition can start tomorrow. The *papaloi* probably realized that I was not to be moved from my purpose, and therefore he gave in. True priest that he was, he still tried to secure something for himself and, through Adelaide, made the condition that I donate twenty dollars for the poor of the community – "the poor" – meant himself, of course! So I sent him the money immediately. Now the black privy councilor will probably be satisfied.

In return he sent me a handful of rotten plants which I was to use for a bath in order to be ordained and become *canzou*. One really is expected to squat forty days in this mud until it has completely evaporated; but a shorter method was permitted me. I threw the stuff out, of course, but, for Adelaide's sake, I ate the second gift– *verver*, a mixture of corn and blood. It tasted abominably. Now I am sufficiently purified to be accepted tomorrow night among the devil priests, the *bizangos* and *quinbindingues*.

November 22.

It costs me an effort to hold my pen. My arm trembles and my hand refuses to obey. Two days I have lain on the couch and even today I walk around in a fever. All my bones seem crushed. Adelaide is still in bed. Small wonder, after that night! If I should report all that happened to my brother, I think the pious gentleman might still return the enclosed check.

God, how my back aches! Each smallest movement makes me scream. I hear Adelaide whimper in her bed. A little while ago I was at her bedside. She said no word; she only cried softly and kissed my hand. And I could hardly realize that this poor little animal was the same cruel priestess with her clawing, blood-stained hands.

I will relate everything quietly

Adelaide left early that morning; I mounted my fallow that afternoon. My two good Brownings were secure in my saddle pocket. This time I knew the way to the *honfoû*, which I reached at sundown. From afar I heard already the noise of excited voices, intermingled with the piercing sound of the *néklésin*. The great clearing was filled with black bodies; they had shed all their clothing and wore only a few knotted red handkerchiefs around their loins. Drinking out of their full-bellied *tafia* bottles, they ran up and down the path along which black and white fowl had been impaled on stakes. Shrieking, they shattered their bottles under the sacred strawberry tree. Apparently I was expected. A few men approached me, tethered my horse to a tree and led me along the path, pouring blood from their vessels over the pitifully cackling and fluttering hens, as if they were so many flower pots. At the entrance to the temple someone pressed an empty bottle into my hand which I shattered under the strawberry tree. We entered the empty room, and everybody pressed after me. Shoved by naked bodies, I came close to the snake basket. Mighty pitch torches were fastened to the beams and sent their soot through the open roof-holes into the night. I was pleased with the red sheen upon the black, glistening bodies; it put me in a good humor.

Next to the snake basket blazed a fire under a huge kettle. Close by the musicians sat upon their drums, *Houn, Hountor* and *Hountorgri*, dedicated to the three apostles, Peter, Paul and John. Behind them I saw a gigantic fellow beating the *Assauntor* drum which is spanned with the skin of a dead *papaloi*. The rhythm became ever faster; ever louder they thundered through the crowded interior.

The acting *avalous* forced the crowd back on both sides and cleared an empty space in the middle. They threw down dry wood and faggots, and poked their burning torches into them. Suddenly a brilliant fire was burning on the stamped floor. Then they led five neophytes, three women and two men, into the circle. These had just finished their forty-days' purification in the mud bath which, fortunately, I had been spared. The drums stopped and the *papaloi* came forth.

He was an old, emaciated negro, clad like the rest in red knotted kerchiefs. He wore a blue ribbon around his forehead, from under which his long, foully clotted hair straggled. His assistants, the *dijons*, handed him a mass of hair, pieces of horn and herbs, which he scattered slowly into the flames chanting incantations to the heavenly twins, *Saugo*, the god of lightning, and *Bado*, the god of winds, that they might fan the flames. Then he ordered the trembling neophytes to jump into the fire. The *dijons* coaxed and pushed the hesitating ones into the flames; it was marvelous to see how they jumped to and fro. Finally they were permitted to emerge again, and now the priest led them to the steaming kettle next to the snake basket. Now he implored *Opété*, the sacred turkey, and *Assougié*, the heavenly chatterbox. In their honor the neophytes had to reach into the boiling water; had to snatch pieces of meat from it which they distributed among the believers on huge cabbage leaves. Time and again the terribly scalded hands reached into the sizzling brew, until even the last one had his leaf. Only then did the measly old man accept them as full-fledged members of his community– in the name of *Attaschollôs*, the great world spirit– and finally he left them to the mercy of their relatives and friends, who anointed their poor seared hands with salve.

I was curious to see whether this benevolent priest would ask a similar ceremony of me, too, but nobody bothered. To be sure, they handed me a piece of meat too, and I ate it just like the rest.

The *dijons* threw more fuel into the fire and arranged a spit over it. Then they dragged in three rams by the horns, two black and one white, and led them before the *papaloi*, who pierced their throats with a powerful knife, and with one mighty thrust severed their heads. With his two hands he held them on high; showed them to the drummers first, then to the believers; and, dedicating them to the god of chaos, *Agaou Kata Badagri*, he threw them into the kettle. In the meantime, the *dijons* caught the blood in huge vessels, mixed it with rum and distributed around to drink. Then they skinned the goats and put them on the spit.

I, too, drank; a sip at first, and then more and more. I felt a strange intoxication rise in me– a wild, lustful drunkenness such as I had never before known. I quite lost consciousness of my part as a disinterested spectator; more and more I entered into this wild world as one who belonged.

With pieces of charcoal the *dijons* drew a black circle on the floor next to the fire, and the *papaloi* stepped into it. And, while the joints roasted and sizzled, he invoked in a loud voice *Allégra Vadra*, the omniscient god. He begged him to enlighten his priests and the trusting community. And, through him, the god answered that enlightenment would come after the goat meat had been consumed. Thereupon the black figures sprang to the spit, tore off the meat with their hands and swallowed it hot and half raw. They broke the bones, gnawing them with their big teeth and throwing them high through the roof-holes into the night– in honor of *Allégra Vadra*, the great god.

And again the drums began to drone. *Houn*, the small one, began; then *Hountor* and *Hountorgri*. And finally, the mighty *Assountor*-drum began to shriek its loathsome song. Ever stronger grew the excitement; ever closer and hotter the black bodies pressed around me. The *avalous* put the spit aside and stamped out the fire. The black crowd surged forward.

And suddenly,– I don't know where she came from– Adelaide, the *mamaloi*, stood upon the snake basket. Like the rest she wore only a few kerchiefs over her loins and her left shoulder. Her forehead was adorned with the blue priest ribbon; her marvelous white teeth shone in the red light of the torches. She was exquisite, absolutely exquisite! With his head bent low, the *papaloi* handed her a big vessel with rum and blood, which she drained in a single draught. The drums were silent. Softly at first, and ever growing in volume she began the great song of the holy snake:

> *Leh! Eh! Bomba, hen, hen!*
> *Cango bafio tè,*
> *Cango mount dè lè,*
> *Cango do ki la*
> *Cango li!*

Twice, three times, she sang the wild words, until, from a hundred drunken lips, it came back to her:

> *Leh! Eh! Bomba, hen, hen!*
> *Cango bafio tè,*
> *Cango mount dè lè,*
> *Cango do ki la*
> *Cango li!*

The small drum accompanied her song, which grew softer again and seemed to die down completely. She rocked to and fro from the hips, bent her head and lifted it, drawing weird snake-lines in the air. And the crowd was silent; breathless in expectation. Softly someone whispered: "Be blessed, *Manho*, our priestess!" And another one: "St. John the Baptist kiss you, *Houangan*, his beloved!" the eyes of the negroes bulged from their sockets. Everybody was staring at the softly humming *mamaloi*.

Then, in a faltering voice, she said quietly: "Come here! *Houedo* hears you, the great snake!"

Everybody pressed close. It was almost impossible for the servants and priests to preserve order.

"Shall I get a new ass this summer?" – "Will my child get well?" – "Will my lover return, whom they made a soldier?" Everyone had a question to ask, a wish to make.

The black Pythia answered, her head sunk deep on her chest, her arms stretched downwards, stiff; her fingers painfully spread apart– perfect oracles which said neither "yes" nor "no," but from which each one could take what he wished to hear. Satisfied, they stepped aside, throwing coppers into the old felt hat which the *papaloi* held. There was silver, too.

Again the drums droned; slowly the *mamaloi* seemed to awaken from her dream. She sprang down from the basket, tore the snake from it and mounted again. It was a long, black and yellow reptile. Confused by the firelight, it thrust its tongue forth and slowly wound itself around the outstretched arms of the priestess. The believers fell to the floor, touching the earth with their foreheads. "Long live the *mamaloi*, our mother and queen! She, *Houndja-Nikon*, our ruler!" And they prayed to the great snake, and the priestess exacted the oath of eternal allegiance. "May your brain rot and your intestines within you if ever you break your oath you swore!" then they chanted: "We swear strong oaths to you, *Houngon-badagri*, St. John the Baptist, you who come to us as *Sobagui*, as *Houedo*, the great voodoo god!"

Now the *mamaloi* opened another basket which stood behind her. From it she drew fowl, black ones and white ones, and thrust them high into the air. The believers jumped up form the soil and grabbed the fluttering animals, tearing their heads off. Greedily they drank the freshly streaming blood that gushed from the fowl. Then they threw them out through the holes in the roof: "For you, *Houedo*; for you *Hougonbadagri*, as a sign that we keep our oath!"

From behind six men pressed around the *mamaloi*. They wore devil's masks; goat furs hung from their shoulders, and their bodies were painted red with blood.

"Fear, fear *Cimbi-Kita!*" they cried. The mob surged back and formed a small opening into which they stepped.

They led a girl of ten years by a rope around her neck. The child looked around, surprised, timid, afraid, but did not cry. It staggered, could hardly stand on its feet; quite drunk with rum. The *papaloi* came close.

"To *Azilit* I give you, and to *Dom Pèdre!* May they carry you to him, the greatest of all devils, to *Cimbi-Kita!*"

He strew herbs into the woolly hair of the child, horn shavings and tufts of hair, and then laid a burning cinder on top of it. But, before the terrified child could reach with its hand into the burning hair, the *mamaloi*, with a horrible shriek, threw herself down from the basket like a maniac. Her fingers closed around the small neck; she lifted the child high up into the air and choked it to death.

"*Aa-bo-bo!*" she shrieked.

It seemed as if she would never let go of her victim. Finally the head priest tore the lifeless child away from her and, as he had done to the rams, cut the head off with one stroke. At the same time the devil-priests with mighty voices chanted their triumphant song:

> *Interrogez le cimetière,*
> *Il vous dira*
> *De nous ou de la mort,*
> *Qui des deux fournit*
> *Les plus d'hôtes.*

Again the *papaloi*, with outstretched arms, showed the head to the drummers; again he threw it into the seething cauldron. Rigid, indifferent, the *mamaloi* stood, while the devil-priests caught the blood in their rum vessels and hacked the body to pieces. Like animals they threw the raw pieces of meat to the believers; the latter fell on them, fought for them, tore at them.

"*Aa-bo-bo! Le cabrit sans cornes!*" they shrieked.

And all of them drank the fresh blood mixed with strong rum. A horrible drink, but one drinks it, one must drink it, more and ever more!

Now one of the devil-priests advanced into the circle next to the priestess. He tore his mask off; threw down his fur. Naked the black man stood there, his body weirdly painted with gore and hands dyed red with blood. Everybody was silent; nowhere was a voice to be heard. Only the small *Houn* drum softly droned to the devil dance, the dance of *Dom Pèdre* which was about to begin.

Motionless the dancer stood, without moving a muscle, for several minutes. Slowly he rocked to and fro; first the head, then the body. All his muscles were tense. A strange excitement seemed to overcome him and to infect everyone like a mystic fluid.

Each one looks at the other, still without moving; but senses how the nerves begin to tingle. Now the priest begins to dance, whirls slowly at first, then ever faster. Louder sounds the *Houn* drum; the *Hountor* drum chimes in. Now life comes into the black bodies; one lifts a foot, another one an arm. They devour each other with their eyes. Two seize each other and join the dance. Now the *Hountorgri*, too, sounds and the mighty *Assauntor* drum; its side of human skin shrieks a terrifying, lashing wail of lust.

Everybody leaps up. They whirl and dance, kick and stamp, jump like goats, cast themselves to the ground, beat the floor with their heads, leap up again, wave their arms and legs, and rave and shriek to the wild rhythm the priestess sings. Proudly she stands in the middle, lifting high the holy snake and singing her song: "*Leh! Eh! Bomba, hen, hen!*" close by her side is the *papaloi*; from huge vats he squirts blood over the black figures which leap ever wilder, chant ever fiercer the song of the queen.

They take hold of one another, tear the red rags from their bodies. Their limbs intertwine; hot perspiration runs from the naked bodies. Drunk with rum and blood, whipped into boundless lust, they tear at each other like animals, throw one another to the ground, lift each other high in the air, thrust their greedy teeth into each other's flesh! And I feel myself drawn irresistibly into this devil-dance of madmen. A crazy lust invades the hall, a bloody delirium of love that transcends all human bounds. They have stopped singing a long time ago; out of their convulsions and delirium only the horrible devil-shout is audible: "*Aa-bo-bo!*"

I see men and women bite each other, possessing each other in every conceivable manner. Blood-thirsty, they thrust their nails into the flesh, tearing deep wounds. The blood lulls their senses. I see men crawl on men, women on women. There, five roll together in a dark knot; here, one, like a dog, stoops over the snake basket. Their mad lust knows no distinction, cannot even mark living from inanimate things.

Two nigger girls fall on me; tear at my clothes. I seize their breasts, throw them to the floor, roll around, bite, shriek– just like all the rest. I see Adelaide indiscriminately possessing one man after the other; and women, too, always fresh ones– her devilish lust unquenchable. She rushes at me naked; red blood trickles from her arms and breasts. Only the blue priest ribbon still adorns her forehead. Like black snakes her thick locks crawl from under it. She hurls me down, takes me by force, rushes up again and thrusts another woman into my arms. And she staggers away, embracing and embraced, ever by other black arms.

And now, all resistance gone, I plunge into the wildest frenzy, into the most unheard of embraces; leap, rage and shriek, wilder and madder than anybody else, the horrible: "*Aa-bo-bo!*"

I found myself outside, lying on the dance-place in a heap of black men and women. The sun was already up. All around me the black bodies lay, groaning and writhing in their dreams. With an immense effort I rose; my clothes hung from me in bloody tatters. I saw Adelaide lying close by, bruised and bloody from head to foot. I lifted her, carried her to my horse. Where I found the strength, I do not know; but I managed to lift her onto the horse's back, and so rode home, holding the senseless woman in my arms. I had her put to bed and went to mine. . .

I hear her whimpering again. I shall go and fetch her a glass of lemonade.

March 7, 1907.

Now months have gone by. As I read over these last pages, it seems to me as if another, not myself, had lived through all this. It seems all so far away and so strange. And particularly when I am with Adelaide, I have to force myself to believe that she was present, too. She, a *mamaloi!* She, this tender, trusting, happy little creature? She has only one thought: our child. will it really be a boy? Surely a boy? A hundred times she asks me that. And is so happy every time I tell her that it will most certainly be a boy. It is too funny: this child that is not even yet come takes up a large part of my thoughts. We have already agreed upon a name; already all the linen is in readiness. And I am almost as worried for the little worm as Adelaide herself.

Incidentally, I have discovered a new extraordinary faculty in her. Now she is a full-fledged department head in my business, and does very well indeed. I have founded a new branch which gives me a lot of amusement. I distill a miracle-water, good for all sorts of things. The recipe is very simple: rain-water colored pink with a little tomato juice. This is poured into little fat bottles which I import labelled from New York. The label is designed after my own directions; it bears *Cimbi-Kita's* bloody axe, and the inscription: *Eau de Dom Pèdre.* The bottles cost me three cents each, and I sell them for a dollar. Moreover, the sales are excellent; the niggers almost fight for it. Since last week I have also begun to ship them into the interior. The purchasers are very well satisfied; they claim that it works marvels for all kinds of ailments. If they could write, I would have quite a collection of testimonials by now. Adelaide, too, is of course convinced of its supernatural powers, and deals in it with real zeal. Her salary and percentage – she also gets a percentage of the sales – is always turned over to me that I may save it for "her boy." She is really charming, this black child. I almost believe I am in love with her.

August 26, 1907.

Adelaide is beside herself with joy; she has her boy! But that isn't all. The boy is white, and that makes her proud beyond belief. All negro children, as is well-known, are not black at birth, but rather pink-looking, just like the children of white people. But, whereas these become white, negro children grow black, or at least brown, in the case of hybrids. Adelaide knew this, of course, and, with tears in her eyes, waited for her child to get black. She never let it from her arms, not even for a second, as if she could prevent it from acquiring its natural color. But hour after hour passed; and day after day; and her child became white and remained white—snow-white in fact, whiter than myself. If it had not had black, kinky hair, nobody would have believed it to be of negro blood! Not until three weeks had passed did Adelaide permit me to take it in my arms. I never held a child in my arms; it was a strange feeling when the little fellow laughed at me and milled about with its little arms. What force he already had in his tiny fingers, particularly in his thumbs – which, of course, have three joints – really a marvelous fellow!

It is a pure joy to watch the mother standing in the store behind the counter, the pink miracle bottles piled up before her. Her strong, black bosom laughs from her red blouse, and the healthy white baby drinks mightily. Really, I feel well in my old days, and as young as ever. In my happiness over the birthday of my son, I have sent a large extra remittance to my dear brother. I can easily afford it; there will always be enough for the boy.

September 4.

I had sworn to myself that I would never again have anything to do with the voodoo crowd, unless it were in connection with my miracle water. Now I had to busy myself once more with them, after all; not as a participant this time, but as an attacker.

Yesterday the old hag who weeds my garden came crying to me. Her great-grandchild had disappeared. I consoled her by saying he probably had run into the woods. She, too, had believed so at first, and had searched for days; but now she knew that the *bidangos* had caught him. He was being held in a hut outside the village and next week he was to be sacrificed in honor of *Cimbi-Kita, Azilit* and *Dom Pèdre*. I promised to help her and rode off on my mission. When I got to the thatched hut a black fellow stepped before me, whom I recognized as the dancer of the devil-priest. I pushed him aside and went inside. There I found the boy squating in a bog box, bound hand and foot. Big pieces of corn-bread soaked in rum next to him. He stared at me from stupid, animal eyes. I cut him loose and took him away, the priest not daring to interfere. I had the boy taken directly aboard a Hamburg-American liner leaving that night. To the captain I gave a letter to a business friend in St. Thomas, who was to take care of the boy. Thus he is safe. Had he remained here he would have fallen victim to the sacrificial knife before long. This voodoo crowd doesn't easily let go of someone they have destined for slaughter. The old crone sobbed with joy when she heard that her only happiness – incidentally, an utterly helpless rascal – was safe aboard ship. Now she has nothing to fear; when he returns he will be a man, capable himself of offering sacrifices.

As a matter of fact, my action pleased me personally, too. It is a sort of revenge for the mulatto boys who disappeared from my courtyard. The old woman has told me they, too, met the fate that was planned for her great-grandchild.

September 10.

For the first time in many months I have had another quarrel with Adelaide. She learned that I had saved Phylloxera's great-grandchild, and asked me about it. The priests of *Cimbi-Kita* had destined the boy to die; how could I dare to tear him from their strong clutches?

In all this time we had never said another word about voodoo, ever since the day, shortly after the sacrificial feast, when she had voluntarily told me that she had resigned her office as *mamaloi*. She could no longer remain a priestess, she said, because she loved me too much. I had laughed at the time, but inwardly I was pleased, nevertheless.

Now she began once more with this terrible superstition. At first I tried to argue with her, but gave it up soon enough, realizing that I could not take away from her a belief which she had absorbed with her mother's milk. Besides that I recognized that her reproaches sprang from her love for me, and not out of her great fear for my safety. She cried and sobbed, and nothing I could do would quiet her.

September 15.

Adelaide is impossible. Everywhere she sees shadows. She remains close by my side, like a dog who wants to protect me. Now this, to be sure, is touching, but also annoying; particularly because the boy, whom she never leaves alone, has quite a remarkable voice. Everything I eat she prepares herself; and, not content with this, she tastes everything before she permits me to eat it. Now I know that these negroes are great poison mixers who know their botany thoroughly, but I don't believe that any one of them would dare to use his science on me. So I laugh at Adelaide– but, nevertheless, I don't feel any too well about it.

September 24.

So they have already taken away from me my "soul"! I know this from Phylloxera; the old lady is no less excited and anxious for me than Adelaide. Today she came to warn me. I wanted to send Adelaide from the room, but she insisted upon listening. It seems that the priests have set afoot the rumor that I had betrayed *Cimbi-Kita*, to whom I had sworn allegiance; that I am a *loup-garou*, a werewolf who sucks the blood of children while they sleep. Thereupon some of the *dijons* stole my "soul" by shaping a likeness of me in clay and hanging it in the temple. This alone would be harmless enough, but it has a rather unpleasant feature: from now on I am a man without a soul, whom anyone may kill. In fact, he who does it accomplishes a good deed.

Nevertheless I do not consider the affair of great importance and do not intend to share the women's fears. So long as my bloodhounds stand before my door, so long as my Brownings are at my bedside and so long as Adelaide prepares my food, I certainly don't fear these black fellows.

"For ages no negro has dared to attack a white man!" I consoled Adelaide.

But she answered: "They no longer consider you a white man! They count you as one of them since you swore allegiance to *Cimbi-Kita*!"

October 2.

I pity the poor woman so much. She follows me like a shadow; not for a second does she leave me out of her sight. She hardly sleeps at night, sitting on a chair at my bedside and guarding my sleep.

She no longer weeps; quietly, silently she walks beside me as if she were wrestling with a great resolution.

How would it be if I gave up my business here? I don't want to go to Germany; not because I fear to collide again with its silly laws– long ago I ceased to bother with other women, since I have had Adelaide and the boy.

But, I really cannot bring a negress along as my wife. I might retire to St. Thomas. Adelaide would certainly feel at home there. I could build a beautiful country seat and might start some new kind of business, if I must have some occupation. If I could only sell my stuff here for a fairly decent sum.

I am writing in my work-room which looks like a fortress. Adelaide has gone out; she did not say where she was going, but I am positive she wants to bargain with the voodoo crowd. The three dogs are in the room before my locked door; my revolver is handy on my desk. It is really ridiculous— as if a nigger would dare harm a hair on my head in broad daylight! But I had to give in to Adelaide's wishes. She went alone; the child lies next to me on the couch and sleeps. I hope she will bring home good news.

October 30.

I think Adelaide has gone mad. She screamed and beat upon the door. I couldn't run fast enough to open it. She rushed directly to the boy, snatched him up and almost smothered him with her caresses. The little fellow began to cry pitifully. But she did not let go of him; kissed him, embraced him, I actually feared she would suffocate him.

Her behavior is really shocking. She says no word, but quite apparently she has been successful. She no longer tastes my meals; her anxiety seems to have disappeared. This surely means that all danger is past. But still she continues to follow me like a dog. At dinner she sat silently by my side without touching a bite; but, not for a second did she take her eyes off me.

Something terrible seems to be brewing in her mind, but she does not speak; not the tiniest word does she say. I don't want to torment her, for I see how the poor woman is consumed with love for me.

I will take every step to get away from here as quickly as possible. I have already spoken with the Hamburg-American agent. He is not opposed to the deal, but he wants to pay hardly one-fourth of what my business is worth, and that only on the installment plan. And yet, I shall probably accept. After all, I have made my share in safety for a long time and can afford to make a transaction at a loss. God, how happy Adelaide will be when I tell her about it! Then I shall marry her, for the boy's sake. She really deserves it. And when everything is in readiness, I shall say: "Now, child, pack your things." She will be mad with joy!

November 11.

My negotiations seem to be progressing satisfactorily. Even the cablegram from the agent's bank has come, stating that they stand ready to advance him the necessary cash. This does away with the principal obstacle; the details can be easily settled, since I am more than willing to compromise. The fellow knows this and insists upon calling me his "friend and benefactor." Well, I don't blame him for not being able to hide his joy over such a marvelous transaction.

It is rather hard for me to keep my secret from Adelaide. Her condition gets worse and worse. Well, she probably will be able to stand it another week, and then her joy will be so much the greater. She called on her voodoo brethren a few times, and each time she returned in a still more desperate condition. I don't understand it at all, since all danger seems to have passed. All doors are now open at night as they used to be and even the cooking she leaves to the other servants. What else can it be?

[100]

She hardly speaks a word now. But her love for me and the boy grows each day, grows almost boundless. This love has something uncanny about it which almost takes my breath away. If I take the boy on my knee and play with him, she shrieks, rushes from the room, throws herself on the bed and sobs as if her heart were breaking.

She must be ill and almost contaminates me with her strange disease. I shall bless the moment when we are able to leave this terrible hole with its horrible secrets.

November 15.

This morning she was quite beside herself. She wanted to do a few errands, taking her child with her. Thus she bid me farewell, but in a most unnatural way. Her eyes had long ago become red and inflamed from crying, but this morning cataracts fell from them. She could not tear herself from my arms; time and again she held the boy for me to kiss— I was quite moved by the scene. Thank God, the Hamburg-American agent came directly afterwards to bring the contracts for my signature. Now the names are affixed to them and the bank check is in my hands. The house is no longer mine; I begged the buyer to permit me to stay for another few days. "Half a year, if you want to!" he said. But I promised that I would not want to stay even another week. Saturday the steamer for St. Thomas is leaving, and by then everything must be ready.

Now I shall put flowers on the table. When she returns, she shall hear the joyous news.

5 P.M.

This is horrible! Adelaide did not come back; she did not come, I say! She did not come! I ran in to town; nobody had seen her. I returned home; she had not arrived. I went to the garden to look for the old hag; she was not there. I ran to the hut— and found her, bound to a pillar.

"At last you have come— at last! Hurry, before it's too late!" I cut her loose; it was difficult to get anything out of the half-crazed woman. "She has gone to the *honfoû*– the *mamaloi*," she stammered. "To the *honfoû* with her child. They bound me so I could not warn you." I ran back to the house to get my pistols. I am writing these lines while my horse is being saddled. Oh, God, what may. . .

Please God . . .!

November 16.

I rode through the woods.

I do not think I thought about anything; only this: you must get there in time— you must get there in time!

The sun had gone down when I crossed the clearing. Two fellows caught hold of my reins. I slashed my whip across their faces. I jumped off, threw the reins over the strawberry tree. Then I rushed into he *honfoû*, thrusting the crowd right and left.

I know I cried out. There in the red light, stood the *mamaloi* on the basket, the snake coiled around her blue ribbon. And, high above her head, she held my child by the throat. And the choked it, choked it, choked it!

I must have shrieked. I tore my Brownings from my pocket and fired. Two shots; one in her face, the other at her heart. She tumbled from the basket. I sprang forward and lifted up the child. I realized immediately that it was dead, but still so warm, so very warm.

[101]

Right and left I shot into the crowd. They pushed and fell aside; they howled, bellowed and shrieked. I tore the torches from the walls and hurled them into the thatch. It burned like tinder.

I mounted my horse and rode back, carrying the dead child home. I did save my child; not from death but from the teeth of those black devils. On my desk I found this letter– I don't know how it got there:

You betrayed *Cimbi-Kita* and they wanted to kill you. But they will spare you if I sacrifice my child. I love it so; but I love you still more. Therefore I will do what *Cimbi-Kita* demands. I know that you will drive me from you when you hear what I have done. Therefore I shall take poison and you will not see me again. For now you are quite safe.

I love you dearly.
Adelaide.

*   *
*

Now my life lies shattered before me. What shall I do? I know no more. I shall put these pages into an envelope and dispatch them. That is one bit of work left to do.

And then?

*   *
*

I answered immediately. My letter was sent in care of the steam-ship agent, with the note: "Please forward." I got it back with another note: "Addressee dead."

The Spider

»Lilith«

And a will therein lieth, which dieth not. Who knoweth the mysteries of a will with its vigor?

Glanville.

Paris, August 1908

The Spider

When Richard Bracquemont, medical student, decided to move into Room No. 7 of the little Hotel Stevens at 6 Rue Alfred Stevens, three people had already hanged themselves from the window-sash of the room on three successive Fridays.

The first was a Swiss travelling salesman. His body was not discovered until Saturday evening; but the physician established the fact that death must have come between five and six o'clock on Friday afternoon. The body hung suspended from a strong hook which had been driven into the window-sash, and which ordinarily served for hanging clothes. The window was closed, and the dead man had used the curtain cord as a rope. Since the window was rather low, his legs dragged on the ground almost to his knees. The suicide must consequently have exercised considerable will power in carrying out his intention. It was further established that he was married and the father of four children; that he unquestionably had an adequate and steady income; and that he was of a cheerful disposition, and well contented with life. Neither a will nor anything in writing that might give a clue to the cause of the suicide was found; nor had he ever intimated leanings toward suicide to any of his friends or acquaintances.

The second case was not very different. The actor Karl Krause, who was employed at the nearby Cirqué Medrano as a lightning bicycle artiste, engaged Room No. 7 two days after the first suicide. When he failed to appear at the performance the following Friday evening, the manager of the theater sent an usher to the little hotel. The usher found the actor hanged from the window-sash in the unlocked room, in identically the same circumstances that had attended the suicide of the Swiss traveling salesman. This second suicide seemed no less puzzling than the first: the actor was popular, drew a very large salary, was only twenty-five years old, and seemed to enjoy life to the utmost. Again, nothing was left in writing, nor were there any other clues that might help solve the mystery. The actor was survived only by an aged mother, to whom he used to send three hundred marks for her support promptly on the first of each month.

For Madame Dubonnet, who owned the cheap little hotel, and whose clientele was made up almost exclusively of the actors of the nearby vaudevilles of Montmartre, this second suicide had very distressing consequences. Already several of her guests had moved out, and other regular customers had failed to come back. She appealed to the Commissioner of the IXth Ward, whom she knew well, and he promised to do everything in his power to help her. So he not only pushed his investigation of reasons for the suicides with considerable zeal, but he also placed at her disposal a police officer who took up his residence in the mysterious room.

[105]

It was the policeman Charles-Maria Chaumié who had volunteered his services in solving the mystery. An old "Marousin" who had been a marine infantryman for eleven years, this sergeant had guarded many a lonely post in Tonkin and Annam single-handed, and had greeted many an uninvited deputation of river pirates, sneaking like cats through the jungle darkness, with a refreshing shot from his rifle. Consequently he felt himself well heeled to meet the "ghosts" of which Rue Stevens gossiped. He moved into the room on Sunday evening and went contentedly to sleep after doing high justice to the food and drink Madame Dubonnet set before him.

Every morning and evening Chaumié paid a brief visit to the police station to make his reports. During the first few days his reports confined themselves to the statement that he had not noticed even the slightest thing out of the ordinary. On Wednesday evening, however, he announced that he believed he had found a clue. When pressed for details he begged to be allowed to say nothing for the present: he said he was not certain that the thing he thought he had discovered necessarily had any bearing on the two suicides. And he was afraid of being ridiculed in case it should all turn out to be a mistake. On Thursday evening he seemed to be even more uncertain, although somewhat graver; but again he had nothing to report. On Friday morning he seemed quite excited: half seriously and half in jest he ventured the statement that the window of the room certainly had a remarkable power of attraction. Nevertheless he still clung to the theory that that fact had nothing whatever to do with the suicides, and that he would only be laughed at if he told more. That evening he failed to come to the police station: they found him hanged from the hook on the window sash.

Even in this case the circumstances, down to the minutest detail, were again the same as they had been in the other cases: the legs dragged on the floor, and the curtain cord had been used as a rope. The window was closed, and the door had not been locked; death had evidently come at about six o'clock in the afternoon. The dead man's mouth was wide open and his tongue hung out.

As a consequence of this third suicide in Room No. 7, all the guests left the Hotel Stevens that same day, with the exception of the German high school teacher in Room No. 16, who took advantage of this opportunity to have his rent reduced one-third. It was small consolation for Madame Dubonnet to have Mary Garden, the famous star of the Opéra Comique drive by in her Renault a few days later and stop to buy the red curtain cord for a price she beat down to two hundred francs. Of course she had two reasons for buying it: in the first place, it would bring luck; and in the second– well, it would get into the newspapers.

If these things had happened in summer, say in July or August, Madame Dubonnet might have got three times as much for her curtain cord; at that time of the year the newspapers would certainly have filled their columns with the case for weeks. But at an uneasy time of the year, with elections, disorders in the Balkans, a bank failure in New York, a visit of the English King and Queen– well, where could the newspapers find room for a mere murder case? The result was that the affair in the Rue Alfred Stevens got less attention than it deserved, and such notices of it as appeared in the newspapers were concise and brief, and confined themselves particularly to repetitions of the police reports, without exaggerations.

These reports furnished the only basis for what little knowledge Richard Braquemont had. He knew nothing of one other detail that seemed so inconsequential that neither the Commissioner nor any of the other witnesses had mentioned it to the reporters. Only afterwards, after the adventure the medical student had in the room, was this detail remembered. It was this: when the police took the body of Sergeant Charles-Maria Chaumié down from the window-sash, a large black spider crawled out of the mouth of the dead man. The porter flicked it away with his finger crying: "Ugh! Another such ugly beast!" In the course of the subsequent autopsy – that is, the one held later for Braquemont – the porter told that when they had taken down the corpse of the Swiss traveling salesman, a similar spider had been seen crawling on his shoulder– But of this Richard Braquemont knew nothing.

He did not take up his lodging in the room until two weeks after the last suicide, on a Sunday. What he experienced there he entered very conscientiously in a diary.

*   *   *   *   *   *   *

THE DIARY OF RICHARD BRAQUEMONT,
MEDICAL STUDENT

Monday, February 28

I moved in here last night, I unpacked my two suitcases, put a few things in order, and went to bed. I slept superbly: the clock was just striking nine when a knock at the door awakened me. It was the landlady, who brought me my breakfast herself. She is evidently quite solicitous about me, judging from the eggs, the ham, and the splendid coffee she brought me. I washed and dressed, and then watched the porter make up my room. I smoked my pipe while he worked.

So, here I am. I know right well that this business is dangerous, but I know too that my fortune is made if I solve the mystery. And if Paris was once worth a mass – one could hardly buy it that cheaply nowadays – it might be worth risking my life for it. Here is my chance, and I intend to make the most of it.

At that there were plenty of others who saw this chance. No less than twenty-seven people tried, some through the police, some through the landlady, to get the room. Three of them were women. So there were enough rivals– probably all poor devils like myself.

But I got it! Oh, I was probably the only one who could offer a "solution" to the police. A neat solution! Of course it was a bluff.

These entries are of course intended for the police, too. And it amuses me considerably to tell these gentlemen right at the outset that it was all a trick on my part. If the Commissioner is sensible he will say, "Hm! Just because I knew he was tricking us, I had all the more confidence in him!" As far as that is concerned, I don't care what he says afterward: now I'm here. And it seems to me a good omen to have begun my work by bluffing the police thoroughly.

Of course I first made my application to Madame Dubonnet, but she sent me to the police station. I lounged about the station every day for a week, only to be told that my application "was being given consideration" and to be asked always to come again the next day. Most of my rivals had long since thrown up the sponge; they probably found some better way to spend their time than waiting for hour after hour in the musty police court. But it seems the Commissioner was by this time quite irritated by my

[107]

perseverance. Finally he told me point blank that my coming back would be quite useless. He was very grateful to me as well as to all the other volunteers for our good intentions, but the police could not use the assistance of "dilettante laymen." Unless I had some carefully worked out plan of procedure. . .

So I told him that I had exactly that kind of a plan. Of course, I had no such thing and couldn't have explained a word of it. But I told him that I could tell him about my plan– which was good, although dangerous, and which might possibly come to the same conclusion as the investigation of the police sergeant– only in case he promised me on his word of honor that he was ready to carry it out. He thanked me for it, but regretted that he had no time for such things. But I saw that I was getting the upper hand when he asked me whether I couldn't at least give him some intimation of what I planned doing.

And I gave it to him. I told him the most glorious nonsense, of which I myself hadn't had the least notion of even a second beforehand. I don't know even now how I came by this unusual inspiration so opportunely. I told him that among all the hours of the week there was one that had a secret and strange significance. That was the hour in which Christ left His grave to go down to hell: the sixth hour of the afternoon of the last day of the Jewish week. And he might take into consideration, I went on, that it was exactly in this hour, between five and six o'clock on Friday afternoon, in which all three of the suicides had been committed. For the present I could not tell him more, but I might refer him to the Book of Revelations according to St. John.

The Commissioner put on a wise expression, as if he understood it all, and asked me to come back in the evening. I came back to his office promptly at the appointed time; I saw a copy of the New Testament lying in front of him on the table. In the meantime I had done just what he had: I had read the Book of Revelations through and– had not understood a word of it. Perhaps the Commissioner was more intelligent than I was; at least he told me that he understood what I was driving at in spite of my very vague hints. And that he was ready to grant my request and to aid me in every possible way.

I admit that he has actually been of very considerable assistance. He has made arrangements with the landlady under which I am to enjoy all the comforts and facilities of the hotel free of charge. He has given me an exceptionally fine revolver and a police pipe. The policemen on duty have orders to go through the little Rue Alfred Stevens as often as possible, and to come up to the room at a given signal. But the main thing is his installation of a desk telephone that connects directly with the police station. Since the station is only four minutes' walk from the hotel, I am thus enabled to have all the help I want immediately. With all this, I can't understand what there is to be afraid of. . . .

Tuesday, March 1

Nothing has happened, neither yesterday nor today. Madame Dubonnet brought me a new curtain cord from another room– Heaven knows she has enough of them vacant. For that matter, she seems to take every possible opportunity to come to my room; every time she comes she brings me something. I have again had all the details of the suicides told me, but have discovered nothing new. As far as the causes of the suicides were concerned, she had her own opinions. As for the actor, she thought he had had an unhappy love affair; when he had been her guest the year before, he had been visited frequently by a young woman who had not come at all this year. She admittedly couldn't quite make out why the Swiss gentleman had decided to commit suicide, but of course one couldn't know everything. But there was no doubt that the police sergeant had committed suicide only to spite her.

I must confess these explanations of Madame Dubonnet's are rather inadequate. But I let her gabble on; at least she helps break up my boredom.

Thursday, March 3

Still nothing. The Commissioner rings me up several times a day and I tell him that everything is going splendidly. Evidently this information doesn't quite satisfy him. I have taken out my medical books and begun to work. In this way I am at least getting something out of my voluntary confinement.

Friday, March 4, 2 P.M.

I had an excellent luncheon. Madame Dubonnet brought a half bottle of champagne along with it. It was the kind of dinner you get before your execution. She already regards me as being three-fourths dead. Before she left me she wept and begged me to go with her. Apparently she is afraid I might hang myself "just to spite her."

I have examined the new curtain cord in considerable detail. So I am to hang myself with that? Well, I can't say that I feel much like doing it. The cord is raw and hard, and it would make a good slipknot only with difficulty– one would have to be pretty powerfully determined to emulate the example of the other three suicides in order to make a success of the job. But now I'm sitting at the table, the telephone at my left, the revolver at my right. I certainly have no fear– but I am curious.

6 P.M.

Nothing happened– I almost write it with regret. The crucial hour came and went, and was just like all the others. Frankly I can't deny that sometimes I felt a certain urge to go to the window– oh, yes, but for other reasons! The Commissioner called me up at least ten times between five and six. He was just as impatient as I was. But Madame Dubonnet is satisfied: some one has lived for a week in No. 7 without hanging himself. Miraculous!

Monday, March 7

I am now convinced that I shall discover nothing; and I am inclined to think that the suicides of my predecessors were a matter of pure coincidence. I have asked the Commissioner to go over all the evidence in all three cases again, for I am convinced that eventually a solution of the mystery will be found. But as far as I am concerned, I intend to stay here as long as possible. I probably will not conquer Paris, but in the meantime I'm living here free and am already gaining considerably in health and weight. On top of it all I'm studying a great deal, and I notice I am rushing through in great style. And of course there is another reason that keeps me here.

Wednesday, March 9

I've progressed another step. Clarimonde–

Oh, but I haven't said a word about Clarimonde yet. Well, she is– my third reason for staying here. And it would have been for her sake that I would gladly have gone to the window in that fateful hour– but certainly not to hang myself. Clarimonde– but why do I call her that? I haven't the least idea as to what her name might be; but it seems to me as if I simply *must* call her Clarimonde. And I'd like to bet that some day I'll find out that that is really her name.

I already noticed Clarimonde the first few days I was here. She lives on the other side of this very narrow street, and her window is directly opposite mine. She sits there back of her curtains. And let me also say that she noticed me before I was aware of her, and that she visibly manifested an interest in me. No wonder– every one on the street knows that I am here, and knows why, too. Madame Dubonnet saw to that.

I am in no way the kind of person who falls in love. My relations with women have always been very slight. When one comes to Paris from Verdun to study medicine and hardly has enough money to have a decent meal once every three days, one has other things besides love to worry about. I haven't much experience, and I probably began this affair pretty stupidly. Anyhow, it's quite satisfactory as it stands.

At first it never occurred to me to establish communications with my strange neighbor. I simply decided that since I was here to make observations, and that I probably had nothing real to investigate anyhow, I might as well observe my neighbor while I was at it. After all, one can't pore over one's books all day long. So I have come to the conclusion that, judging from appearances, Clarimonde lives all alone in her little apartment. She has three windows, but she sits only at the one directly opposite mine. She sits there and spins, spins at a little old fashioned distaff. I once saw such a distaff at my grandmother's, but even my grandmother never used it. It was merely an heirloom left her by some great-aunt or other. I didn't know that they were still in use. For that matter, Clarimonde's distaff is a very tiny, fine thing, white, and apparently made of ivory. The threads she spins must be infinitely fine. She sits behind her curtains all day long and works incessantly, stopping only when it gets dark. Of course it gets dark very early these foggy days. In this narrow street the loveliest twilight comes about five o'clock. I have never seen a light in her room.

How does she look?– Well, I really don't know. She wears her black hair in wavy curls and is rather pale. Her nose is small and narrow, and her nostrils quiver. Her lips are pale, too, as it seems as if her little teeth might be pointed like those of a beast of prey. Her eyelids throw long shadows; but when she opens them her large, dark eyes are full of light. Yet I seem to sense rather than know all this. It is difficult to identify anything clearly back of those curtains.

One thing further: she always wears a black, closely-buttoned dress, with large purple dots. And she always wears long black gloves, probably to protect her hands while working. It looks strange to see her narrow black fingers quickly taking and drawing the threads, seemingly almost through each other– really almost like the wriggling of an insect's legs.

Our relations with each other? Oh, they are really quite superficial. And yet it seems as if they were truly much deeper. It began by her looking over to my window, and my looking over to hers. She noticed me, and I her. And then I evidently must have pleased her, because one day when I looked at her she smiled. And of course I did, too. That went on for several days, and we smiled at each other more and more. Then I decided almost every hour that I would greet her; I don't know exactly what it is that keeps me from carrying out my decision.

I have finally done it, this afternoon. And Clarimonde returned the greeting. Of course the greeting was ever so slight, but nevertheless I distinctly saw her nod.

Thursday, March 10

Last night I sat late over my books. I can't truthfully say that I studied a great deal: I spent my time building air castles and dreaming about Clarimonde. I slept very lightly, but very late into the morning.

When I stepped up to the window, Clarimonde was sitting at hers. I greeted her and she nodded. She smiled, and looked at me for a long time.

I wanted to work, but I couldn't seem to find the necessary peace of mind. I sat at the window and stared at her. Then I suddenly noticed that she, too, folded her hands in her lap. I pulled at the cord of the white curtain and – practically at the same instant – she did the same. We both smiled and looked at one another.

I believe we must have sat like that for an hour.

Then she began spinning again.

Saturday, March 12

These days pass swiftly. I eat and drink and sit down to work. I light my pipe and bend over my books. But I don't read a word. Of course I always make the attempt, but I know before-hand that it won't do any good. Then I go to the window. I greet Clarimonde, and she returns my greeting. We smile and gaze at one another– for hours.

Yesterday afternoon at six I felt a little uneasy. Darkness settled very early, and I felt a certain nameless fear. I sat at my desk and waited. I felt an almost unconquerable urge to go to the window– certainly not to hang myself, but to look at Clarimonde. I jumped up and stood back of the curtain. It seemed as if I had never seen her so clearly, although it was already quite dark. She was spinning, but her eyes looked across at me. I felt a strange comfort and a very subtle fear.

The telephone rang. I was furious at the silly old Commissioner for interrupting my dreams with his stupid questions.

This morning he came to visit me, along with Madame Dubonnet. She seems to be satisfied enough with my activities: she takes sufficient consolation from the fact that I have managed to *live* in Room No. 7 for two whole weeks. But the Commissioner wants results besides. I confided to him that I was tracking down a very strange clue. The old fool believed all I told him. In any event I can still stay here for weeks– and that's all I

care about. Not on account of Madame Dubonnet's cooking and cellar–
God, how soon one becomes indifferent to that when one always has
enough to eat!– only because of the window, which she hates and fears, and
which I love so dearly: this window that reveals Clarimonde to me.

When I light the lamp I no longer see her. I have strained my eyes
trying to see whether she goes out, but I have never seen her set foot on the
street. I have a comfortable easy chair and a green lampshade whose glow
warmly suffuses me. The Commissioner has sent me a large package of
tobacco. I have never smoked such good tobacco. And yet I cannot do any
work. I read two or three pages, and when I have finished I realize that I
haven't understood a word of their contents. My eyes grasp the significance
of the letters, but my brain refuses to supply the connotations. Queer! Just
as if my brain bore the legend: "No admittance." Just as if it refused to
admit any thought other than the one: Clarimonde. . . .

Finally I push my books aside, lean far back in my chair, and dream.

Sunday, March 13

This morning I witnessed a little tragedy. I was walking up and down in
the corridor while the porter made up my room. In front of the little court
window there is a spider web hanging, with a fat garden spider sitting in
the middle of it. Madame Dubonnet refuses to let it be swept away: spiders
bring luck, and Heaven knows she has had enough bad luck in her house.
Presently I saw another much smaller male spider cautiously running
around the edge of the web. Tentatively he ventured down one of the
precarious threads toward the middle; but the moment the female moved he
hastily withdrew. He ran around to another end of the web and tried again
to approach her. Finally the powerful female spider in the center of the
web seemed to look upon his suit with favor, and stopped moving. The
male spider pulled at one of the threads of the web– first lightly, then so
vigorously that the whole web quivered. But the object of his attention
remained immovable. Then he approached her very quickly, but carefully.
The female spider received him quickly and let him embrace her delicately
while she retained the utmost passivity. Motionless the two of them hung
for several minutes in the center of the large web.

Then I saw how the male spider slowly freed himself, one leg after
another. It seemed as if he wanted to retreat quietly, leaving his companion
alone in her dream of love. Suddenly he let her go entirely and ran out of
the web as fast as he could. But at the same instant the female seemed to
awaken in a wild rush of activity, and she chased rapidly after him. The
weak male spider let himself down by a thread, but the female followed
immediately. Both of them fell to the widow-sill; and, gathering all his
energies, the male spider tried to run away. But it was too late. The female
spider seized him in her powerful grip, carried him back up into the net,
and set him down squarely in the middle of it. And this same place that had
just been a bed for passionate desire now became the scene of something
quite different. The lover kicked in vain, stretched his weak legs out again
and again, and tried to disentangle himself from this wild embrace. But the
female would not let him go. In a few minutes she had spun him in so
completely that he could not move a single member. Then she thrust her
sharp pincers into his body and sucked out the young blood of her lover in
deep draughts. I even saw how she finally let go of the pitiful,

unrecognizable little lump– legs, skin and threads– and threw it contemptuously out of the net.

So that's what love is like among these creatures! Well, I can be glad I'm not a young spider.

Monday, March 14

I no longer so much as glance at my books. Only at the window do I pass all my days. And I keep on sitting there even after it gets dark. Then she is no longer there; but I close my eyes and see her anyhow. . . .

Well, this diary has become quite different than I thought it would be. It tells about Madame Dubonnet and the Commissioner, about spiders and about Clarimonde. But not a word about the discovery I had hoped to make.– Well, is it my fault?

Tuesday, March 15

Clarimonde and I have discovered a strange new game, and we play it all day long. I greet her, and immediately she returns the greeting. Then I drum with my fingers on my window-pane. She has hardly had time to see it before she begins drumming on hers. I wink at her, and she winks at me. I move my lips as if I were talking to her and she follows suit. Then I brush the hair back from my temples, and immediately her hand is at the side of her forehead. Truly child's play. And we both laugh at it. That is, she really doesn't laugh: it is only a quiet, passive smile she has, just as I suppose mine must be.

For that matter all this isn't nearly as senseless as it must seem. It isn't imitation at all: I think we would both tire of that very quickly. There must be a certain telepathy or thought transference involved in it. For Clarimonde repeats my motions in the smallest conceivable fraction of a second. She hardly has time to see what I am doing before she does the same thing. Sometimes it even seems to me that her action is simultaneous with mine. That is what entices me: always doing something new and unpremeditated. And it's astounding to see her doing the same thing at the same time. Sometimes I try to catch her. I make a great many motions in quick succession, and then repeat them for the fourth time, but change their order, introduce some new motion, or leave out one of the old ones. It's like children playing Follow the Leader. It's really remarkable that Clarimonde never makes a single mistake, although I sometimes change the motions so rapidly that she hardly has time to memorize each one.

That is how I spend my days. But I never feel for a second that I am squandering my time on something nonsensical. On the contrary, it seems as if nothing I had ever done were more important.

Wednesday, March 16

Isn't it queer that I have never thought seriously about putting my relations with Clarimonde on a more sensible basis than that of these hour-consuming games? I thought about it last night. I could simply take my hat and coat and go down two flights of stairs, five steps across the street, and then up two other flights of stairs. On her door there is a little coat-of-arms engraved with her name: " Clarimonde. . ." Clarimonde what? I don't know what; but there the name Clarimonde is clearly there. Then I could knock, and then. . .

That far I can imagine everything perfectly, down to the last move I might make. But for the life of me I can't picture what would happen after that. The door would open– I can conceive that. But I would remain standing in front of it and looking into her room, into a darkness– a darkness so utter that not a solitary thing could be distinguished in it. She would come; as a matter of fact, there would be nothing there. Only the black impenetrable darkness.

Sometimes it seems as if there could be no other Clarimonde than the one I play with at my window. I can't picture what this woman would look like if she wore a hat, or even some dress other than her black one with the large purple dots; I can't even conceive her without her gloves. If I could see her on the street, or even in some restaurant, eating, drinking, talking– well, I really have to laugh: the thing seems so utterly inconceivable.

Sometimes I ask myself whether I love her. I can't answer that question entirely, because I have never been in love. But if the feeling I bear toward Clarimonde is really – well, love – then love is certainly very, very different than I saw it among my acquaintances or learned about it in novels.

It is becoming quite difficult to define my emotions. In fact, it is becoming difficult even to think about anything at all that has no bearing on Clarimonde– or rather, on our game. For there is truly no denying it: it's really the game that preoccupies me– nothing else. And that's the thing I understand least of all.

Clarimonde– well, yes, I feel attracted to her. But mingled with the attraction there is another feeling– almost like a sense of fear. Fear? No, it isn't fear either: it is more a temerity, a certain inarticulate alarm or apprehension before something curiously passionate that keeps me at a distance from her and at the same time draws me constantly nearer to her. It is as if I were going around her in a wide circle, came a little nearer at one place, withdrew again, went on, approached her again at another point and again retreated rapidly. Until finally– of that I am absolutely certain – I *must* go to her.

Clarimonde is sitting at her window and spinning. Threads– long, thin, infinitely fine threads. She seems to be making some fabric– I don't know just what it is to be. And I can't understand how she can make the network without tangling or tearing the delicate fabric. There are wonderful patterns in her work– patterns full of fabulous monsters and curious grotesques.

For that matter but what am I writing? The fact of the matter is that I can't even see what it is she is spinning: the threads are much too fine. And yet I can't help feeling that her work must be exactly as I see it– when I close my eyes. Exactly. A huge network peopled with many creatures– fabulous monsters, and curious grotesques. . .

Thursday, March 17

I find myself in a strange state of agitation. I no longer talk to any one; I hardly even say good morning to Madame Dubonnet or the porter. I hardly take time to eat; I only want to sit at the window and play with her. It's an exciting game. Truly it is.

And I have a premonition that tomorrow something must happen.

Friday, March 18

Yes, yes. Something must happen today. . . I tell myself – oh, yes, I talk aloud, just to hear my own voice – that it is just for *that* that I am here. But the worst of it is that I am afraid. And this fear that what has happened to my predecessors in this room may also happen to me is curiously mingled with my other fear– the fear of Clarimonde. I can hardly keep them apart.

I am afraid. I would like to scream.

6 P. M.

Let me put down a few words quickly, and then get my hat and coat.

By the time five o'clock came, my strength was gone. Oh, I know now for certain that it must have something to do with the sixth hour of the next to the last day of the week. . . . Now I can no longer laugh at the fraud with which I duped the Commissioner. I sat on my chair and stayed there only by exerting my will power to the utmost. But this thing drew me, almost pulled me to the window. I had to play with Clarimonde– and then again there rose that terrible fear of the window. I saw them hanging there– the Swiss traveling salesman, a large fellow with a thick neck and gray stubble beard. And the lanky acrobat and the stocky, powerful police sergeant. I saw all three together, hanging from the same hook with open mouths and with tongues lolling far out. And then I saw myself among them.

Oh, this fear! I felt I was as much afraid of the window-sash and the terrible hook as I was of Clarimonde. May she forgive me for it, but that's the truth: in my ignominious fear I always confused her image with that of the three who hanged there, dragging their legs heavily on the floor.

But the truth is that I never felt for an instant any desire or inclination to hang myself: I wasn't even afraid I would do it. No– I was afraid only of the window itself – and of Clarimonde – and of something terrible, something uncertain and unpredictable that was now to come. I had the pathetic irresistible longing to get up and go to the window. And I *had* to do it. . . .

Then the telephone rang. I grabbed the receiver and before I could hear a word I myself cried into the mouthpiece: "Come! come at once!"

It was just as if my unearthly yell had instantly chased all the shadows into the farthest cracks of the floor. I became composed immediately. I wiped away the sweat from my forehead and drank a glass of water. Then I considered what I ought to tell the Commissioner when he came. Finally I went to the window, greeted Clarimonde, and smiled.

And Clarimonde greeted me and smiled.

Five minutes later the Commissioner was here. I told him that I had finally struck the root of the whole affair; if he would only refrain from questioning me today, I would certainly be able to make some remarkable disclosures in the very near future. The queer part of it was that while I was lying to him I was at the same time fully convinced in my own mind that it is the truth– against my better judgment.

He noticed the unusual condition of my temper, especially when I apologized for screaming into the telephone and tried to explain– and failed to find any plausible reason for my agitation. He suggested very amiably that I need not take undue consideration of him: he was always at my service– that was his duty. He would rather make a dozen useless trips over here than to let me wait for him once when I really needed him. Then he invited me to go out with him tonight, suggesting that that might help distract me– it wasn't a good thing to be alone all the time. I have accepted his invitation, although I think it will be difficult to go out: I don't like to leave this room.

Saturday, March 19

We went to the Gaieté Rochechouart, to the Cigale, and to the Lune Rousse. The Commissioner was right: it was a good thing for me to go out and breathe another atmosphere. At first I felt rather uncomfortable, as if I were doing something wrong, as if I were a deserter, running away from our flag. But by and by that feeling died; we drank a good deal, laughed, and joked.

When I went to the window this morning, I seemed to read reproach in Clarimonde's look. But perhaps I only imagined it: how could she know I had gone out last night? For that matter, it seemed to last for only a moment; then she smiled again.

We played all day long.

Sunday, March 20

Today I can only repeat: we played all day long.

Monday, March 21

We played all day long.

Tuesday, March 22

Yes, and today we did the same. Nothing, absolutely nothing else. Sometimes I ask myself why we do it. What is it all for? Or, what do I really want, to what can it all lead? But I never answer my own question. For it's certain that I want nothing other than just this. Come what may, that which is coming is exactly what I long for.

We have been talking to one another these last few days, of course not with any spoken word. Sometimes we moved our lips, at other times we only looked at one another. But we understand each other perfectly.

I was right: Clarimonde reproached me for running away last Friday. But I begged her forgiveness and told her I realized that it had been very unwise and horrid of me. She forgave me and I promised her never again to leave the window. And we kissed each other, pressing our lips against the panes for a long time.

Wednesday, March 23

I know now that I love her. It must be love– I feel it tingling in every fiber of my being. It may be that with other people love is different. But is there any one among a thousand millions who has a head, an ear, a hand that is like anyone else's? Everyone is different, so it is quite conceivable that our love is unlike that of other people. I know that my love is very singular. But does that make it any less beautiful? I am almost happy in this love.

If only there would not be this fear! Sometimes it falls asleep. Then I forget it. But only for a few minutes. Then it wakes up again and will not let me go. It seems to me like a poor little mouse fighting against a huge and beautiful snake, trying to free itself from its overpowering embrace. Just wait, you poor foolish little fear, soon our love will devour you!

Thursday, March 24

I have made a discovery: I don't play with Clarimonde– *she plays with me.*

It happened like this.

Last night as usual, I thought about our game. I wrote down five intricate movements with which I wanted to surprise her today. I gave every motion a number. I practiced them so as to be able to execute them as quickly as possible, first in order, and then backwards. Then only the even numbers and then the odd, and then only the first and last parts of each of the five motions. It was very laborious, but it gave me great satisfaction because it brought me nearer to Clarimonde, even though I could not see her. I practiced in this way for hours, and finally they went like clock-work.

This morning I went to the window. We greeted each other, and the game began. Forward, backward– it was incredible to see how quickly she understood me, and how instantaneously she repeated all the things I did.

Then there was a knock at my door. It was the porter, bringing me my boots. I took them; but when I was going back to the window my glance fell on the sheet of paper on which I had recorded the order of the movements. *And I saw that I had not executed a single one of these movements.*

I almost reeled. I grabbed the back of the easy chair and let myself down into it. I couldn't believe it. I read the sheet again and again. But it was true: all the motions I had made at the window, not a single one was mine.

And again I was aware of a door opening somewhere far away– her door. I was standing before it and looking in . . . nothing, nothing– only empty darkness. Then I knew that if I went out, I would be saved; and I realized that now I *could* go. Nevertheless I did not go. That was because I was distinctly aware of one feeling: that I held the secret of the mystery. Held it tightly in both hands. –Paris– I was going to conquer Paris!

For a moment Paris was stronger than Clarimonde.

Oh, I've dropped all thought of it now. Now I am aware only of my love, and in the midst of it this quiet, passionate fear.

But in that instant I felt suddenly strong. I read through the details of my first movement once more and impressed it firmly in my memory. Then I went back to the window.

And I took exact notice of what I did: *not a single motion I executed was among those I had set out to do.*

Then I decided to run my index finger along my nose. But instead I kissed the window-pane. I wanted to drum on the window-sill, but ran my hand through my hair instead. So it was true: Clarimonde did not imitate the things I did: on the contrary, I repeated the things she indicated. And I did it so quickly, with such lightning rapidity, that I followed her motions in the same second, so that even now it seems as if I were the one who exerted the will power to do these things.

So it was I – I who was so proud of the fact that I had determined her mode of thought– I was the one who was being so completely influenced. Only, her influence is so soft, so gentle that it seems as if nothing on earth could be so soothing.

I made other experiments. I put both my hands in my pockets and resolved firmly not to move them; then I looked across at her. I noticed how she lifted her hand and smiled, and gently chided me with her index finger. I refused to budge. I felt my right hand wanting to take itself out of my pocket, but I dug my fingers deep into the pocket lining. Then slowly, after several minutes, my fingers relaxed, my hand came out of the pocket, and I lifted my arm. And I chided her with my index finger and smiled. It seemed as if it were really not I that was doing all this, but some stranger whom I watched from a distance. No, no– that wasn't the way of it. I, I was the one who did it– and some stranger was watching me. It was the stranger – that other me – who was so strong, who wanted to solve this mystery with some great discovery. But that was no longer I.

I– oh, what do I care about the discovery? I am only here to do her bidding, the bidding of my Clarimonde, whom I love with such tender fear.

Friday, March 25

I have cut the telephone wire. I can no longer stand being perpetually bothered by the silly old Commissioner, least of all when the fateful hour is at hand. . . .

God, why am I writing all this? Not a word of it is true. It seems as if some one else were guiding my pen.

But I do— I do want to set down here what actually happens. It is costing me a tremendous effort. But I want to do it. If only for the last time to do– what I really want to do.

I cut the telephone wire . . . oh . . .

Because I had to. . . . There, I finally got it out! Because I had to, I had to!

We stood at the window this morning and played. Our game has changed a little since yesterday. She goes through some motions and I defend myself as long as possible. Until finally I have to surrender, powerless to do anything but her bidding. And I can scarcely tell what a wonderful sense of exaltation and joy it gives me to be conquered by her will, to make this surrender.

We played. And then suddenly she got up and went back into her room. It was so dark that I couldn't see her; she seemed to disappear into the darkness. But she came back very shortly, carrying in her hands a desk telephone just like mine. Smiling, she set it down on the window-sill, took a knife, cut the wire and carried it back again.

I defended myself for about a quarter of an hour. My fear was greater than ever, but that made my slow surrender all the more delectable. And I finally brought my telephone to the window, cut the wire and set it back on the table.

That is how it happened.

I am sitting at the table. I have had my tea, and the porter has just taken the dishes out. I asked him what time it was– it seems my watch isn't keeping time. It's five fifteen . . . five fifteen . . .

I know that if I look up now Clarimonde will be doing something or other. Doing something or other that I will have to do too.

I look up anyhow. She is standing there and smiling. Well... if I could only tear my eyes away from her! . . . now she is going to the curtain. She is taking the cord off– it is red, just like the one on my window. She is tying a knot– a slipknot. She is hanging the cord up on the hook in the window-sash.

She is sitting down and smiling.

. . . No, this is no longer a thing one can call fear, this thing I am experiencing. It is a maddening, choking terror– but nevertheless I wouldn't trade it for anything in the world. It is a compulsion of an unheard of nature and power, yet so subtly sensual in its inescapable ferocity.

Of course I could rush up to the window and do exactly what she wants me to do. But I am waiting, struggling, and defending myself. I feel this uncanny thing getting stronger every minute . . .

    *   *   *   *   *   *   *

So, here I am, still sitting here. I ran quickly to the window and did the thing she wanted me to do: I took the curtain cord, tied a slipknot in it, and hung it from the hook . . .

And now I am not going to look up any more. I am not going to stay here and look only at this sheet of paper. For I know now what she would do if I looked up again– now in the sixth hour of the next to the last of the week. If I see her, I shall have to do her bidding . . . I shall have to . . .

I shall refuse to look at her.

But I am suddenly laughing– loudly. No, I'm not laughing– it is something laughing within me. I know why, too: it's because of this "I will not . . ."

I don't want to, and yet I know certainly that I must. I must look at her . . . must, must do it . . . and then– the rest. I am only waiting to stretch out the torment. Yes, that is it . . . For these breathless sufferings are my most rapturous transports. I can remain sitting here longer . . . in order to stretch out these seconds of torture, which carry the ecstasy of love into infinity . . .

More . . . longer . . .

Again this fear, again! I know that I shall look at her, that I shall get up, that I shall hang myself. *But it isn't that that I fear.* Oh, no– that is sweet, that is beautiful.

But there is something else . . . something else associated with it– *something that will happen afterward.* I don't know what it will be– but it is coming, it is certainly coming, certainly . . . certainly. For the joy of my torments is so infinitely great– oh, I feel it is so great that something terrible must follow it.

Only I must not think . . .

Let me write something, anything, no matter what. Only quickly, without thinking . . .

My name– Richard Bracquemont, Richard Bracquemont, Richard– oh, I can't go any farther– Richard Bracquemont– Richard Bracquemont– now – now I must look at her . . .Richard Bracquemont– I must –no – no, more– more . . . Richard . . . Richard Bracque——

    *   *   *   *   *   *   *

The Commissioner of the IXth Ward, after failing repeatedly to get a reply to his telephone calls, came to the Hotel Stevens at five minutes after six. In Room No. 7 he found the body of the student Richard Bracquemont hanging from the window sash, in exactly the same position as that of his three predecessors.

Only his face had a different expression; it was distorted in a horrible fear, and his eyes, wide open, seemed to be pushing themselves out of their sockets. His lips were drawn apart, but his powerful teeth were firmly and desperately clenched.

And glued between them, bitten and crushed to pieces, there was a large black spider, with curious purple dots.

On the table lay the medical student's diary. The Commissioner read it and went immediately to the house across the street. There he discovered that the second apartment had been vacant and unoccupied for months and months . . .

The Box of Counters

»Letzte Kultur«

Om dat de werelt is soe ongetru
Daer om gha ie in den ru.
Brueghel the Elder

In the Atlantic, on board the "König Wilhelm II."
March, 1908

The Box of Counters

I had been waiting a very long time that evening for Edgard Widerhold. I was lying in a long chair, where the boy behind me slowly pulled the punkah. The old fellow had Hindoo boys, who had followed him here a long time ago. And now their sons and grandsons served him too. They are good servants, and know how to wait on us.

"Go on, Dewla, tell your master I am waiting."

"Atcha, Sahib." Without a sound he glided away.

I was lying on the terrace, and, like a vision, I saw the "Clear Stream" beneath. An hour ago the week-old clouds had dissolved; an hour ago the tepid rain had stopped falling, and the broad shafts of low light from the evening sun made bars across the violet mists of Tonkin.

Below the junks were riding at their moorings, and stirring from their sleep. The crews crawled out on deck; with round shovels, floor cloths, and tamarind-brooms they sluiced out the water and cleaned the sampans. But no one talked; they worked so quietly it was all but impossible to hear them; hardly a sound rose up to disturb the leaves and tendrils on the bank. A large junk sailed past, closely packed with légionnaires. I waved to the officers lying in the campan; they returned my salute wistfully. I dare say they would have rather sat with me on the spacious verandah of Edgard Widerhold's bungalow than have sailed up the river for days and weeks through the hot rain, up to their miserable station. I counted— there were at least fifty légionnaires on the junk. A few were Irishmen and Spaniards; a few Flemings and Swiss, no doubt. . . and all the rest were Germans. Who may they be? No teetotalers, but boys after the heart of Tilly or of mad Duke Christian. There are sure to be some incendiaries amongst them, robbers and murderers— what better could be chosen for the purposes of war? They know their trade, you may believe me. There are others, too, from amongst the upper ten, those who disappear from society, to go under in the troubled waters of the Légion— clergymen and professors, members of the high nobility and officers. A bishop was killed in the storming of Ain-Souf; and how long ago is it that a German man-of-war came from Algiers for the corpse of another légionnaire and rendered to it all the honors due to a prince of the blood?

I lean over the balustrade: "Vive la Légion!" And they answer back, bawling loud from their raucous drinkers' throats, "Vive la Légion! Vive la Légion!" They have lost their country, their family, their home, their honor, and their money. They have got only one thing left, which has to do duty for it all, *esprit de corps*—— "Vive la Légion!"

I know them. Drinkers and gamblers, souteneurs, deserters from camps all over the world. Anarchists all of them– who do not know what anarchism is, who rebelled and fled from the oppression of some insupportable compulsion. Half criminals and half children, small brains and big hearts– real soldiers. Landknechts with the right instinct, that sacking and violating women is a fine thing, their very own profession: for they have been hired for killing, and he who may do the greater thing should also be allowed to do the lesser one. They are adventurers who were born too late into this world of ours, who were not strong enough to hew out their own pathways. Each one of them has been too weak for that, has collapsed in the undergrowth, and can move no further forward. A flickering will o' the wisp has led him astray long ago from the beaten track, and he was not able to find a way of escape. Something went wrong, but he does not know where. Each one of them has been stranded, a miserable and helpless wreckage. But they find each other, they close the ring, they build a new pride of their own: "Vive la Légion!" It is mother and home and honor and country to them, all in one. Listen to their shouts: "Vive, vive la Légion!"

The junk draws away into the evening, westward, where at the second turn the Red River rolls into the Clear Stream. There she disappears, steers deep into the mist, far into this country of violet poisons. But they do not fear anything, these fair, bearded men; not fever, not dysentery, and least of all the yellow rebels. Have they not got alcohol enough and opium and their trusted Lebel rifles? What more could they want? Forty of the fifty will have to die; but never mind, whoever comes back signs on again, for the glory of the Légion, not for that of France.

Edgard Widerhold entered the verandah. "Have they passed?" he asked me.

"Who?"

"The légionnaires!" He went to the balustrade and looked down the river. "Thank goodness, they have gone. The devils take them; I cannot stand seeing them."

"Is that so?" I said. Of course, like everybody else in the country, I knew the peculiar relations between the old fellow and the Legion, and I tried to fathom it. That's why I feigned surprise. "Is that so? And still the whole Légion adores you. A captain of the second Légion told me of you at Porquerolles, years ago: if ever I came to the Clear Stream I was to be sure and visit Edgard Widerhold."

"That must have been Karl Hauser, of Muhlhausen."

"No; it was Dufresnes."

The old man sighed. "Dufresnes, the Auvergnat! It's many a glass of Burgundy he drank here."

"Like all the rest, no doubt."

Eight years ago, the house nicknamed "Le Bungalow de la Légion," had closed its doors; and Mr. Edgard Widerhold, "le bon Papa de la Légion," had instituted his depot of supplies in Edgardhafen. That was the small harbor of Widerhold's farm, two hours down river. The old man had persisted in having even the postal designation *"Edgardhafen,"* on the stamp, and not "Port d'Edgard." For though his house had indeed been closed to the Légion since that time, neither his heart nor his hospitality had been lacking. Every passing junk of the Légion called at Edgardhafen, and the manager took a few cases of wine aboard for officers and men. With it went always the old man's visiting card with the message: "Mr. Edgard Widerhold regrets greatly not being able to see the gentlemen this time. He begs of them to accept kindly the present gift, and is drinking to the health of the Légion." And every time the officer in command would express thanks for the kind present and the hope of being able to thank the giver in person on his return. But it never went any further; the doors of the spacious house near the Clear Stream remained closed to the Légion. Sometimes a few officers still paid a call, old friends, whose wine-gladdened voices had rung often enough through the rooms. The boys took them to the verandah and put the choicest wines in front of them; but the officers would never be able to see the old man. Consequently they stayed away; slowly the Légion got used to the new way. There were already many who had never seen him, who only knew that at Edgardhafen it was the thing to call, to take wine aboard, and to drink to the health of a mad old German. Every one of them looked forward to this, the only break of the hopeless journey through the rain on the Clear Stream, and Edgard Widerhold was as much liked in the Légion as before.

When I came to him I was the first German he had talked to for years—of course he had seen many of them down the river. I am certain the old fellow hides behind a curtain and looks down whenever a junk of the Légion passes. But to me he talked again in German. I think that's the reason why he keeps me here, always finding some new reason for postponing my departure.

The old fellow does not belong to the shouting kind. He abuses the German Empire like a pick-pocket. He is very old, but must needs live ten times as many years to suffer all the penalties which his crimes of *lèse majesté* alone would cost him. He curses Bismarck, because he allowed the continuance of the Kingdom of Saxony and did not annex Bohemia, and he curses the third Emperor because he allowed himself to be cheated into swapping the East African Empire for Helgoland. And Holland! We must have Holland if we mean to live on, Holland and her Sunda Islands. It's got to be, it cannot be helped; we shall go to the devil if we do not get it. Then of course the Adriatic! Austria is a calculated piece of nonsense, an idiocy which is a blot on any self-respecting map. Ours are her German provinces, and, as we cannot allow them to shut the door in our face, we have to have the Slavonic districts which keep us from the Adriatic as well, Carniola and Istria. "The Devil take me!" he shouts; "I know we shall get lice in our furs with them! But rather a fur with lice from them than being frozen to death without a fur!" Already today he sees himself sailing under the black-white-and-red from a German Trieste to a German Batavia.

Then I ask him, "And what about our friends, the English?"

"The English!" he bawls: "they shut up if you hit them square in the jaw!"

He loves France, and is glad for her to have a spacious place in the sun; but he hates the English. Such is his way; if a German pours poisonous abuse over Emperor and Empire, he rejoices in it and laughs. And if a Frenchman jokes at our expense, he laughs, but is not slow in paying him back by recalling the latest idiocies of the Governor at Saigon. But if an Englishman dares so much as make the most innocent remark about the most idiotic of our consuls, he waxes furious. That was the reason that he had to leave India. I do not know what the English colonel said, but I know that Edgard Widerhold lifted up his riding whip and knocked one of his eyes out. That is now as many as forty years ago, maybe fifty or sixty. He had to flee, went to Tonkin, and was squatting on his farm long before the French came into the country. Then he hoisted the Tricolore on the Clear Stream, sad that it was not the black-white-and-red flag that waved to the breeze, but still glad that at least in was not the Union Jack.

Nobody knows how old he actually is. Whom the tropics do not devour in his younger years they desiccate. They make him weatherproof and hard, and give him a mail of yellow leather, which defies all corruption. Such an one was Edgard Widerhold. An octogenarian, perhaps a nonagenarian, he was six hours daily in the saddle. Long and narrow was his face, long and narrow his hands, every finger armed with big yellow nails, each longer than a match, hard as steel, sharp and curved like the claws of a wild animal.

I offered him my cigarettes. I had long ago given up smoking them, the sea air had spoiled them. But he loved them— they had been made in Germany.

"Won't you tell me for once why you banished the Légion from your bungalow?"

The old fellow did not go away from the balustrade. "No!" he said. Then he clapped his hands. "Bana! Dewala! wine, glasses!" The boys set the table; he sat down near me, and pushed the papers towards me. "There," he went on, "have you read the *Post*? The Germans gained a splendid victory in the motor race at Dieppe. Benz and Mercédès or whatever make they are. Zeppelin has finished has airship– he promenades over Germany and Switzerland, wherever he wants. There, look at the last page– chess tournament at Ostend. Who has won the prize? A German! Really it would be a joy to read the papers if only they had not to chronicle the doings of the lot in Berlin. Look at their idiocies——."

But I interrupted him. I did not care to hear any more about the diplomatic stupidities of these gigantic asses. I drank to him "Good health! Tomorrow I have got to go."

The old man pushed his glass away. "What— tomorrow?"

"Yes; Lieutenant Schlumberger will pass with part of the third battalion. He is going to take me along."

He gave the table a blow with his fist. "That is a dirty trick!" — "What?"

"That you want to go tomorrow, to the devil! A low down trick I call it."

"Well, after all, I cannot stay here forever!" I laughed. "It will be two months, next Tuesday—"

"That's just it! Now that I've got used to you. Had you ridden away after an hour, I should not have cared."

But I would not give in. Good Lord, had he not had people staying with him often enough and seen them leave again, one after the other? Until some fresh ones arrived.

That made him start. In olden times, yes, indeed, in olden times he would not have lifted a finger to keep me. But now, who was there to see him now? Two people a year, and once every five years a German, ever since he could not bear any longer to see the légionnaires.

There I got him again. And I told him I would stay another week if he told me why—

That, again, he called a low down trick– what, a German poet bartering his ware, like a tradesman?

I argued upon that. "Raw material," I said. "Wool from the peasant. But we spin the threads and weave the colored rugs."

He liked that; he laughed. "For three weeks I shall sell the story."

I have learned bargaining at Naples. Three weeks for a story– most expensive. And then, I told him, it meant buying a pig in a poke without knowing whether the stuff was any use at all. At the best I would get two hundred marks for the story, and I had been here already two months, and he wanted me to stay for another three weeks– and all the time I had not produced as much as a line. And, after all, there would have to be something for myself, and as I was always out of pocket, and, in short, he was ruining me.

But the old fellow looked after his own. "The twenty-seventh is my birthday," he said. "I do not want to spend it by myself. Well, then, eighteen days– that's the best I can do! I will not tell the story for less."

"All right, then," I sighed, "that is a bargain!"

The old fellow shook hands. "Bana," he called, "Bana! Take away the wine. Bring shallow glasses and champagne."

"Atcha, Sahib, atcha."

"And you, Dewla, get Hong-Dok's box and the counters."

The boy brought the box, and at a nod of his master's put it in front of me, pressing a spring so that the lid moved back. It was a big box made of sandalwood, the delicate scent of which filled the air in a moment. The wood was closely inlaid with the tiniest leaves of mother o' pearl and ivory, the sides were carved with elephants, crocodiles, and tigers set in scroll-work. But the lid showed a picture of the Crucifixion; it may have been copied from an old print. Only the Saviour was beardless, had a round, or rather full, face, which, however, betrayed an expression of the most terrible suffering. There was no wound in the side of the body, neither was there a proper cross; this Christ seemed to have been nailed to a flat board. The tablet at His head did not show the letters I.N.R.I., but others, viz., K.V.K.S.II.C.L.E.

This presentiment of the Crucified God had an uncanny realism; I could not help being reminded of Matthias Grünewald's painting, although they had nothing at all in common. The innermost conception was radically different: this artist did not seem to have derived his powers of attaining the extreme limit of realism in portraying the terrible from an immense pity or from a capability of understanding, but rather from a passionate hatred, a voluptuous submersion in the torments of the sufferer. The work had been executed with an immense amount of pains; it was the masterpiece of a great artist.

The old fellow saw my enthusiasm. "You have it," he said quietly.

I grasped the box with both hands. "Do you want to make a present of it to me?"

He laughed. "Present– no! But I have sold you my story, and the box you hold– is my story."

I was burrowing amongst the counters– round, triangular, and rectangular pieces of mother o' pearl of a deep metallic iridescence. Each single one showed on both sides a little picture, the contours cut out, the details finely chased.

"Will you give me the key to it?" I asked.

"You are playing with the key there! If you put the counters in order nicely, as they follow each other, you may read my story as in a book. But now close down the lid and listen. Fill up, Dewala!"

The boy filled the glasses and we drank. Then he charged the short pipe of his master, handed it to him and put a light to it.

[127]

The old fellow inhaled the acrid smoke and blew it out sharply. Then he leant back and motioned to the boy to start the punkah.

"You see," he began, "it is quite correct what Captain Dufrenes or whoever else it was told you. This house well deserved being called the bungalow of the Légion. Up here the officers sat and drank– and the privates down below in the garden; often enough I invited the latter also to come up on the verandah. You know, the French do not have those ridiculous notions of class difference as we have them; off duty the ranker is as good as his general. Most of all this holds good in the colonies, and particularly in the Légion, where many an officer is a peasant, and many a ranker a gentleman. I used to go down and drink with the men in the garden, and whoever I liked I asked to come upstairs. Believe me, I met in those days many a curious beggar, many a hard-boiled sinner, and many a babe longing for his mother's apron strings. That was my great museum, the Légion, my great big book, which told me new fairy tales and adventures over and over again.

"For the boys used to tell me things; they liked to get me by myself and to open their heart to me. You see, it is quite true, the légionnaires loved me, not only because of the wine and the few days' rest which they got here. You know the kind of people they are, and that each considers his rightful property whatever he claps his eyes on; that it is not safe for either officer or ranker to leave the smallest thing lying about, for it would disappear in the twinkling of an eye. Well, then, in over twenty years it happened only once that a légionnaire stole something from me, and his comrades would have killed him had I not interceded myself on his behalf. You do not believe that? Neither should I if somebody else told me, and still it is literally true. The boys loved me because they were well aware that I loved them. How did it all come about? Good Lord, as the time went on. No wife, no child, and quite by myself out here through all the years. The Légion– well, it was the only thing, that gave me back Germany, that made the Clear Stream German for me, in spite of the Tricolore. I know, the law-abiding citizens at home call the Légion the foulest dregs and scum of the nation. Gaol fodder dregs which Germany spat out contemptuously on to these latitudes, outcasts, of no use any longer in the beautifully regulated home land, contained dross of such rare color that my heart laughed with joy. Dross indeed! Not worth a farthing for the jeweler, who sells big diamonds set in heavy rings to prosperous butchers. But a child would pick it up on the sands. A child and old fools like myself, and mad poets like yourself, who are both– children and fools! For us this dross is valuable, and we do not want at all that it should perish. But it perishes. Without help, one piece after another – and their manner of perishing, pitifully, miserably, through long tortures, that's what I cannot bear. A mother may see her children dying two or three. She is sitting there, her hands in her lap, and cannot help them; she cannot. But all that passes, and the day will come when she will get the better of her pain. But I – the father of the Légion – have seen a thousand children die, each month, nearly every week they died away. And I had no power to help them, none at all. You see now why it is I do not collect dross any longer; I cannot go on seeing my children die.

"And how they died! In those days the French had not penetrated the country as far as today. The furthest outpost was only three days' sail up the Red River, and there were exposed posts in and around Edgardhafen. Dysentery and typhoid were the usual and expected thing in those damp camps, and side by side with both tropical anæmia cropped up here and there. You know this particular illness: you know how quickly it kills. Quite a light, weak attack of fever, that scarcely makes the pulse go quicker, day and night. The patient does not want to eat any longer; he gets capricious, like a fine lady. But he wants to sleep, sleep all the time– until at last the end comes slowly, the end that he welcomes because at last he will get his fill of sleep. Those who died of anæmia were the lucky ones, they and the others who fell fighting. God knows, it is no fun to die of a poisoned arrow, but, after all, it is a quick job over a few hours. But how few were there who died like that– scarcely one amongst a thousand. And for their luck the others had to pay heavily enough, those who happened to fall alive into the hands of those yellow devils. There was Karl Mattis, who had deserted from the Deutz-Cuirassiers, corporal in the first company, a broth of a boy, who would not be deterred by the maddest danger. When the Gametta station was attacked by a force of a thousand times superior in numbers, he undertook with two others to slip through and to take the news to Edgardhafen. During the night they were attacked, one of them was killed, Mattis was shot in the knee. He sent on his comrade and covered his flight for two hours against the Black-flags. At last they caught him, tied his hands and legs together, and tied him to a tree trunk, over there on the shallow banks of the stream. For three days he was lying there, until the crocodiles devoured him, slowly, bit by bit, and still they had no more pity than their two-legged fellow countrymen. Half a year later they captured Hendrik Oldenkott, of Masstricht, a seven-foot giant, whose incredible strength had been his ruin; in a state of heavy intoxication he had killed his own brother with his bare fist. The Légion saved him from the gaol, but not from the judges he found over here. Down there in the garden we found him, still alive. They had cut his belly open, filled the abdominal cavity with rats, and neatly sewed it up again. Lieutenant Heudelimont and two privates had their eyes picked out with red hot needles; they were found in the woods half dead of starvation. They hacked off Sergeant Jakob Bieberich's feet and made him play Mazeppa on a dead crocodile. Near Edgardhafen we fished him out of the river; for three cruel weeks he lived on in the hospital before he died.

"Is the list long enough for you? I can go on, string name on name. One does not cry out here any longer– but had I shed a few tears for each of them they would fill up a barrel bigger than any in my cellar. And the story contained in this box of counters is only the last little drop which made the full barrel run over."

The old fellow pulled the box towards himself and opened it. With his long nails he searched among the counters, picked out one, and passed it to me. "There, look you; this is the hero of the story."

The round mother o' pearl counter showed the picture of a légionnaire in his uniform. The full face of the soldier showed a striking likeness to the image of Christ on the lid; the reverse showed the same inscription as over the head of the crucified figure: K.V.K.S.II.C.L.E. I read K. von K., soldier, second class, Légion Etrangére.

"That's correct!" said the old fellow. "That's he: Karl von K——" He interrupted himself. "No, never mind about the name. If you want, you could find it easily enough in an old Navy List. He was a naval cadet before he came over here. He had to leave the service and the fatherland at the same time; I believe it was that foolish paragraph 218 of the previous criminal code which brought about his prosecution. There is no paragraph in that code too idiotic to win recruits for the Légion.

"Dear me, he was a joy to look at, the naval cadet! They all called him that, comrades and officers alike. A desperate fellow, who knew that he had gambled away the chances of his life, and now got his sport by playing the Limit all the time. In Algiers he had defended a camp by himself; when every officer and non-com had fallen he assumed the command of ten légionnaires and a few dozen goumiers, and stuck to the hole, until relief came up a few weeks after. That was when he got promoted for the first time; three times he was promoted, and as many times reduced to the ranks again. That's their way in the Légion– sergeant today and private again tomorrow. As long as they are out in the open it's all right; but this unbounded liberty cannot stand the atmosphere of the towns; they get into some nasty trouble in a moment. It was also the naval cadet who in the Red Sea jumped after General Barry when he slipped on the gangway and fell into the water. Amid the cheers of the men he fished him out, regardless of the giant sharks.

"His faults? He drank heavily– like every légionnaire. And, like all of them, he was forever after the women, and at times he forgot to ask nicely for permission first. And then– well, he treated the natives a good deal more *en canaille* than was absolutely necessary. But otherwise a magnificent fellow, for whom no apple was hanging too high. He was clever; in a few months he spoke the gibberish of the yellow scoundrels better than I had learned to in all the years I have been living here in my bungalow. His comrades thought I was making a fool of myself over him. Well, well, it was not quite as bad as that; but I was very fond of him, and he, too, stood closer to me than the rest. A whole year he was in Edgardhafen: and he drank a mighty gap into my cellar. He did not say, 'No, thanks!' when he had only got to the fourth glass, as you do! Go on, drink! Bana, fill up!

"Then he went to Fort Valmy, which was the furthermost station in those days. Four days you have to sail up river in a junk, crawling through the never-ending bends of the Red River. But it is much nearer as the crow flies; on my waler mare I can ride up there in eighteen hours. In those days he came here only very seldom; but, nevertheless, I saw him sometimes when I used to ride there to pay a visit to another friend of mine.

"That was Hong-Dok, the maker of this box.

"You smile? Hong-Dok– a friend of mine? That's what he was, all the same. Believe me, there are people out here quite your equals– few, very few, I must own. But he was one of them, Hong-Dok. And perhaps he was more than my equal. Fort Valmy– we shall ride out there one of these days; the Marines are quartered there now– no légionnaires any longer. It is an ancient, incredibly dirty town; the small French fortress rises above it on a hill near the river. Narrow, muddy streets, poor miserable houses. But that is only the town of today. In olden times, many centuries ago, it must have been a big, beautiful city, until the Black-flags came from the north, those cursed Black-flags, who give us so much trouble still. The heaps of *débris* around the town are six times as large as the town itself; whoever wants to build there can get the material cheap enough. But right amongst these miserable ruins there stood a big old building – you might have called it a palace – close to the river: Hong-Dok's house. It had been there from time immemorial, and the Black-flags had spared it out of some kind of religious fear.

"In that house used to live the rulers of this country, Hong-Dok's ancestors. He had a hundred generations of ancestors, and still another hundred, and yet a third hundred – more than all European dynasties put together – but he knew them all. Knew their names, knew what they had done. Princes they had been and emperors, but Hong-Dok was a wood carver, as his father had been, and his grandfather and great-grandfather. Because the Black-flags had spared the house, it is true, but nothing further, and the rulers were reduced to beggarly poverty like the least of their subjects. Thus the old stone house fell to pieces amongst the red blooms of the hibiscus bushes. Until a new glamor lit it up when the French arrived. For Hong-Dok's father had not forgotten the history of his country, as had done all those who ought to have been his subjects. And when the Europeans took possession of this country he was the first to give them greeting on the Red River. He rendered invaluable services to the French, and in recognition he was given land and cattle and a small stipend, and was made a kind of civil prefect of the town. That was the last little piece of good fortune that the ancient family experienced. Today the house lies in ruins, like the surroundings. The légionnaires smashed it; they did not leave one stone standing upon the other; they avenged on it the murder of the naval cadet, because the murderer had escaped them.

"Hong-Dok, my great friend, was the murderer. Here is his portrait."

The old man handed me another counter. It showed on one side in Roman letters Hong-Dok's name; on the other the picture of a native of the noble classes in native costume. But its execution was careless and lacking in detail, not approaching the beautiful work of the other counters.

Edgard Widerhold read my thoughts. "You are right," he said: "it's no good, this counter, the only one amongst the lot. It is very curious, just as if Hong-Dok did not care to call even the least attention to his own person. But have a look at this little gem!"

With the claw of his forefinger he shot another counter in my direction. It showed the portrait of a young woman who was beautiful even according to European notions; she was standing in front of a hibiscus bush, a little fan in her left hand. It was a masterpiece of unsurpassing perfection. The reverse showed again the name, Ot-Chen.

"This is the third figure in the tragedy of Fort Valmy," continued the old man. "Here you see a few minor actors and supers. He pushed a few dozen counters across the table; they showed on both sides crocodiles in all sort of positions; some of them swimming in the river, others sleeping on the bank, a few with jaws wide open, others again whipping their tails or raising themselves high up on their forelegs. A few were conventionalized; most of them, however, realistic; they all showed an extraordinary observation of the animal's habits.

Another lot of counters slid across to me, impelled by the yellow claws of the old man. "The venue," he said. One counter showed a big stone building, evidently the home of the artist; on others were representations of rooms and vignettes of a garden. The latter gave views of the Clear Stream and of the Red River– one of them as seen from Widerhold's verandah. Every one of these wonderful counters called forth unbounded delight in me; I actually took sides with the artist and against the naval cadet. I stretched out my hand for more counters.

"No!" said the old man; "wait! You shall see it all in proper order, each in its turn. As I have told you, Hong-Dok was a friend of mine, as his father had been. Both of them had worked for me through all those years. I was practically their only customer. When they became rich they kept on cultivating their art– only they would not take money any longer. The father even went so far as to insist on returning to me the last farthing of the money which I had paid him one time or another, and I had to accept it, if I did not wish to offend him. Thus, indeed, the contents of all the cupboards which you are so fond of admiring did not cost me a farthing.

"Through me the naval cadet became acquainted with Hong-Dok; I took him there once myself. I know what you are going to say: the naval cadet was a petticoat-hunter, and Ot-Chen was a most desirable quarry. Is not that it? And I might have thought that Hong-Dok would not just sit there and look on? No, no; there was nothing I could foresee. You might, perhaps have thought that; but not I, who knew Hong-Dok so well. When all had happened, and Hong-Dok told me the story, up here on the verandah– oh, in a far more quiet and collected way than I do at present– it appeared to me, nevertheless, so unlikely that I found it scarcely possible to believe him. Until, right in the middle of the river, a proof came swimming along, which admitted of no more doubt. I have often thought about the matter, and I think I know now some of the curious reasons which impelled Hong-Dok to his deed. A few, but who could read everything in a brain that carried the impress of a thousand generations and was saturated to the full with power, with art and with the all-penetrating wisdom of opium?

"No, no; there was nothing I could have foreseen. If anybody had asked me then, 'What would Hong-Dok do, if the naval cadet seduced Ot-Chen or any of his other nine wives?' I would have answered without fail, 'He would not even look up from his work!' Or even, if he is in a good temper, he will make a present of Ot-Chen to the naval cadet. Thus must have acted the Hong-Dok I used to know, thus and not otherwise. Ho-Nam, another one of his wives, he caught once with a Chinese interpreter; he thought it below his dignity to say as much as a single word to either of them. Another time it was Ot-Chen herself who deceived him. So you can see that there was not a particular preference just for this woman by which he was actuated. The almond eyes of one of my Indian boys who had ridden with me to Fort Valmy had fascinated little Ot-Chen, and even if the two were not able to say a word to each other, they soon were in sweet agreement. Hong-Dok caught them in his garden; but he never lifted a hand against his wife, neither would he allow me to punish the boy. All that touched him no more than if a dog had barked at him in the street– he would scarcely turn his head. There doesn't seem to me the most remote possibility that a man of Hong-Dok's unshakable philosophic calm should have lost his head for a moment and have acted in a sudden ebullition of temper. And, quite apart from that, the severe investigations which we held after his flight amongst his wives and servants showed clearly that Hong-Dok had deliberated and carefully executed even the smallest detail of his deed. Thus it would appear that the naval cadet was a constant visitor to the stone house for three months, and kept up all this time his relations with Ot-Chen, relations of which Hong-Dok was told after the first few weeks by one of his servants. But, in spite of it all, he let them go on with it quietly, rather using the time to mature the cruel manner of his vengeance, which I feel certain he must have decided to take from the first moment.

"But why did he resent as a bitter insult what the naval cadet did, when the same action committed by my Indian boy made him scarcely smile? I may be mistaken, but I think I have found the torturous path of his thoughts after a prolonged search. Hong-Dok was a king. We laugh if we find on our coins the letters D.G., and most of our European princes deride no less their tenure by the Grace of God. But imagine a ruler who believes in it, whose conviction that he is the Lord's anointed is really as firm as the rocks. I know the comparison does not quite fit, but there is a certain likeness. Hong-Dok, of course, did not believe in a god, he only believed in the precepts of the great philosopher; but that his family was a thing apart, sky high above everybody else, of that he was – and quite rightly so – firmly convinced. From ages without origin his ancestors had been rulers, monarchs of unlimited power. A prince with us, if he has got a scrap of intelligence, knows quite well that there are many thousands in his country who are very much more clever and a great deal better educated than is he himself. Hong-Dok and all his ancestors were equally certain of the contrary; a gigantic chasm had always separated them from the great masses of their people. They alone were rulers, while all the rest were abject slaves.

"They alone had wisdom and knowledge– they came in contact with their peers only on those rare occasions when ambassadors arrived from the neighboring kingdom on the sea, or from Siam far away in the south, or even Chinese mandarins across the mountains of the savage Meos. We would say, Hong-Dok's ancestors were gods amongst men. Theirs was a different kind of life: they felt themselves men amongst dirty animals. Do you see the difference? A dog barks at us– we scarcely turn our heads.

"Then arrived the barbarians from the north, the Black-flags. They took the country and destroyed the town, and many other towns in these regions. Only the house of the ruler they would not touch; they did not hurt as much as a hair on anyone's head who belonged to the ruler's house. Where peace and quiet had been ruling the country now echoes for ever with murder and killing; but the turmoil did not reach the palace on the Red River. And Hong-Dok's ancestors despised the savage hordes from the North as much as they had despised their own people; nothing could have bridged the colossal chasm. Animals they were, exactly as the others; but they themselves were men who knew the wisdom of the philosopher.

"Then lightning cleft the mists of the river. From far distant shores strange white beings arrived, and Hong-Dok's father saw with joyous surprise that they were men. He could see, of course, the difference between himself and the strangers; but this difference was infinitely small, compared with that which separated him from the people of his own country. And, like so many others among the nobles of Tonkin, he felt at once that he belonged to them, and not to the others. Hence his ever ready assistance from the first moment, consisting chiefly in teaching the French to discern between the quiet, peaceful aborigines and the bellicose hordes of the north. And when he was appointed civil prefect of the country the population continued to see in him their real, native sovereign. It was he who had freed them from the nightmare of the Black-flags; the French had only been his tools, foreign warriors he had called into the country. Thus

[133]

he was considered as ruler by his people, with powers quite as unrestricted as once his ancestors, of whom they were told half-forgotten tales.

"Thus grew up Hong-Dok, the son of a prince, destined to rule himself. Like his father, he considered the Europeans men, and not silly animals. But now that the good fortune of the old palace had been built up again he had more leisure for looking closely at these strangers, for finding out the differences existing between them and himself, also amongst them. Being in constant touch with the Légion, he acquired as sure a knowledge as my own in recognizing the private who was a gentleman and the officer who was a serf, in spite of the gold lace. Indeed, all through the East it is far more education than birth which distinguishes the gentleman from the serf. He was well aware that all these warriors towered high above his people– but not above himself. While his father had considered every white man as his equal, Hong-Dok did not do so any longer, and the closer and the more intimate his acquaintance with them the fewer he found who could be considered his equals. He agreed they were wonderful, unconquerable warriors– each single one of them worth more than a hundred of the dreaded Black-flags– but was that fame? Hong-Dok despised soldiering as much as any other profession. They all were able to read and write– their own characters, it is true, but he did not mind that; but there was scarcely one amongst them who knew the meaning of philosophy. Hong-Dok did not demand that they should know the great philosopher, but he expected to find some other foreign wisdom, equally profound. And he found nothing. These white men knew less of the ultimate origin of all things than the lowest smoker of opium. But there was one thing which caused him surprise and greatly lowered his esteem for them: the attitude they assumed in their religion. It was not the religion itself which he disliked, and he thought the Christian creed as good as the others he knew of. Now, our légionnaires are anything but religious, and no clergyman, mindful of his duty, would allow any of them to partake of the Sacrament. And yet at times, in moments of great danger, a mutilated prayer for help tore itself from their hearts. Hong-Dok had noticed that– and he found that these people actually believed that an impossible help might be sent to them by some unknown power. Now he went on with his investigations– did I tell you that Hong-Dok spoke a better French than I?– and made friends with the kindly military chaplain of Fort Valmy. And what he discovered then corroborated more and more the conviction of his own superiority. I remember quite well still, how he talked to me about these matters one evening in his smoking-rooms, how he smiled when he told me that now he knew how Christians really looked at their cult, and that even the priest had no understanding for the symbolical.

"The worst of it was that he was right; I had not a word to say to him. We Europeans are believers– or we are not believers. But for Christians in Europe who guard the faith of their fathers with loving care like a beautiful raiment covered with profound symbols, you may look with the lantern of Diogenes, and you may be quite sure you will find not a single one out here in Tonkin. But just some such conception was the most natural thing for this Eastern sage, a thing that goes by itself, indispensable for the man of real education. And when he discovered its downright absence, and was not even understood by the priest in thoughts which he considered the most simple, he lost a great deal of his admiration and esteem. In many things the Europeans were his superiors– things, however, which he thought of scarcely any value. In others, again, they were his equals: but in the matter most important of all, the profoundest recognition of all life, they stood far, far below him. And as the years went on, this contempt gave birth in him to a hatred that slowly grew, the more the foreigners became the actual rulers of the country, the more they advanced, step by step, uniting all power in their strong hands. Already in his country they did not need any longer that mediating semblance of power which they had given to his father, and later on to himself: he felt strongly that his father had been mistaken, and that the old stone house near the river was out of it forever. I do not believe that, for all that, bitterness crept into the mind of this philosopher, who took life as it came: on the contrary, the consciousness of his own superiority may have been for him a source of joyous satisfaction. The modus of living with the Europeans which evolved in the course of the years was very simple; he retired into himself as much as he could, but treated them in all externals quite sincerely as his equals. But he closed to everybody the gates and windows of the house behind his angular yellow forehead, and if he opened them at times to me, that was owing to a friendship which he had practically imbibed with his mother's milk, and which was ever kept alive by my vivid interest in his art.

"Such a one was Hong-Dok. Not for a moment could it stir him, when his wives compromised themselves with the Chinese interpreter or one of my boys. Had there been any results of these trifling escapades, Hong-Dok would simply have had the brats drowned, not out of hatred or revenge, but just as one drowns puppies– simply because they are not wanted. And had the naval cadet, when he took a liking to Ot-Chen, asked him for her as a present, Hong-Dok would have given her to him at once.

"But the naval cadet came to his house like a gentleman– and he took away his wife like a scullion. On the first evening already Hong-Dok recognized that this légionnaire was made of finer stuff than most of his comrades; I could see that, because with him he came out a little from the shell of his courteous reserve. And during their further relations with each other – all that is only surmise on my part – the naval cadet most probably treated Hong-Dok exactly as he would have treated some country gentleman in Germany whose wife he admired. He brought into play the whole range of his glittering amiability, and I am sure he succeeded in fascinating Hong-Dok as much as he had always fascinated me and all his superiors: you simply could not help liking this clever, fresh, and attractive boy. That's what Hong-Dok did, to the extent of descending from his elevated throne, he, the ruler, the artist, the wise disciple of Confucius, to the extent of making friends with the légionnaire and loving him, certainly loving him more than anybody else.

"Then a servant brought him the news, and he saw from his window how the naval cadet took his pleasure with Ot-Chen in the garden.

"So, that was the reason of his coming to him. Not in order to see him– only because of her, a woman, an animal! Hong-Dok felt shamefully deceived– oh! not at all like a European husband. But that this foreigner should have feigned friendship for him, and that he should have given him his friendship, that was the point. That he, in all his proud wisdom, should have been fooled by this base-born soldier who, secretly, like a scullion, went after his wife. That he should have wasted his love on something so miserable, so far below him. You see, that's what this proud yellow devil could not get over.

[135]

*   *   *   *   *   *

"One evening his servants carried him to the bungalow. He descended from the palanquin and came smiling up the verandah. As usual, he brought me a few presents, little fans, beautifully carved in ivory. A few officers were also here, Hong-Dok greeted them most amiably, sat down with us, and was silent; he scarcely spoke three words until they left an hour afterwards. He waited until the sound of their horses' trot lost itself along the river; then he spoke up, quite calmly, quite sweetly as if he had to give me the best of news: 'I have come to tell you something. *I have crucified the naval cadet and Ot-Chen.*

"Although Hong-Dok was not at all in the habit of making jokes, this astounding piece of news caused me but one sensation; there must be some good fun behind it all. And I liked his dry, casual way of speaking so much that I entered into it right away, and asked him, in the same quiet strain, 'Is that so? And what else have you done with them?'

"He answered. 'I have had their lips sewed up!'

"This time I laughed. 'Really, you do not say so! And what other kindnesses have you bestowed on them?– And why?'

"Hong-Dok spoke quietly and seriously, but the sweet smile did not leave the corners of his mouth. 'Why? I caught them in the act.'

"This expression he liked so much that he repeated it. He had heard or read it somewhere, and he thought it very ridiculous that we Europeans should attach particular importance to catching a rogue exactly at the moment of his deed; just as if it mattered in the least whether he is caught in it, or before or afterwards. He said it with an accent of feigned importance, with an easily noticeable exaggeration, which showed better than anything else his bitter contempt. 'Am I not right in thinking that in Europe the deceived husband has the right to punish the thief of his honor?'

"This sweet sneer sounded so sure that I could not find words to answer him. He continued therefore, still with the same friendly smile, as if he was recounting the simplest thing in the world: 'Consequently I have punished him. As he is a Christian, I thought it best to choose a Christian manner of death; I assumed this would suit him best. Have I done right?'

"I did not care at all for this curious way of joking. Not for a moment did I think he might speak the truth; but I began to feel uncomfortable, and wished he would be done with his story. Of course I believed him when he told me the naval cadet had got entangled with Ot-Chen, and I thought he wanted by means of this occurrence to reduce once more *ad absurdum* our European notions of honor and morals. So I said only: 'But certainly! Quite right! I am sure the naval cadet valued greatly this little courtesy.'

"But Hong-Dok shook his head, sadly nearly: 'No, I do not think so. At least he never said a word about it. He only cried.'

"'He cried?'

"'Yes,' said Hong-Dok, with an expression of sweet melancholy and regret, 'he cried very much. Far more than Ot-Chen. He kept on praying to his god, and in between he cried. Much worse than a dog which is being killed. It was really very disagreeable. And that's why I had to have his mouth sewn up!'

"I had had more than enough of these jokes, and wanted to get him to stop. 'Is that all?' I interrupted him.

[136]

"'Yes, that's all. I had them seized and tied and then stripped. Then I had their lips sewn up and had them crucified, throwing them in the river afterwards.'

"I was glad that he had done. 'Well, and what about it all?' At last I thought to hear the explanation.

"Hong-Dok looked at me with big eyes, as if he did not quite understand what I wanted. 'Oh, it was only the vengeance of the poor deceived husband!'

"'All right,' I said, 'all right! But now do tell me what you actually mean! What is the point of your joke?'

"'The point?' He showed a happy smile, just as if this word came exactly at the right moment. 'Oh, please just wait a little!' He leant back in his chair and was silent. I did not feel the least desire to urge him further, so I followed his example; let him finish his idiotic murder-story when he wanted.

"Thus we sat down for half an hour, neither saying a word. Inside, in a room, the time-piece struck six o'clock. 'Now they must come,' said Hong-Dok quietly. Then he turned to me: 'Will you kindly ask the boy to fetch your telescopes?'– I called Bana; he brought my telescopes. But before Hong-Dok got hold of one of them he jumped up, leaned far out over the balustrade. He pointed his arm towards the right, in the direction of the Red River, and shouted triumphantly, 'Look, look! There it is coming, the point of my joke!'

"I took my telescope and looked intensely through it. Far, far up river I noticed a little speck drifting in the middle of the current. It came nearer, I saw a little raft. And on the raft two people, two naked people. Without thinking, I ran to the extreme edge of the verandah, so that I might see better. There was a woman, lying on her back her black tresses hanging into the water; I recognized Ot-Chen. And, upon her, a man. I did not see his face, but the reddish, fair color of his hair– ah, the naval cadet, the naval cadet! Long iron hooks had fixed hands upon hands, feet upon feet, driven deeply into the boards; then dark streaks of blood were running over the white wood. At this moment I saw how the naval cadet lifted his head, shaking it, shaking it wildly. I was certain he wanted to make me a sign– they were still alive, still alive!

"I dropped the telescope; for a second I lost consciousness. But only for a second. Then I shouted, bawling like a madman, for the servants: 'Down and man the boats!' I ran back along the verandah. There stood Hong-Dok, smiling sweetly, amiably. Just as if he wanted to ask me: 'Now then, is the point of my joke not very good?'

"You know, people have often made fun of my long nails. But at that moment, I give you my word, I realized what they were good for. I got hold of the yellow blackguard's throat and shook him to and fro. And I felt how my claws sank deeply into his cursed throat–

"Then I let him go. Like a sack he fell down on the ground. Like one possessed, I tore down the stairs, all my servants after me. I ran down the bank to the river, and was the first to cast off one of the boats. One of the boys jumped in, but he went right through the bottom at once, standing up to his hips in water; the center plank had broken out. We went to another one, a third one– all along; they were full of water up to the gunwale; out of all of them long planks had been cut. I ordered the servants to get the big junk under way; pell mell we climbed into her. But, as in the boats, we found the bottom perforated with big holes, and had to wade through deep water– quite impossible to get the junk even a yard away from the bank.

"'Hong-Dok's servants!' exclaimed my Indian overseer. 'They have done it! I saw them slink around near the river!'

"We jumped back on the bank. I gave the order to pull one of the boats ashore, to bail it out, and nail quickly a plank on the bottom. The boys ran into the water, pulled, shoved, pushed, nearly collapsed under the load of the big craft. I kept on shouting to them, and in between I looked out on the river.

"The raft came past quite close, alas! scarcely fifty yards away from the bank. I stretched out my arms, as if I could grasp it, like that, with my hands—

"What do you say? Swimming? Quite so– on the Rhine or the Elbe! But on the Clear Stream? And it was June, I tell you, June! The river was swarming with crocodiles, particularly as the sun was just setting. The loathsome brutes swam closely round the small raft; I saw one of them lifting itself up on its forelegs, and knocking its long, black snout against the crucified bodies. They could scent their quarry, and went along with it impatiently, down river—

"And again the naval cadet shook his head desperately. I shouted to him we were coming, coming—

"But it was as if the cursed river was in league with Hong-Dok; it grasped the boat firmly in tough fingers of mud and would not let go. I also jumped into the water and pulled with the boys. We tore and pushed, we were scarcely able to lift it, inch by inch. And the sun was sinking and the raft was drifting away, further and further.

"Then the overseer brought along horses. We put ropes round the boat and whipped up the animals. Now things moved. One other effort, and yet another, shouting, whipping! The boat was on the bank. The water ran from it; the boys nailed new planks on the bottom. But the dark night had fallen long ago when we started.

"I took the helm, six men bent heavily over the oars. Three were kneeling on the bottom, bailing out the water which kept on coming in. In spite of it all, it rose, until we sat up to the calves in water. I had to tell off two, and yet another two, from the oars for bailing. We advanced with painful slowness—

"I had big pitch torches for searching. But we did not find anything. Several times we thought we could see a raft far away; when we got near, it was a drifting tree trunk or alligator. We found nothing. We searched for hours and found nothing. I went ashore in Edgardhafen and gave the alarm. The commander sent out five boats and two great junks. They searched the river for three days. But they had no better luck than we. We despatched wires to all stations down river. Nothing– nobody saw him again, poor naval cadet!

"——What do I think? Well, the raft got stuck somewhere on the bank. Or it drifted against a tree trunk and got smashed. One way or the other, the black reptiles got their prey."

*　*　*　*　*　*

The old man emptied his glass and held it out to the boy. And emptied it once more, quickly, in one draught. Then he stroked his dirty grey beard with his long claws.

"Yes," he went on, "that's the story. When we returned to the bungalow Hong-Dok had disappeared, and with him his servants. Then came the investigation– I told you about it already. Naturally nothing new was brought to light.

"Hong-Dok had fled. And never again did I hear anything from him, until one day this box with the counters arrived; somebody brought it in my absence. The boys told me it came from a Chinese merchant. I had investigations made, but in vain. There you are, take your box; look at the pictures which you do not know yet."

He pushed the mother o' pearl counters towards me. "This one shows Hong-Dok being carried to me by his servants in the palanquin. Here you see me and himself on the verandah; here you see him, how I grasp him by the throat. These are several counters showing show how we try to get the boat clear, and here are others recording our search through the night on the river. One counter shows Ot-Chen and the naval cadet being crucified, the other one how they have their lips sewn up. This is Hong-Dok's flight; here you see my clawing hand, and on the reverse his neck with the scars."

Edgard Widerhold relit his pipe. "Now take away your box!" he said. "May the counters bring you good luck on the poker table! There is blood enough sticking to them."———

And this is a true tale.

The Execution of Damiens

Ich glaube daher, daß die Sinnesempfindungen noch etwas mehr enthalten, als die Philosophen sich einbilden. Sie sind nicht bloß leere Wahrnehmungen von gewissen im Hirn gemachten Eindrücken: sie geben der Seele nicht nur Ideen von Dingen; sondern sie stellen ihr auch wirklich Gegenstände vor, die außer ihr existieren, ob man gleich nicht begreifen kann, wie dies eigentlich zugehe.

Leonhard Euler, Briefe an eine Deutsche
Prinzessin. Bd. II, S. 68.

The Execution of Damiens

Sprawled in leather chairs they sat in the lobby of the Spa Hotel and smoked. Music drifted to them from the ballroom.

Erhardt drew out his watch and yawned. "Late enough," he said. "They could stop now."

At this moment the young Baron Grödel walked up. "I have become engaged, gentlemen!" he yapped.

"To Evelyn Ketschendorff?" asked fat Dr. Handl. "It took long enough."

But Brinken said: "Take care, my boy! She has pinched, set, English lips."

The handsome Grödel nodded: "Her mother was an Englishwoman."

"I thought so," said Brinken. "Take care, my boy!"

But the Baron did not listen; he placed his glass on the table, and ran back to the ballroom.

"You don't like Englishwomen?" asked Erhardt.

Dr. Handl laughed; "Don't you know that? He hates all women with a bit of race or class; especially if they're English! Only fat, dumb, silly women find favor in his eyes— geese and cows."

Aimer une femme intelligente est un plaisir de pédèraste!" cited Count Attems.

Brinken shrugged his shoulders. "Whether it is just that, I don't know. Besides, it is not quite right to say that I hate intelligent women; if they have nothing else, they can appeal to me, too. It is those who have a soul, feeling, fantasy that I fear in the affairs of love. Cows and geese are respectable animals: they eat corn and hay, and not their fellows."

The others were silent, so he continued:

"I can explain further, if you like. Early this morning I went for a walk through the morning sun; there, in Val Madonna, I saw a pair of lovesick snakes: two steel-blue fat adders; each a meter and a half long. It was a pretty game. They glided between the stones, went back and forth, hissed at each other. At length they intertwined, and stood rocking on their tails, upright, closely embraced. The heads pressed against each other, the jaws opened wide, the forked tongues darted through the air. Oh, nothing is more beautiful than such nuptial play! The golden eyes shone— it seemed to me as if they both carried scintillating crowns on their heads!

"Then they fell away from each other, exhausted by their wild play; lay there in the sun. The female soon recovered; slowly she moved towards the dead-tired bridegroom, seized him by the head and devoured him, powerless as he was. Choked, choked, millimeter by millimeter, infinitely slowly she devoured the body of her mate. It was a frightful work; one saw how all her muscles worked to swallow the animal which was larger than

[143]

herself. The jaws jerked almost from their sockets; she bent herself back and forth, drew her husband even deeper within. At last only his tail stuck out a hand's length from her mouth— farther he could not go. She lay plump, ugly, unable to stir."

"Was there no stick or stone?" cried Dr. Handl.

"What for?" said Brinken. "Should I punish her? Nature after all, is the devil's work, not God's— Aristotle already said that. No, I seized the tail sticking out of the mouth and drew the miserable lover out of his too gluttonous idol. They lay then half an hour next to each other in the sun: I would like to know what they thought the while. Then they crept into the bushes, he to the left, she to the right; for even a snake-lady cannot eat her spouse twice. But perhaps the poor fellow, after this experience, will take care when he wanders again awooing."

"That was nothing out of the ordinary," said Erhardt; "every female spider devours her male after the mating."

Brinken continued, "The mantis *religiosa*, the Worshipper-of-God, doesn't wait first for the end. You can observe this here on the Adriadic island every day. She skilfully turns her neck round, seizes with her terrible pincers the head of the lover seated upon her, and calmly begins to consume him— in the midst of the mating. Nowhere, gentlemen, will you find more atavism in mankind than in sexual life. I, for my part, have no use for the soulful paroxysms of the most beautiful houri, who suddenly discloses herself as a snake, spider, or Worshipper-of-God."

"I have never met one!" remarked Dr. Handl.

"That doesn't mean that you may not meet her tomorrow," answered Brinken. "Have a look at the anatomy collection of any university: there you will find crazier combinations of atavistic monstrosities than the fantasy of the average man could picture. You can find in human shape the entire animal kingdom. Many such creatures live seven years, twelve years, and still longer. Children with a hare-lip, with a split palate, with tusks, and those with pig's heads; children with webs between all their fingers, between their arms and their legs, with a frog's mouth, or a frog's head, or a frog's eyes; children with horns on their heads, not only stag's horns, but with the pincer horns of a stag-beetle. If you can see such monstrous atavisms everywhere, is it not to be wondered at that a few singular characteristics of this or that animal be repeated in human soul life?

"When you see such wild atavism everywhere, is it astonishing that some peculiar qualities of this or that animal should also be found in human souls? It is only remarkable that we don't stumble over them more often; but the reason may lie in that no one speaks willingly about them. You can associate intimately with a family for years without learning that one of the sons is a complete cretin put away in some institution."

"Granted!" said Erhardt. "But still you haven't explained your grudge against dangerous women. Tell us, who was your Worshipper-of-God."

"My Worshipper-of-God," said Brinken, "prayed to God every morning and every evening, and even succeeded in getting me to pray with her. Don't laugh, Count, it is literally as I say. My Worshipper-of-God went twice every Sunday to church, and to chapel every day. Three days a week she visited the poor. My Worshipper-of-God—"

He interrupted himself, mixed a whisky, and drank.

Then he continued:

"I was just eighteen years old, an undergraduate on my first vacation. During my years at school and at university my mother always sent me abroad for my holidays— she believed it good for my education. This time I was staying in England with a school master in Dover, where I was thoroughly bored. By chance I made the acquaintance of Sir Oliver Bingham, a man of forty, who invited me to visit him at his place in Devonshire. I accepted at once, and departed with him a few days later.

"Bingham castle was a magnificent country seat, four hundred years or more in the possession of the family. There was a large and well-cultivated park with golf-links and tennis-courts; a little river, where row-boats lay, flowed through the grounds. Two dozen hunters in the stables. And all this at the disposal of the guests. It was the first time I had enjoyed English hospitality with its liberality; my youthful joy was boundless.

"Lady Cynthia was the second wife of Sir Oliver. He had two sons by the first marriage; both were at Eton. I perceived at once that this wife was a wife only in name. Sir Oliver and Lady Cynthia lived side by side as two complete strangers; between them there was nothing but an extremely careful and often somewhat unnatural politeness, which, nevertheless, was scarcely forced. Inborn and acquired convention helped both easily over all stiles.

"Not until much later did I understand that Sir Oliver, before he presented me to his wife, had intended to warn me. At that time I did not notice it. He said: 'Look here, my boy! Lady Cynthia, now see— well, take care of yourself!' He could not quite speak openly what he thought; and, as I said, I did not understand him.

"Sir Oliver was a real country gentleman of the old style, as you might find in a hundred English novels: Eton, Oxford, sport and a little politics. He took pleasure in his estate and was a capable farmer. Everybody at Bingham Castle loved him— men, women and animals. He was a powerful, blond, brown and healthy, large and open-hearted. For his part he loved no less those around him, and demonstrated this kind of rural love more especially and rather indiscriminately to the younger female servants. This happened without the slightest hypocrisy and quite obviously: Lady Cynthia alone seemed not to notice it.

"It was this unconcealed faithlessness to his wife which deeply grieved me. If ever a woman, it seemed to me, had earned the full and implicit love of a man, she was this Lady Cynthia; if ever adultery was a treacherous and repulsive crime, so it was against this woman.

She must have been about twenty-seven years old. If she had lived during the Renaissance in Rome, or Venice, one would see her portrait today in many a church. I never saw another woman who was so like a Madonna. She wore her gold-shimmering brown hair parted in the middle. Her features were of perfect regularity. Her eyes seemed to me like seas of amethyst dreams; her long, narrow hands were of an almost transparent whiteness; her throat, her neck— ah, it seemed to me as if this woman were scarcely earthly. You never heard her step. It was as though she floated through the rooms.

"No wonder I fell in love. At this time I wrote sonnets by the dozen; at first in German, then in English. They were probably extremely poor— but if you could read them now, gentlemen, you would certainly be able to picture, from their minute descriptions, Lady Cynthia's unusual beauty and at the same time my state of soul.

"And this woman was deceived by Sir Oliver, who did not even give himself the trouble to conceal the fact. I couldn't even prevent it, I had to hate him. He noticed that: once or twice he attempted to speak to me about it, but he could not find the right opening.

"I never saw Lady Cynthia laugh— nor weep. She was unusually silent; like a shadow she glided through the park and the house. She did not ride, nor play golf, nor did she indulge in any sport. Neither did she ever trouble herself with the household; this was left entirely to the old butler. But as I have said, she was very religious— attended church regularly and visited the poor of the villages. She said grace before every meal. Every morning and every evening she went to the castle chapel and knelt down to prayers. Never did I see her read a paper, and seldom a book. On the other hand, she embroidered a great deal, made laces, rosepoint and edging. At times she sat at the piano in the music-room, played also the organ in the chapel. While she plied her needle she would often sing softly, almost always a simple folk-tune. Only many years later did it occur to me how absurd it was that this woman, who had never had a child, should prefer to sing cradle-songs. At the time I took it for dreamy wistfulness, which I found fascinating.

"Our relationship was determined from the first day: she was the mistress and I was her obedient page, hopelessly enamored, but very well behaved. At times she let me read to her— Walter Scott's novels. She suffered me about her while she played or sewed, and she often sang for me. At mealtimes I sat next to her. As Sir Oliver was often away, we were frequently alone. Her sentimentality had taken possession of me: she seemed to be sorrowing silently over something; and I held it to be my duty to sorrow with her.

"Often late in the afternoon she stood at the narrow window of the tower room. I could see her from the park: sometimes I went into the room at this hour. A boyish shyness kept me from speaking; I crept on tiptoes down the stairs into the garden, hid myself behind a tree, and sent longing glances to the window from the distance. She would stand there a long time, not moving. Often she would clench her hands, and a quiver would fly over her face; but the deep amethyst eyes would stare out motionless. She seemed to see nothing, her glance sped over trees and bushes strangely possessed.

"Once, I know, I dined alone with her at night. We talked long after the meal, then went into the music room. She played for me. It was not the music which made me flush; I stared at those white hands, those fingers which were not human. As she finished, she half turned to me. I seized her hand, bent over it, and kissed her finger-tips. At this moment Sir Oliver walked in. Lady Cynthia, polite as always, wished him good evening. Then she went out.

"Sir Oliver had seen my movement, he also saw my excited eyes, which cried aloud how it stood with me. He strode up and down the room once or twice with long strides, suppressing with difficulty a few good curses. Then he came to me, clapped me on the shoulder, said: 'For Heaven's sake, my boy, take care! I tell you— no, I beg you, beseech you— take care. You—'

"Here Lady Cynthia returned to the room to fetch her rings, which she had left on the piano. Sir Oliver broke off abruptly, squeezed my hand strongly, bowed to his wife and went out. Lady Cynthia came to me, slipped, one after the another, her rings on her fingers. Then she held out both her hands to me for a goodnight kiss. She said not a word, but I felt what was commanded. I bent down and covered her hands with hot kisses. She let me hold them long, finally she freed herself and left.

"I had the feeling that I had committed a grievous wrong to Sir Oliver, as if I were in honor bound to tell him about it. It seemed to be easier to do it in writing; so I went into my room and sat down at the desk. I wrote one letter, two letters, three letters; each seemed more stupid than the other. At length I decided to speak to him, so I went out to look for him. To avoid losing my courage again, I ran up the steps as fast as I could; before the door of his smoking-room, which was wide open, I suddenly stopped. I heard voices in there: first the jovial, somewhat broad laugh of Sir Oliver, then a woman's voice.

"'But, Sir Oliver. . .' said the voice.

"'Go on, don't be a little fool,' laughed Sir Oliver, 'don't take on so.'

"I turned on the spot, crept down the steps. It was Millicent's voice— that of one of the parlormaids.

"Two days later, Sir Oliver went to London. I remained alone at Bingham Castle with Lady Cynthia.

"At this time I was in wonderland, in an Eden that the Deity created for me alone. It is difficult to describe the witchery of the dream in which I lived. I tried to describe it in a letter to my mother. When I visited her, a few months ago, she showed me the old letter, which she had faithfully preserved. The envelope bore on the back the words 'I am very happy!' The letter itself contained this astonishing gush of feeling: "Dear mother: you ask how I feel, what I do? Oh, mother! Oh, mother, mother!' And a dozen times more, 'Oh, mother!' Nothing more.

"With these words, of course, one might express the deepest pain, the wildest despair, as well as the extremest delight; but something superlative it must be!

"I remarked early in the morning when Lady Cynthia went into the chapel, which lay a short distance from the castle by the side of a stream. Then I waited until she came out, and accompanied her to breakfast. One morning she made a sign; I understood it, without her having to speak. I followed her, therefore into the chapel; she knelt to pray, and I knelt behind her. From that time I always went with her into the chapel. At first I did nothing but stare at her; but gradually, I did what she did— prayed. Just imagine, gentlemen, I praying— a German student! And surely a heathen! I don't know what or to whom I prayed; but it was some sort of thanksgiving for so much happiness and a shower of burning wishes for this woman.

"I rode a good deal; somehow or other my foaming blood had to calm down. Once I had ridden out fairly early, lost myself in the country, and was in the saddle for many hours. When at last I found my way back to the castle a raging thunderstorm broke, a regular cloud-burst. I came back to the stream and found the wooden bridge washed away; to get to the nearest stone bridge I would have to make a considerable detour. I was wet through as it was, so I jumped into the swollen stream. I got across, though I had considerably overestimated the strength of my worn-out mare, and was carried downstream a good way.

"Lady Cynthia awaited me in her sitting-room. I hurried, therefore, to my room, bathed and changed. Perhaps I looked a little tired; at all events, she insisted that I should lie on the couch. Then she sat beside me, stroked my forehead, and sang:

> *Rockaby, baby, on the tree-top—*
> *When the wind blows, the cradle will rock,*
> *When the bough breaks, the cradle will fall,*
> *Down will come baby, cradle and all!*

"She stroked my forehead and sang; it was as though I lay in a magic cradle, which hung on the high bough of a tree. The wind blew and sang, and my cradle rocked in the breezes. If only the bough does not break! I thought.

"Well, gentlemen, my bough broke; and I fell down, hard enough. At any time Lady Cynthia would give me her hands— but only her hands. I trembled for her shoulders, her forehead— oh! of her lips I dared not think. I never spoke about it, but my glances offered her my heart and my soul— everything, every day and every hour. She took everything, and gave me her hands.

"Sometimes on late afternoons when I had sat for hours at a time with her, when my blood screamed from all my pores, she would stand up and say quietly: 'Now to riding.' She went to her tower room, and softly I followed her, peered through the hangings. She took a little book bound in old brocade, then she sat down, read only for a few minutes, then stood up again, went to the window, stared out. I went to the stables, saddled my horse, rode through the park, then out to the fields. Like a madman I galloped through the dusk. A cold bath when I returned; thus I found a little rest before supper.

"Once I had ridden out earlier and came back at tea-time. I met her in the hall, as I was going to my bath.

"'Come,' she said, 'when you are ready! Hurry; tea awaits in the tower.' I was in my kimono.

"'I must dress myself,' I answered.

"'Come as you are,' she said.

"'I jumped into the tub, turned on the shower; in a few minutes I was ready. I went to the tower room. She sat on the couch, her little book in her hand; she laid it aside as I entered. She was like myself, in a dressing-gown— a wonderful kimono, purple with flowers of dull gold. She poured my tea, buttered my toast. Not a word did we say. I gulped down the toast, poured down the hot tea. I trembled in every limb. At length tears ran into my eyes. I knelt before her, took her hands, buried my head in her lap. She let me do it.

"At length she stood up. 'You may do everything— everything. But you must not utter a word. Not a word, not a word!"

"I did not understand what she meant: but I got up and nodded. Slowly she stood up and went to the narrow window. I hesitated, did not quite know what I should do. Finally I followed her, stood behind her. I knew I must not speak.

"I stood undecided, motionless like her. I heard her light breathing. Then I bent down, very slowly; I touched her neck with my lips. Oh, so tenderly: no butterfly could kiss more tenderly. Then I felt she felt the kiss. A gentle shiver ran over her skin.

"I kissed her shoulder, her scented hair, her sweet ear— only gently, very softly, page-like, embarrassed. My fingers sought, found her arms, caressed them up and down. A sigh escaped her lips, floated far out into the evening.

"I saw the high trees without, heard the song of a late nightingale.

"I shut my eyes. Nothing was between us but a little silk. I breathed deeply and heard her breathing. My body thrilled down to the toes, and I felt how she trembled in my arms. Faster went her breath, and faster; a hot quivering seized her body. Then she seized my hands, pressed them against her breast.

"I embraced her, clasped her tightly, held her, I don't know how long. Then her hands dropped, she threatened to swoon, and hung for awhile in my arms. Then she pulled herself together.

"'Go,' she said softly.

"I loosened my hands as she commanded; left her, crept outside on tiptoe.

"That evening I did not see her again, I was alone for supper. Something had happened, but I did not know what it was. I was rather young in those days.

"Next morning I waited before the chapel. Lady Cynthia nodded to me as she went in. She knelt down and prayed as she did every morning.

"A few days later — and then again and yet again — she said 'Come tonight!' But she did not forget to add, 'Not a word must you speak, not a word!'

"Eighteen years old I was, and very gauche and inexperienced. But Lady Cynthia was very wise, and all happened as she wished. Her mouth spoke no word and my mouth spoke no word— only her blood spoke to my blood.

"Then Sir Oliver returned. We sat at supper, Lady Cynthia and I: I heard Sir Oliver's voice in the hall. I let my fork drop; I believe I was whiter than the damask tablecloth. Not fear— it was certainly not that! But I had, by this time, completely forgotten that this man was still in the world— Sir Oliver!

"Sir Oliver was in a good humor this evening. He certainly noticed my embarrassment; but he did not betray this knowledge by the slightest gesture. He ate, drank, talked of London, spoke of theaters and horses. He excused himself immediately after the meal, clapped me on the shoulder, bade his wife in a chosen phrase, goodnight. Yet he waited a moment or so as if he were observing me. I did not know what to do, so I stammered that I was tired, kissed Lady Cynthia's hands, and went.

"That night I didn't sleep a wink. I had a continuous feeling that Sir Oliver would come to me: I listened for every step in the castle, certain that he would come. But he did not. At length I undressed and went to bed. I contemplated what now must happen— what had happened during his absence.

"One thing seemed to be clear: I must tell Sir Oliver everything, must place myself at his disposal. But to what end? I knew that there was no more dueling in England, that he would laugh at me if I just mentioned such a thing. But— what else? Would he drag me before a Court of Justice? He— me? that was even more laughable, and quite certainly no satisfaction for him. Fisticuffs? He was much bigger, much broader and stronger than I, one of the best amateur boxers in the country. I hadn't the

[149]

slightest idea of this sport; the little I knew he, himself, had taught me. Nevertheless, I ought to let him challenge me, come what might.

"But then, if I spoke, wasn't it an infamous betrayal of Lady Cynthia? If he crippled me, what did it matter! But she— sweet, holy woman, she— What would become of her? For she was not guilty. All the guilt was mine, mine alone; I felt that in every fiber of my being. I had come into her house. I had loved her from the first moment. I had stalked her, lain in wait for her, followed her wherever she went. Not content that she gave me her white hands, I had desired her more and more, more ardently every day— until—

"True, I had not spoken. But had my blood not cried for her every hour? What use were my words, when my eyes sang, when my body trembled at the very sight of her? She, brutally flung aside by her husband, betrayed every day and insulted before all eyes, tortured and bearing these tortures and insults like a saint— oh, not a shadow of guilt fell upon her! Small wonder that she had finally fallen to the temptations of a seducer, who followed her step by step—

"And even then, even then she remained the saint she was. She gave her body more out of goodness of heart, out of pure pity for the youth who was devoured by longing for her. She gave herself to me as she gave to the poor she visited, and, in spite of it, remained pure. And so great was her sweet shame that she forbade me to speak in those hours, that she did not once turn around, did not once look into my eyes—

"I understood everything now. I alone bore all the guilt. I was the seducer the wretched scoundrel. And I was now to crown this work, stand before Sir Oliver and tell him— No, no! Then, again, something had to be done! I did not know what. The night passed— I found no way!

"I breakfasted in my room. Then the butler came: Sir Oliver inquired whether I would play golf with him. I nodded, dressed myself, went down, met him outside.

"I have never played good golf. But this time I dug holes in the turf instead of hitting the ball.

"Sir Oliver laughed. 'What's the matter' he said.

"I said something. But as my shots became worse, he grew serious.

"Suddenly he came to me and asked, 'Is it— Were you— at the window, young man?'

"Now it had gone too far. I let my golf club fall; he might as well kill me with his iron.

"I nodded. 'Yes,' I said tonelessly.

"Sir Oliver whistled. He tried to talk— but said nothing. He whistled again. Then he turned, went slowly to the castle. I followed him at some distance.

"I did not see Lady Cynthia that morning. When the gong rang for lunch, I forced myself to go down.

"Before the dining-room I met Sir Oliver; he came to me and said, 'I would rather you did not speak alone with Lady Cynthia today.' Then he waved me through the door.

"During the meal I spoke scarcely a word to Lady Cynthia. Sir Oliver led the conversation, what there was of it. Afterwards Lady Cynthia ordered the carriage: she was going to visit her poor.

"She gave me her hand, which I kissed, and said: 'Tea at five o'clock.'

"She did not return until six: I stood at my window as her carriage drew up. She looked up to me. 'Come,' said her glance. At the door I met Sir Oliver.

"'My wife is back,' he said; 'we'll have tea with her.'

"'Now it's coming,' I thought.

"Only two cups stood on the little table. It was obvious that Lady Cynthia awaited me only, and not her spouse. But she rang at once and had another cup brought. Again Sir Oliver endeavored to carry on the conversation, but his efforts were even less successful than at the luncheon. At length no one said a word.

"Then Lady Cynthia went. Still Sir Oliver did not speak; silently he sat there, whistling lightly through his teeth. Finally he sprang up, as if he had a sudden idea. 'Please wait for me!' he cried, and hurried out.

"I did not have to wait long; after a few minutes he was back. He beckoned me to go with him. We went through a few rooms— to the tower room. Sir Oliver drew back the curtains, looked into the room; then he turned to me and said: 'Bring me the little book on that stool.'

"I obeyed. I slipped through the hangings. At the window stood Lady Cynthia. I felt I was committing treachery, but I could not grasp how or why. Very softly I went to the stool, took the tiny brocade-bound book, that I had so often seen in her hand, crept back again, and gave it to Sir Oliver. He took it, slipped his arm through mine and whispered: 'Come along, my boy!'

"I followed him down the steps, across the courtyard, into the park.

"He seized my arm, his other hand gripping the red book. At length he began: 'You love her? Very much? Very much, my boy? But he did not wait for an answer. 'It is not necessary to speak! I also loved her— perhaps more than you; I was twice as old as you. Not for Lady Cynthia's sake am I speaking to you, but for your own sake!'

"Again he was silent, led me through the avenue, then to the left up a small side path. There stood a bench under the old elms, he sat down and motioned for me to sit beside him. Then he raised his hand, pointed upwards: 'Look! There she stands.'

"I looked up, There stood Lady Cynthia at her window. 'She will see us,' I said.

"Sir Oliver laughed aloud. 'She won't see us. Not if a hundred people sat here— she would see none, hear none! This book she sees, this she feels— and nothing else!'

"He gripped the little volume in his strong hands. 'It is cruel to show it to you, my poor youth— very cruel, I know. But it must be for your own sake. Then— read!'

"I opened the book. It only held a few pages of strong handmade paper. It was not printed, but written, and it was in Lady Cynthia's handwriting.

"I read:

'THE EXECUTION OF ROBERT FRANÇOIS DAMIENS
ON THE PLACE DE GRÊVE. . .IN PARIS
MAY 28TH, 1757
ACCORDING TO THE TESTIMONY OF AN EYEWITNESS
THE DUKE OF CROY'

"The letters flickered before my eyes; what, what had that to do with the woman who stood at the window? I stuttered. I could not recognize the words; I let the book fall.

"Sir Oliver picked it up, and began to read in a loud voice:

"'According to an eye-witness, the Duke of Croy—'

"I rose. Something drove me. I had a feeling I must fly, hide myself in the thickest bushes like a wounded animal. But the strong hand of Sir Oliver seized my arm. And his inexorable voice went on:

"'Robert Damiens, who on January 5th, 1757, attempted to assassinate His Sacred Majesty King Louis XV of France, and on that day at Versailles wounded him in the left side with a dagger thrust, was compelled to expiate his guilt on May 28th, 1757.

"'The same sentence was executed upon him as upon the murderer of King Henri IV, François Ravaillac, on May 17th, 1610.

"'On the morning of the day of execution, Damiens was stretched on the rack; his arms, thighs and calves were ripped open with red-hot hooks, and into the wounds was poured molten lead, boiling oil and burning pitch, mixed with wax and sulphur. At three in the afternoon, the muscular delinquent was led to the Cathedral of Notre Dame and thence to the Place de Grêve. The streets were filled with a mob which took sides neither for or against the criminal. The aristocratic world, ornamented and dressed as for a festival, elegant ladies and gentlemen of nobility, crowded the windows, playing with their fans and holding their smelling salts in case of fainting. At half past four the great spectacle began. In the middle of the square a stage had been erected, to which Damiens was brought. With him, the executioners and two father confessors ascended the platform. This huge man betrayed neither surprise or fear, but merely expressed a wish to die quickly.

"'Six assistant executioners now bound his trunk to the boards with iron chains and rings, so that he could not move his body. Then his right hand was seized and burned slowly in a fire of sulphur, while Damiens gave voice to a horrible shrieking. It was seen that the hair on his head stood up stiffly, while his hand was being burnt. The iron hooks were made glowing hot, with them large pieces of flesh were ripped out of arms, legs and breast. In the fresh wounds were poured liquid lead and boiling oil. The atmosphere on the whole square was befouled by the stench of burning.

"'Now, strong ropes were bound round the upper arm and upper thigh, the wrists and ankles, to which were harnessed four strong horses, one at each of the four corners of the stage. The horses were then whipped forward, with the intention of tearing the wretch apart. For a full hour the horses were spurred and whipped yet they did not succeed in wrenching off either an arm or a leg. Above the blows of the whips and the shouting of the executioners could be heard the terrible yells of pain of the man in his sickening torment.

"'Then six more horses were harnessed on, and all the horses were whipped together. The cries of Damiens increased to a mad bellowing. At length the executioners obtained permission from the judges present to make incisions in the joints, in order to lighten the work of the horses. Damiens raised his head to see what was being done to him, but he did not cry out while they cut through his joints. He turned his head to the crucifix held before him and kissed it while the two confessors exhorted him to repent. Then the blows once more rained down on all the horses at once, and at last, after one and a half hours, they succeeded in pulling off the left leg.

"'The people in the square and the aristocrats in the windows clapped their hands. The work was continued.

"'When the right leg was torn off, Damiens once more began to scream wildly. The shoulder joints were then cut, and the horses were again whipped up. As the right arm was wrenched off, the cries of the wretch grew weaker. His head began to droop, but only when the left arm was detached did his head fall right backward. Now only the palpitating trunk remained, with the head upon which the hair had turned white. But this trunk and his head lived yet.

"'Now his hair was cut off and his limbs collected together, while the father confessors approached him once more. Henri Samson, the chief executioner, held them back, however, saying that Damiens had drawn his breath. Thus was the believing criminal denied the last spiritual consolation, for the trunk could be seen turning itself here and there, while the lower jaw moved itself to speak. This trunk still breathed: the eyes turned upon the bystanders.

"'What remained was burned upon a pyre and the ashes scattered to the winds.

"'Thus was the end of a wretch who suffered the greatest torment that ever a man suffered; in Paris, before my own eyes and those of many thousands of people, including those of many noble and beautiful women who stood at the windows.'"

"Do you wonder, gentlemen," Brinken concluded, "that since that evening I have been a little frightened of woman who have feelings, souls, imagination? And especially if they are English?"

www.ingramcontent.com/pod-product-compliance
Lightning Source LLC
Chambersburg PA
CBHW060403030726
47497CB00003B/829